Sandcastles

By Suzie Carr

ι

Also by Suzie Carr:
The Fiche Room
Tangerine Twist
Two Feet off The Ground
Inner Secrets
A New Leash on Life
The Muse
Staying True
Snowflakes
The Journey Somewhere

Keep up on Suzie's latest news and projects:
www.curveswelcome.com

Follow Suzie on Twitter:
@girl_novelist

For you, my friend.

Sandcastles are temporary. Trying to build them into permanent structures is an impossible dream. They fall down quickly, with little warning. The comfort comes when one realizes that when they crumble and fall back into the sea, they become the foundation for something else in the waiting.

Acknowledgements

I have so many people to thank for helping me to write this book. With your guidance, I learned a lot of valuable lessons in writing and in life. Dorina, my beautiful twin soul, your feedback fueled my creativity and drove me to seek truths. Alak, your knowledge in Ayurveda Medicine helped teach me how to take charge of my own health and gave lift to the many lessons found in Sandcastles. Susan Duggan, I am eternally humbled to have met you, and am grateful to you for making my acupuncture journey a powerful, life-changing one. Dr. Rao, your dedication to functional medicine and educating patients on proactive approach is so inspiring. I will forever be indebted to you for the gift of empowerment. Diane Marina, Angela, Bethany, and Felicia, thank you for your insights and honesty. You give me confidence to share my writing with others, and I cherish you for this. To my better half, thank you for having patience with me while I dove into character mode each and every day. Your support gives me the freedom to soar. And to Pat, thank you for sharing your insights with us while you were here. I hope you know how much we miss you.

Chapter One
Lia

I ran out of the flea market like my life depended on it. I tripped over the ramp leading out to the parking lot, and coins, along with my favorite lipstick, spilled out of my pocketbook. I kept running, past the security guard with the dropped jaw and the crying kid with orange hair and freckles.

I dashed out in front of a car, carrying my portable air compressor like a running back in a football game. The driver honked his horn and yelled something out of his window in Spanish. With no time to apologize, I flew through the parking lot, kicking up stones and dirt along the way.

I stopped at the edge of the lot and stared at the line of traffic coming toward me on Pulaski Boulevard. I peeked over my shoulder and saw my assistant, Dean, and that blast from my past, Willow, in the entranceway, bending down to collect my stuff.

With no time to waste, I flung an arm up in the air and commanded the traffic to stop. A minivan screeched to a halt. I offered a nod and crossed out in front of it only to be faced with a line of cars barreling down the opposite lane. With traffic stopped in my lane, I waited for a clear path so I could dash toward my truck and arrive in time.

Two Hours Earlier

I stood in front of my window and stared out at the crowded street below, wishing I didn't have to go out there.

My father would only turn sixty once in his lifetime, and he wanted that damned air compressor from his good friend, Ernie, at the flea market in Bellingham. I skived flea markets ever since I found a cockroach in a bar of taffy I bought with my allowance when I was just eleven years old. My father, despite that, loved them and befriended vendors.

The trip would require support, and so I called out to Dean.

My door flew open. "What's up, boss?"

I continued to stare out to the street below, watching a delivery truck narrowly miss side-swiping a Volkswagen Beetle. "I need to run an errand." I turned to face him. "Want to take a ride?"

He leaned against the doorframe, twisting his mouth. "Why do I have the feeling saying yes to this is going to end in some sort of regret?"

"I'm not taking you to Six Flags again. I promise." I walked over to my desk and undocked my laptop. "Trust me, that excursion pained me far more than it did you." My eardrums still hadn't fully recovered from his screams at the top of the double loop coaster. "I'll even treat you to lunch."

He tapped his chin with a pen. "As much as it pains me to miss out on the fun of a potential adventure, I have to respectfully decline." His face contorted into a wince. "Maybe next time." He darted out of the doorframe. His black hair swayed in the wake.

"Hey, hang on." I brushed past my chair. "Why do you always assume I'm going to pull the rug out from under your feet?"

He stopped, turned, and faced me. He lifted his chin and looked down at me under the rim of his Calvin Klein mahogany frames. "Because, Lia, you've literally pulled the rug out from under my feet before."

I nodded, and a smile crept onto my face.

He remained stoic even in the foreshadowing of my impending tease.

"I sense an eminent assault of laughter aimed at me," he said. "So, if you'll excuse me, I'm going to return to the five foot pile of paperwork you tossed on my desk yesterday morning. After all, that is why I'm here on a Saturday morning when the rest of the office staff is probably enjoying a beautiful, sunny day free of marketing jargon." He bowed, tipped an imaginary hat, and whisked away.

"Come on now," I said, catching up to him and spinning him around on a quick tug. "Admit it. You're the one who set yourself up for that rug pulling."

He didn't flinch at my mocking, something I admired about him and incessantly needed to test. "You asked me to sample carpet remnants under my chair. I didn't think I'd have to take out an insurance policy for my safety."

"It's not my fault that you're extremely gullible." I patted his upper arm. "Let's go. We'll go to your favorite spot and get Indian buffet." Nothing riled him up like Naan and curry.

"No."

I folded my arms over my chest. "Well, that's an order."

He tilted his head back and scanned the drop ceiling above, taking in every nook and cranny on the tiles. A smile emerged as he lowered back to meet my gaze. "I want the Indian buffet on Hope Street or you've got no deal."

I dropped my arms. "Fine. Let me get my laptop and close up my office."

He narrowed his eyes. "You do plan to come back and work, right?"

"I wasn't planning on it. Do I need to?"

"We've got to go over the project timeline for Monday morning's meeting still."

"I've got to get to my parents right after I drop you back off. Just copy what we did for Shine Salon and change the header to say Chic Spot."

He stared at me like I had ten heads.

"That'll work, right?"

"Copy? We don't copy here. We're unique. That's your motto."

"I don't have time to be unique today." I couldn't skip the party. My mother planned it for weeks. "Can you work your magic? Please?"

He rolled his eyes. "I suppose that's why you pay me the big bucks."

"I don't know what I'd do without you." I searched his gaze for a hint of understanding, waiting for him to acknowledge that I was a serious business owner. Life had just served me another dodgeball I had to deal with.

"I suspect you'd get along just fine." He folded his arms over his chest.

3

I arched my eyebrow, then headed back to my office. "I'll just be a moment."

A few minutes later, laptop in hand, Dean opened the door for me. "Where are we going, anyway?"

"To get my dad a birthday gift." I marched toward the elevator. Taking him to a flea market was going to be like taking a child to a penny candy store. He'd get overexcited and embarrass himself for sure.

I'd keep my sanity for as long as possible by keeping our destination a surprise.

The elevator chimed and the doors opened. Dean stood in the doorframe to keep them open. "Why do I need to come?"

"Can't I just simply ask you to come along because I enjoy your company? Does there have to be a reason?"

The elevator closed and for twenty long seconds we rode down to the first floor on silent mode, something Dean required after that one time he got stuck for three hours on the elevator during Rhode Island's one and only noticeable earthquake.

The elevator chimed again, and the door opened up to the office building's sunny foyer. "With you," he said, waving me off the elevator as he straddled the frame, "there's always a reason."

I pushed through the front door. The fragrant fresh blooms of lilacs woke me up. I inhaled the spring air, savoring it as I led us to my brand new silver Tacoma four door, long bed pickup truck. "If I tell you why, then you'll know where we're going, and that'll just ruin the surprise."

"And that would be a shame because I live for surprises." His sarcasm dripped in sweet, reliable rhythmic beats, a sound I'd grown fond of over the past two years.

We drove to the Bellingham Flea Market and fought about what to listen to the entire time. I wanted lite seventies and he kept changing it to heavy metal. When we arrived, we still hadn't listened to a full song of either genre.

"I love flea markets," Dean said, sticking his nose against the window.

"The place is packed." My heart tightened. I drove past the parking lot entrance, thankful he agreed to come along.

4

"You just missed that spot right up front." He pointed to a spot in between two beat up old sedans.

"No way. Not with my brand new truck." I stopped and let a couple wearing colorful ponchos cross the street. "It won't hurt us to walk a little."

I parked my brand new truck along a remote edge of Pulaski Boulevard, removed from the threat of other cars and inconsiderate people.

We hiked to the entrance, me shouldering my pocketbook and Dean smearing a stupid smile clear across his youthful face. One would've thought we entered Disney World the way his eyes opened wide in delight at the chaos that presented itself to us upon entering the crammed building.

I pushed us through the crowd, detangling from their clumsy arms and feet with each step. "The tools are in the back," I yelled over my shoulder to Dean.

He clung to the back of my shirt, smiling in his goofy wide-toothed way as he scanned the scene.

I cleared our path with more determined strokes. We passed a man with wiry white hair and a fruit stained t-shirt. He held up a bag of mangos. "Get yours now. Only a dollar. Get them while they're fresh."

Dean stopped me. "We have to get some."

I grabbed his wrist and led him away. "We're not here to buy soggy mangos."

The man continued his chant. "Get yours now. Only a dollar. Get them while they're fresh."

Dean stopped again. "This is snack time, Lia. I'm getting mangos." He reached into his jacket and pulled out his wallet. "Shall I get you some too?"

The man grinned, exposing a wad of chewing tobacco. My stomach rolled. "That would be a big no."

I turned away and headed over to a table of cleaning products. A young teenaged girl popped up from a chair. "Can I help you?"

"I'm just looking."

She nodded and plopped down again, sitting on her hands. Poor kid looked about ready to cry.

"Maybe I'll get this bottle of Windex."

She popped up again. "That'll be six dollars, please." She folded her hands in front of her, squeezing them until they turned white.

"For Windex?"

She shrugged and her bottom lip trembled.

"I'll give you three dollars." I took the bills out of my pocketbook and offered them to her. "Six is ridiculous. You should tell your parents a customer said so."

She reached out with shaky hands for my dollars. "Okay."

Dean stepped up to an adjacent table, plucking up a terry cloth hand towel. "I need these." He picked up a pack of white ones, then yellow, and continued scanning the table. "Oh look, they come in red, too." He shoved those under his arm. "What color do you want for the kitchen at the office?"

The young girl and I shared a goofy smile before I turned from her and removed the white pack from under his arm, placing it back in its rightful spot. "Pace yourself."

He dragged me around that flea market as if on a treasure hunt for the world's most rare and valuable items. Everywhere my eyes landed, I saw nothing but junk. His eyes grew larger by the second. He had to touch everything. Every bottle of disinfectant, every piece of fabric, every picture frame and knick-knack.

I had brought Dean to the ultimate paradise for someone obsessed with secondhand junk. Table after table housed the most hideous, most random items known to mankind. Who the hell in his right mind would walk into that place, pick up a pair of white and orange striped tube socks and travel back home a happy person?

Dean would.

His arms overflowed as we headed to the tool section.

The place stunk. It smelled like mothballs, leather, and aftershave. People laughed and smiled, shoving loads of faded blue jeans, underwear without packaging, and used toys under their arms as if they were uncovering mega deals at Ozzy World's semi-annual sale.

They bumped into me without apology, shoving past us as if we didn't exist. One older lady with a random curler on her forehead even stole the last bottle of Avon's Skin-So-Soft right out of Dean's hands. Instead of fighting back for it, he shrugged it off and moved on to the next exciting item, a tube of extra-soft, strawberry scented, hand lotion.

I grabbed his arm. "You're just going to let her take the Skin-So-Soft?

"She needs it more than me, surely."

I stared at the lady, hobbling as she inched her way down a table of cosmetics whose lids were missing and labels half-scratched off. I would have wrestled her for the bottle had I not been in Dean's company. A tiff would've charged me and caused my skin to prickle. The scrapper inside of me would've danced to a new beat and wanted to find more tiffs. I wanted a fight ever since talking with my mother earlier that morning about my father's gift. *Your father wants an air compressor, but only from his loyal customer Ernie. You've got to get it from him. I've already called him up and told him to put one aside for you.*

I dragged Dean away from the cosmetics. "Come on. We've got an air compressor to buy."

He stopped at a grandfather clock, tracing his finger along its botched up wooden surface. "You're getting your father an air compressor?" He squinted his eyes and examined the gold-plated hands of the clock.

"Yes. He wants one." I tried to nudge him forward, but he remained firm.

"Did you know at one time in history only the nobility owned grandfather clocks? Owning one symbolized wealth." He over pronounced the end of the word like a snob.

"And here it sits in the middle of junk heaven." I gazed out over the sea of junk in search of Ernie's booth. "Come on. This place creeps me out with all its old smells. It reminds me of summers at my aunt's house when she didn't have air conditioning and kept her windows sealed shut."

"You were afraid to come here by yourself." His voice rose up in a challenge. "That's why you asked me to tag along."

"Let's just get the compressor and get out of here." I brushed past him, snaking my way through the blockades of people browsing the junk. I traveled halfway through the cluttered room before realizing I had been dragging one of those terry cloths under my feet.

A satisfied grin sat on Dean's face as he offered me his shoulder. "You look ridiculous. Better get that off your foot before you embarrass yourself."

I peeled it off my shoe. "That's disgusting." I flung it to the sticky concrete.

"No," he said, wiping the grin from his face. "That's fucking hysterical."

"That coming from a man who enjoys eating soggy mangos in a baggy and buying up a lifetime supply of terry cloth hand towels." I waved him ahead of me. "After you."

He marched past me with his head high and took his sweet time browsing car radios as if fascinated with such devices.

I waited patiently, with my hand gripping my hip and my teeth biting down on the inside of my cheek. I looked up past the radios and noticed an odd looking lady standing beside a pub style table. She wore a rainbow-colored jumpsuit that puffed out as if inflated with helium. Her eyes, shadowed in sparkly blue, flickered when she caught my eye, and a chill coursed through me.

She stared at me. I snapped away and focused back on Dean. He stuck his nose in some megaphone attached to a turntable. "Fascinating." His voice echoed.

The lady's eyes bore into me with magnetic force. I struggled to keep my grounding.

"Let's go." I yanked him.

Dean didn't resist. He followed in step beside me. Then, in his typical curious fashion, he locked eyes with the lady. "I've always wanted to get a palm reading."

She continued to stare at me, looking right past the crowds who passed in front of us and right into my eyes. The faint sound of theatrical music drifted in and out.

My head clouded with a euphoric sense. The space between me and the lady shrank, forming a tunnel where Dean's excitable jibber jabber and the chatter of hundreds of flea marketers quieted. Even though a good fifteen feet of distance separated me from that lady with mysterious eyes, wearing earrings far too large for the saggy earlobes she carried around on her raisin head, her energy gripped me.

The little hairs on my arm rose.

A hollow gap in time and space sucked the air from my lungs. I tugged at Dean, urging him away with me, away from the weird lady. But Dean and his curious soul stood firm, now staring at her with the wide eyes of someone seeing a UFO. I pushed him forward, but he remained glued with that mischievous grin I've learned to love so much.

"Let's see what she has to say."

"We came to buy an air compressor."

I pulled him away, and he followed me like a puppy.

We walked a few tables over and found the air compressor booth and a man, with a huge nose and even bigger ears, hunched over the counter reading *The Providence Journal.*

"Are you Ernie?" I asked.

He looked up from the newspaper, offering me a welcome smile. "Yes I am. The one and only." He stood up and opened his arms up to me. "You look just like your father. My God. It's uncanny." He walked up to me and took me in his arms, squeezing me in a bear hug. "Your mother told me I should be expecting you."

"Yes. Apparently, my father only wants your air compressor."

His face lit up. "Smart man." He winked and turned to the corner of his booth where a shiny red cylinder sat. "Last time I went to your father's garage to get my tires rotated, we talked about it."

"I'm glad I'll get him a gift he's going to like," I said.

"It's the last one I have in stock. So, he's going to be a happy man. They don't manufacture them like this model anymore."

9

"Fantastic." I handed him my credit card.

Once we finished our transaction, I carried the compressor under my arm and braced for the bumps and shoves of the crowd.

We walked past the psychic, and her eyes bore into mine again. I shivered.

Dean veered off in her direction, stranding me in a sea of stupid people who banged into me and ushered me along like a rotten log in a dirty river.

I backed away, tearing myself from her eyes. I hid behind a rack of lip-glosses, taking in the full side view of them both beginning their dance of curiosity. I watched as the weird lady charmed Dean with a crooked smile. She took his palm and studied it.

"You have allergies, I see," she said, speaking with a serious tone.

Dean arched his eyebrow. "No. You're wrong on that one."

She shook her head. "No. I'm not wrong. You have allergies."

"Tell me more, then."

She dropped his hand and pointed to her tabletop sign. "I can do a basic life reading for ten dollars. But if you want to find the root cause of that allergy, I'll have to do the more intense Tarot Card Reading for forty-five dollars." She pointed her eyes at him. "It's the only way to know for sure what's going on."

I charged toward them. "Don't throw your money away, Dean."

The lady smiled up at me.

I looked down at Dean. "This is ridiculous."

"She's got me curious. I can't leave now." Dean stretched his eyes up at me. "I could have allergies I don't know about."

"You're going to pay her forty-five dollars to tell you you're allergic to a tree?"

"Well, yeah."

"Maybe I pay you too much money."

Just then a cute blonde, with a set of eyes as blue as the Caribbean, walked out from behind the booth's back curtain. "Auntie, just do his palm reading. I'm sure you can figure out his allergy from it. Even I can."

10

"My niece, she's cute as anything, but a real know-it-all," she said, whispering to Dean.

Dean, being the true gentleman, leaned into her and handed her a fifty. "I want the entire story."

I bit my lip, placed my Windex and air compressor on the sticky ground, and settled in for what I could only guess would be one of the most ridiculous ten minutes of our lives.

The blonde smiled at me with an apology written all over her pretty face. "I tried."

We lingered on a gaze, and in those few seconds, familiarity worked its way in. "I know you from somewhere."

An awkward clench to the jaw replaced her smile. "Yes, you do." She met my eye again. "I'm Willow. Willow from Bowdish Lake Campground."

The past crash-landed in front of me. Willow. Braces, coke bottle glasses, pimply faced, weirdo Willow. "Wow. You look different."

She smirked and tossed her hair over her golden shoulder. "And, you look the same."

"Thanks," I said, prematurely accepting that as a compliment.

She mocked me with an arched eyebrow. The same arched brow she had used on me many times over at the campground when I'd laugh at her predictions. She'd predicted when the wind would blow, who would win the potato sack race, how many fish people would catch. She'd freaked us all out when she had predicted the campground owner would receive a call that his father had suffered a heart attack, and he did.

"How have you been?" I asked to be polite, eyeing Dean's psychic reading progress.

She hugged herself and looked around the booth with a wishful smile. "I'm doing fantastic."

11

"I can see that." I scanned the booth with all its eccentrics—a colorful pie chart of the zodiac signs, a sculpted hand detailing palmistry that sat on top of a column, the likes of which you'd find on an old historic building, a sculpted head with hollowed eyes detailing phrenology, and another chart, this one so colorful it hurt the eye, detailing some weird thing called Hemphta.

She hugged herself tighter, warming into a smile. "My aunt and I set up this booth a few years back, and it's working out pretty good I have to say. Her wife owns a wellness center, and we tried to talk her into setting up there, but she says it's not spontaneous enough for her taste." She rolled her eyes and chuckled. "I'm a yoga instructor there, and I love it. She doesn't know what she's missing."

Her face lit up in the most beautiful glow when she laughed. Even her eyes smiled. She locked onto my gaze, and I fluttered inside.

I tore away and landed back on Dean.

Her aunt narrowed her eyes, staring at Dean with great concern. "The silver truck."

"That's not mine. It's hers." Dean cocked his head at me.

"What about the silver truck," I asked, stepping up to them.

"Someone's trying to steal it." She dropped Dean's hands and sat back. "You should go. Go now."

I turned to Willow. "Is she for real?"

"He's smashing your window right now," the aunt said.

Willow stepped forward. "You should go."

I reached down for my air compressor and cradled it like a football. "This is silly."

"You've got a purple hangtag with the letter E on it," her aunt said. "And the hoodlum has your laptop on the ground already."

Fuck.

I dashed off, leaving the Windex behind. I ran through the crowd, stomping on feet and pushing people out of the way.

When I broke through the exit, my pocketbook flew off my shoulder, spilling some change and a tube of lipstick. I grabbed my pocketbook, tossed it over my head and shoulder, and gripped the air compressor tighter under my arm. I tore off through the lot.

Please God, let that wacko be wrong.

# #

I stood in front of a minivan, blocking its way. Finally, I saw my break in the southbound lane and went for it, running across. Dean called out to me. I looked over my shoulder and saw the panic stretch across his face. Then Willow threw her hands up to her pretty face in horror. That's when I heard the horn wail from a truck that had come out of nowhere in the southbound lane. I dropped the compressor and leaped forward, catapulted by superhuman force, and shoulder rolled off the road and onto the dusty grass. My father's compressor flew through the air as the truck ran over it. It flew straight up and over me, landing in the trees a dozen feet away.

The sting of the gravel on my face didn't hit me until the truck, and the ones following it, skidded to halt. A bird chirped above my head on the telephone line. A car door opened and slammed shut. Dean yelled out to me. "Good God woman! What were you thinking?"

"Go," I yelled to him. "Run to my truck before the hoodlum steals it."

He gripped his hair as if he had just survived the near wreck. "Nobody is breaking into your precious truck," he yelled to me. "The lady played us for a few bucks is all."

"My aunt seldom gets these things wrong," Willow said, catching up to Dean. He scanned the road as he crossed it. Panic returned to his face. "Shit." He ran off toward my truck, kicking up dust with his dress shoes. I looked past his skinny body and saw what he saw, my truck door wide open and the shadow of a man's head in my rear window. I rose to my feet and sprinted ahead, forgetting my pocketbook on the side of the road and my father's birthday present in the trees.

"Hey," Dean yelled out as he bolted down the road.

The man swung his head around, then hopped out of my truck and ran down Pulaski Boulevard, clutching his pry bar and pulling up his saggy pants.

Dean got to my truck first and fell against it, panting.

Willow and I ran up to him, doubling over in equal panting.

Sweat rolled down his cheeks. "Holy shit," he managed, steadying against the truck. "I wonder if this means I really do have allergies."

I noticed my laptop case on the ground. "Oh thank God." I reached down for it.

Dean gulped. "Really? You've got blood dripping from your mouth and you're worried about a laptop?"

I tasted the blood, suddenly. "I'm bleeding?"

He handed me one of his terry cloth towels. "It's dripping down your chin."

I pressed it against my lip and watched as the traffic began to move again. A few cars passed us by, yelling out their windows at us.

"Never just a typical day at the office with you, is it?" He took over nursing my cut, dabbing the towel against it with great care. "This package of cloths is the only one I managed not to drop on Pulaski Boulevard."

"I'll buy you more," I said.

Willow brushed past us and sat in my driver's seat. She gripped the steering wheel and shook it.

Dean pressed my lip harder, and I winced.

"I've got to stop the bleeding somehow. You can dash out in front of a tractor trailer truck but you can't handle a little compression?"

I trusted Dean. He looked out for me. He enjoyed playing the wise assistant, and I couldn't bring myself to ruin that for him. The day he stopped jeering me would be the day I would no longer trust him. In all of my thirty-one years, I'd never met someone I could trust more.

"No lectures or else you'll never come back to this place with me again," I said.

He stared at me with blankness, undeterred by my empty threat, as he continued to try and fix me as he always did.

14

"Looks like he broke your steering column," Willow said, sliding out of the front seat. "You're not going to be able to drive it."

I stepped back from Dean, pressing the cloth to my lip myself now. "I just canceled my roadside assistance the day I bought this."

"I'll call your insurance company and see if they can send someone to help." Dean pulled out his cell phone.

Willow placed her hand on my arm, and her eyes twitched slightly as if something important just dawned on her. "I don't mind driving you somewhere."

"I don't want to put you through the trouble," I said, trying to be polite.

"It'll give me a good excuse to get away for a few hours." She eased her hand down the length of my arm, then playfully wrestled with a smile. "You're not going to deprive me of that, are you?"

Her challenging gaze and teasing question stirred me in a strange, unsettling way. It tickled the dormant parts of me, somehow reaching down into my soul and bringing me out of the depths of a sensual hibernation I didn't realize I had even entered.

Chapter Two
Willow

The first time I caught a glimpse into the future, I was attending Christmas Eve mass at Saint Ann's Catholic Church with my parents. My mother leaned over and asked me, "Would you please pass me the songbook?"

When I handed it over, she smiled and patted my leg. Her hand warmed me, even through my thick wool pants. Then, the church and all its people blurred, leaving only my mother in my view. A bright halo of white surrounded her, and I had the peaceful sense that angels were among us, blanketing me in peace. Then, I looked down to her lap and saw a cute baby wearing a pink dress and a white bonnet. The baby sucked her thumb and gurgled. I sensed my mother's love for her, and a weird jealousy poked at me.

I looked back up at my mother's face. Her smile vanished. She tugged at my sleeve and wore the same face she did whenever I got hurt or came down with a fever. "Are you okay?"

I looked in her lap. "Where did the baby go?"

"What baby?"

My father shushed us.

"The baby in your lap."

"I wasn't holding a baby, sweetheart." Panic traced her voice.

My father grabbed her wrist and pulled it, flashing us both a stern look. "That's enough. We're in church."

She snapped her eyes away from me and looked up at the altar and at the priest who recited the offertory hymn.

I stared at her, at her trembling lips and the red blotches that popped up all over her face and neck, and wondered where the white halo, the peace, and the cute baby

17

had gone to. Later when we walked out to the car, I clasped onto my mother's hand. "I saw a baby. I swear, I did."

She shushed me and pushed me along.

Her eyes flashed a fear I'd only seen the time that old man rear-ended us on the way back from the beach the summer before.

My father pointed his stern gaze straight ahead, ignoring me as usual.

We didn't speak another word about that day. In the months that followed, my mother and I baked cakes, painted Easter eggs, went shopping for pretty dresses, and never once did she talk about the baby growing in her belly. I never asked about it either, out of fear she'd look at me again with that awful fear in her eye.

Later that year, on a sweltering hot day in August, when my mother and father first introduced me to my baby sister, Mary Rose, I kept my mouth shut about how I had already met her eight months earlier in the pew at St. Ann's Catholic Church.

My mother adored Mary Rose. Her perky giggles and pretty blonde curls placed her far above me, the one who freaked her out. When she cried, my mother laughed. When she threw a tantrum, my mother smiled. When she broke my favorite doll by smashing it against the ceramic floor, my mother pinched her cheek and cooed, "You're my little doll smasher, aren't you?" She rubbed her nose against the tip of Mary Rose's.

Not long after Mary Rose turned a year, I caught my second major glimpse into the future. It came to me the day I sat in a circle with my mother and Aunt Lola and urged Mary Rose to take her first step. We sang *put one foot in front of the other, and soon you'll be walking across the floor.* Mary sat in the middle of our circle and giggled. I wanted her to walk to me first, mainly because if she did, my mother would be equally as happy with me as with her.

Mary Rose didn't disappoint. She did it. She stood up, wobbled a bit, and then headed straight toward me. I opened my arms up wide and sang louder. She giggled, wobbled, and landed in my arms.

18

She hugged me, and immediately the room turned foggy. The same peaceful, white-glowing haze from the day I saw Mary Rose as a baby on my mom's lap in church filled the room, and suddenly, I found myself sitting on my front porch, struggling with a jigsaw puzzle. I looked up and saw a young girl riding her big wheel bike in our front yard. She waved at me as she passed by the porch. I waved back. One moment I saw her pretty blonde curls blowing in the wind, the next she disappeared. She drove off the tall wall that separated our yard from the street below. I sat still, scared, not knowing if the girl had cracked open her skull and died right there on Third Avenue.

I opened my mouth to scream for help, but my voice got caught in my throat. I closed my eyes, steadying to push out the scream. When I opened them back up again, I sat in a circle with my mother and aunt on the floor in my living room, hugging Mary Rose.

I stared into her big blue eyes. She pulled my hair, bringing me back to the present moment, to our circle, to the joy of her first steps. I hugged her again. I couldn't stop the tears.

"Why are you crying?" Aunt Lola asked, scooting in closer and turning our circle into a lopsided triangle.

"I saw Mary Rose on a big wheel falling off a high wall."

My mother pointed her finger at me. "Stop talking that kind of nonsense." That same dreadful fear I'd heard in her voice that day in the church now stretched into every line on her face. "I mean it. Stop it."

I shrank backward and released Mary Rose into the safety of Aunt Lola's arms.

After that incident, I saw visions all the time. I only had to touch certain objects and I'd see scenes of someone's life. Some were fun to watch, and others scared me. I learned how to escape out of them when one time, a man with a long straggly beard looked right at me in one of those visions and I told him to *stop it* just like my mother had told me. It worked. The man disappeared in a flash, and I reentered the present.

I only had to say *stop it,* and I'd snap out of it.

Overall, I kept my visions to myself. Only once I weakened and told my mother about a scary vision I had of a little boy being taken away by a clown in a van. I ran to her and started crying, wishing she'd protect me and erase the visions for good. She helped me in her own way by marching me into the bathroom and sticking a bar of soap in my mouth to cleanse my sinful thoughts. She cried along with me, telling me we needed to pray as hard as possible for my soul. She pulled out her rosary beads and recited the prayers while I stood in front of her with a bar of soap.

I never told her about another vision again.

Instead, I turned to Aunt Lola.

"Are you scared of these visions?" Aunt Lola asked me one afternoon when she treated me to McDonald's for vanilla shakes.

I sat across from her, struggling with brain freeze, and nodded. "A little."

"You don't have to be. The angels blessed you with the gift of helping people."

My 'gift' as my Aunt Lola called it, was more like a curse. "I'd rather have roller blades."

She laughed and slurped her milkshake.

"You don't understand it now, but one day you will."

I rolled my eyes. "I'd still rather have roller blades."

"The angels blessed me with the same gift."

I stopped slurping. "They have?"

She explained to me that she was a clairaudient psychic, which meant she could hear voices and sounds from the spirit world. She could also catch visuals from time to time. She told me I had the gift of psychometry. Pretty much through the sense of touch, I could see, smell, hear and taste the past, present and future.

After our shakes that day, we walked through the park and sat under a big tree.

"This is my favorite tree," she said, staring up at it. Her long braid swept the ground below. "When I was a kid I used to read books under it. My mother would take me and your mother to the library right across the street, and we'd sit here for hours reading." She smiled and her whole face glowed. She raised her head upright, and her braid fell against the back of her flowery shirt.

"It's beautiful."

"It's called a weeping willow, and when I was just about your age, I remember declaring that I would one day name my daughter Willow."

I hugged her, sinking into her safety. "Willow. I like it. I wish that was my name."

"It could be my nickname for you. Would you like that?"

I nodded. "Yes."

Later that afternoon, I told my mother, "Aunt Lola renamed me to Willow."

"Your name is Catherine. It will always be Catherine. Do you understand me?" She pointed that finger of hers at me again. I feared a bar of soap would soon follow if I didn't agree.

"But it's just a nickname."

"Your Aunt Lola is weird. She scares people with pretending she can tell the future and read their mind. I don't want you hanging around her anymore. From now on, no more milkshakes with her. She's not right in the head. If she's not careful, she'll end up being jailed in one of those mental institutions. You don't want that for yourself. Do you?" She scanned my face.

I pictured doctors and needles, and being chained to a bed just like in that movie I peeked in on when I fooled my parents by pretending to be asleep.

"Well do you?" she yelled.

"No," I cried. "I'm not like that. I don't see things anymore. I don't need to go to jail."

She exhaled and stared me down.

The tears began to leak down my cheeks.

In a matter of seconds, she softened and drew me into her arms. "That's my sweet girl."

I loved hearing those words. I tightened my grip around her, wanting to stay swaddled in that moment forever. I always wanted my mother to love me, and I never wanted her to fear me the way she did my aunt.

For several years, I kept quiet. I pretended to be a normal preteen kid who didn't see things that weren't real. When I'd get a happy vision, I'd giggle and smile over it by myself. When I'd get a bad vision, I'd point my finger at it and say *stop it.*

When the holidays swung around and Aunt Lola came by, I'd hide from her. I didn't want to talk about my 'gift' with her. Things were going great between me and my mother. She began to relax around me and not wear that fear on her face anymore. She even trusted me to watch my sister in the yard while she cooked dinner or folded laundry. I felt normal, and I didn't want that to end.

Life was cruel, though, and didn't always work that way. I stole those words from my father. He spoke them most every day. I finally understood what he meant.

I was sitting on my front porch playing with a puzzle. Mary Rose rode her big wheel bike out front. She pedaled by me, waving. Then, just like in my vision from when she took her first steps as a baby, she disappeared over the wall. An eerie silence filled the neighborhood as if everyone stopped breathing, talking, and laughing all at once. Dread engulfed me.

I stood up and screamed for my mother. She ran out of the front door wearing her rollers. Panic dripped down her face. She wore her housecoat and still had dough smeared on her hands. I just pointed to the wall.

She screamed and ran to the wall. "Oh God. Oh no. No. Please no." Her screams rose even louder when she bent over to see Mary Rose.

I couldn't talk. The fright in those few fragile seconds of when my mother dove off the wall to when I heard Mary Rose's first blood curdling screams snuffed out the air. My mother yelled out for someone to help. Soon, the next door neighbors, two teenaged boys, dashed off their front porch and jumped off the wall to help. The three of them carried a very bloody faced and panic-stricken Mary Rose to our porch. Her two front teeth were missing and blood poured out of her mouth like someone turned a faucet on in the back of her throat.

I feared the worst. I feared my mother would send me off to a mental hospital and have me locked away for good, far away from them all.

But, she surprised me. When my mother tucked me into bed that night, she spoke to me with a sweet quality. "Can you see what's going to happen to me?"

I shook my head. "What do you mean?"

She kissed my cheek, and my heart ached suddenly. A sadness filled me, and I wanted to cry.

"It's nothing, Catherine. Just go to sleep now and have pleasant dreams."

I couldn't fall asleep that night. The sadness wrapped itself around my heart and tightened with each beat. I sensed a terrible gloom, one that I didn't understand.

The following week my mother landed in the hospital because she fainted. After that, she needed to sit down after standing for not more than five minutes. She could barely get through cooking dinner most nights. My father worked harder because of the medical bills, so I'd end up mixing up macaroni and cheese a lot while my mother collapsed on the couch in a cold sweat. Six months later, lying in a hospital bed, she asked me to come close to her so she could tell me something.

Her breath hit my ear in short, punctuated beats. "I'm glad you couldn't see this the way you saw Mary Rose fall off the wall."

"See what, Mom?"

She drew a long, shallow breath as she smiled at me with tired eyes. "This moment when I have to leave you."

I waited for her to breathe again. She didn't.

I stared at her mouth, willing it to move.

It sat still. The air in the room stopped circulating. My father sniffled. Mary Rose clung to his leg and cried.

I wanted to yell *stop it* and escape the nightmare. Only I couldn't. I witnessed it in real time, not the past or the future. But right then and there.

23

She never took another breath. She simply closed her eyes on a smile and never opened them again.

In the weeks that followed, my father called on my Aunt Lola to help him out with us because he had no one else to turn to. He never brought up our psychic abilities, and neither did we. We simply went on living our lives as normal as possible, eating hot dogs and going to the movies, riding bikes, and taking walks in the park. Aunt Lola would take me and Mary Rose to Sand Hill Cove Beach every Tuesday when my father had to work second shift, and we'd collect seashells.

Now, at thirty two years old, almost twenty years later, I still met with my Aunt Lola weekly. Only now instead of collecting seashells, we worked a booth together at the Bellingham Flea Market every Saturday and Sunday.

On occasion, I'd run into people from my past at the booth and be surprised at how much they had changed since the last time I saw them. Some got fatter or skinnier and some lost their good looks or gained some. But opening up that booth curtain and seeing Lia Stone standing before me surprised me in the biggest of ways. Lia Stone hadn't changed one bit. She still wore her hair cropped and sexy, kept her same toned body, and still didn't need an ounce of makeup to bring out her God-given features. That same enigmatic force laced her eyes and pulled me in with its lure. Just like an unopened present under the Christmas tree, she challenged my inner desires to peel away her façade and discover once and for all what waited inside.

I used to dream about kissing her when I first met her as a teenager. I saw the way she looked at other girls with a curiosity, and longed for her to look at me like that. I'd go back to my aunt's Winnebago, a few campsites down from the rec hall at the lake, and pretend we snuggled up against each other, kissing, running our fingers through our hair, and whispering sweet things to each other.

All of that halted the day she laughed at me in front of her sister and all of her friends.

I was walking past her to buy a soda at the refreshment stand. As I drew closer, I smiled. One of the friends yelled, "Do it." Then, next thing I knew, I tripped over the stick that Lia placed out in front of me. I fell flat on my face, scraping it on the gravel. They laughed at me. I looked up at Lia, the same pretty girl I dreamed of kissing every night that entire summer, and she turned ugly to me.

I hated to be laughed at like some weak, powerless girl.

"How dare she?" I said to my aunt later when I returned to her camper.

"She has no idea how special you are." My aunt gripped my shoulder, and a power surged through me.

That power surge marked the moment when I viewed my gift as a true treasure and no longer a curse. After that, I modeled after my Aunt Lola, embracing my gift.

I predicted things at the campground, and they came true. Instead of laughing at me, the other kids would ask me to read their thoughts and predict the future. They took interest in me. And I liked it.

They respected me. If they were playing the Ms. Pac-Man machine when I walked into the rec hall, they'd clear a path for me and let me take over the play. If I stood behind them in line for refreshments, they'd let me get ahead of them.

I reigned supreme in the social circle at Bowdish Lake Campground, except with Lia's adopted sister, Anna. She feared me, and often begged her friends to not talk to me. But, they stopped listening to her, and started listening to me.

Life was great.

Then one day I caught Lia peeking up at me over the rim of her diet soda. My tummy flipped. She curled up her finger and motioned for me to come over to her. I floated in her direction, swept up in a deep and poignant dance between longing and trepidation.

She stared at me. My mind blanked. I reached around for something witty and bold, or heck, even half-normal. "I like your hair."

She narrowed her eyes at me. "I don't really care."

The unexpected blow buckled me, popping my inflated ego. Its hiss echoed in the silence that followed.

I needed to correct that, so I sidestepped her insult and asked her, "How about a piece of gum for a sip of your soda?"

She handed me the can. "It's yours now." She stood up and scoffed. "I always knew you were a fake."

I placed my lips on the rim of the can where her lips had been two seconds earlier. I suddenly sensed her fear, even though she stood before me smirking with the upper hand. I imagined her hunched over in the corner of a tiger's cage, arms over her head in a protective pose. She cowered in the corner without protection from her friends, fearing that the tiger would come in and expose her weak skin by ripping through its delicate layers with one quick, easy swipe.

Lia feared me.

Now, so many years later, driving down Pulaski Boulevard with Lia Stone in my passenger seat, I wondered how she'd react to the emotional vision I got of her when I touched her arm on the roadside.

"Thanks again for driving us back," Lia said, once I pulled into the parking lot of her building.

"No problem." I smiled through my nerves.

She opened the door and went to climb out, but I placed my hand on her wrist to stop her. "So what is it you do up there behind those windows?"

The guy in the backseat leaned forward. "She drives us all crazy is what she does. When she's not doing that, I suppose one could say she creates award-winning marketing advertisements."

"Don't listen to him." A casual grin surfaced on Lia's face. "I create award-winning marketing *campaigns*."

"I stand corrected," he said.

I sensed a playful comradeship that served them both in ways no one outside of themselves would truly fit into or understand.

"Marketing, huh?" I paused to pretend I weighed a burning question. "The wellness center sure could use some help with that."

She locked eyes with me, and in her powerful gaze I found that appeal I used to dream about as a naïve teenager, the one that would set my heart racing and my inner thighs screaming for her touch.

She reached into her pocketbook, now scratched from the roadside catastrophe of an hour ago, and handed me her business card. "Call the number. Dean will set something up for us."

She climbed out of the car, but before closing the door, she leaned back in and whispered, "I'm guessing you're not a fake after all." She winked and closed my door.

I guarded my smile until she turned away, then I accelerated with an energy that surprised even me.

Chapter Three
Lia

Three years ago

I met Dean when he first arrived in the country. He moved to the United States from India as a young professional looking for a new opportunity. He arrived at the marketing firm of Edwards and Harding as my marketing assistant right off the cusp of failing India's premier and highly sought after Exams for Civil Services Program. Apparently, out of four hundred fifty thousand people who tested for that elite program, only twelve hundred passed and moved onto the next grueling test phase.

Dean did not pass.

So, he applied at our firm and our boss assigned him to my team.

At first, I felt sorry for him. He just came in, sat at his desk, and did his work quietly. Not until we initiated bagel Wednesdays did he start to open up to a few of us. He carried the weight of his future around like a bag full of bricks, always talking about how his parents expected him to come back to visit India one day as a success story.

He'd say things like, "Well, sometimes life tosses a person curves, and those curves force him off the promise road and unto one far less predictable." We'd nod and sink our teeth into the soft, warm bagels and agree.

He spoke with such eloquence, so much so, that I started to search for equally intelligent words only to come up short.

Well, the day had arrived when Dean finally lost his knack for eloquence when our boss, a big, tall, goofy-eyed man in his late forties, confronted him. I'd never seen Dean look so frightened.

The day started off as any other in the marketing firm with me prepping a cup of coffee in the kitchen. Then, Dean entered. He darted his eyes down to me, smiled, and got about his business of microwaving his curry chickpeas and jasmine rice breakfast.

I stood staring at the back of his head as he watched his white bowl go round and round in the microwave, wondering if he'd ever consider eggs instead. Then, in walked our big, goofy boss, Mr. Edwards. He wore an emerald green suit, which only served to showcase the extreme wideness of his body. He looked like a giant green bean plumped up with too many salty fluids.

He walked right up to Dean. "What did you do to Mr. Allen's logo?" He spoke slowly, deliberately, as if Dean couldn't hear him.

Dean's face flashed a dangerous shade of red. "His logo?"

"Yes, his logo."

Dean blinked a few too many times. "I fixed it for him."

Oh fixed. Not a good word choice.

Mr. Edwards got right up in Dean's face. "Did I permit you to access his account?"

"I was just trying to make it better, Mr. Edwards." Dean swallowed hard.

Make it better? Yikes. Nothing eloquent about that.

"Did I tell you that you could redesign his logo?" Mr. Edwards nudged his right shoulder, and Dean arched backwards against the counter. "Well, did I?" His voice grew too loud for the small kitchen nook.

The man sure had a temper and loved to wear it like a sick badge of honor.

"It wouldn't have resized correctly in its current state." Dean stuttered and darted his eyes to me, blinking again as if signaling for help in Morse code.

"I should fire you."

Dean's eyes twitched.

I had to do something to save the poor guy. "I told him to redesign the logo," I said. My words pinged against the orange cabinets and reverberated back against my clouded mind.

Mr. Edwards glared at me. "Why would you redesign anything without my permission?"

"Because I'm the marketing manager, and that's what I do." I spoke slowly and deliberately to him now.

A smirk surfaced on his cracked, chubby lips. He moved in closer, so close I could smell his cigarette breath. "You walk around this place barking out design orders like you're the queen of the marketing world. Frankly, I find that incomprehensible." His eyes flashed anger. "You're not the marketing manager anymore."

I stepped back, absorbing the impending gravity of the situation. "What do you mean, exactly?"

"You're fired."

"I'm fired?" My voice echoed in my head, banging around like a tin can gone wild in the back of a pickup truck bed.

"Fired." He seethed, and backed up. "Enjoy your curry, Dean." He walked away and waved at everyone who he passed like he *was* the Jolly Green Giant.

I couldn't be fired. I had plans. I needed a job, a steady paycheck, and the dignity that came along with that. My girlfriend, Sasha, and I had just secured a new apartment in the city. We purchased a new ergonomic massage chair from Brookstone, and the first payment was due in three weeks. I finally convinced Sasha that I could, too, manage my half of the responsibilities, even though she made almost double what I did as a life coach.

Dean and I just stood staring at each other in disbelief.

The buzz from the coffee pot filled the space, followed by a few too many rapid inhales and dramatic exhales from Dean.

Finally, he stopped hyperventilating and hung his jaw. "Why did you do that?"

I'd never seen such gratitude and relief shining in a person's eyes the way I did in that moment. That had to count for something, right? "Because it was the right thing for me to do."

"What are you going to do now?"

The air in my lungs vanished.

My God. I just lost my job. How would I ever tell Sasha that news? Or my parents? My father would pretend the news didn't bother him, but deep inside the wrinkles lining his smiling face would lurk the evidence of his disappointment. I'd once again sit behind his prized adopted daughter, Anna, in the great game of life.

The room swayed. The air grew stale. The smell of curry sat heavy in between us.

"I'll get a new job."

He regarded me with authority. "Go back out there and tell him the truth." He pointed toward Mr. Edward's office.

"It's not going to happen," I said. "I'm not going to beg. And besides, he's had it out for me ever since I—well, ever since I turned him down." I twisted my mouth to drive home the point.

"You can use that as leverage."

"No proof."

He paced the kitchen area. "I owe you in a very big way."

"Don't be so melodramatic." I brushed past him.

He grabbed my wrist. "I just got you fired. I need to repay you somehow."

I just got fired. I no longer had a job. I just destroyed my career.

The first sting of bitter tears hit the back of my eye. "You can repay me by not letting him ruin you too."

I left him with those words, and a few minutes later, with a box of my possessions bundled in my arms, I left him and everyone else behind to fend for themselves.

Numb as ever, I walked across the street to my favorite park. I sat down on my usual bench and gazed out at the geese floating on the pond.

Within five minutes, a very humble Dean sat next to me, staring down at the birds gathered at our feet.

We didn't talk right away. He understood without my having to say anything that I needed some space to let the news sink in. Then, finally, he spoke as he tossed a rock in the pond. "I wish he would've fired me too."

I chased his rock toss with a longer one. "That's the stupidest thing I've ever heard."

"Guilt is sitting on my shoulders right now and it's already too heavy."

"Well brush it off. He's a jerk and I'm happy to get away from him."

"I'm going to help you find a new job."

"I'll be fine." My voice cracked, and I coughed to cover it up.

"Yes," he said. "Yes, you certainly will be fine. If anyone would be fine after such an ordeal, it would be you."

I shivered, despite the overheated day. I tossed another rock. "I can do better than this place."

His eyes penetrated straight into me. "Of course you can."

"I can apply to many marketing firms."

He stared at me long and hard. "Why don't you just open up your own marketing firm?"

I shrugged and looked down at the geese pecking the grass. "Do you think I really could?"

"Do you really think you couldn't?"

I shrugged.

"I'll work for you."

I laughed. "I don't have a penny to my name."

"So? You live in America, the land of opportunity. Surely, a way has to exist. Hell, look at any convenience store and what do you see?"

I laughed again. "Immigrants running them."

"Exactly. If we can leave our country, safety, and family, and manage to sacrifice for a little while as we catch our bearings and start a business, surely, you can too." A sternness traced his words, a sharp contrast to his usual quiet demeanor. "Do you want your own business?"

"Yes." I'd give anything to serve my parents that kind of news. "I've always wanted to run my own show."

"If that idiot Mr. Edwards can run a business, you certainly can. It can't be that difficult."

True. How hard could it be? Open a line of credit with the bank, rent some space, buy some second hand office equipment, and open the doors. My mood started to perk up.

He sat up tall. "You've got the brains and the talent. You've been a remarkable boss, standing up for me like you did. People take notice. People admire you. You'll succeed."

His words pumped me up. "Yes, I can succeed."

"Let me help you research what you need to do. I'm resourceful and good at analyzing data and breaking it down into digestible chunks."

"I'm capable of doing that myself."

"With all due respect, you tend to get a little overwhelmed in stressful situations."

His straight face caught me off guard. "I don't get overwhelmed."

"You get overwhelmed. Your eye is twitching, and you haven't even been without a job for fifteen minutes."

I covered my twitching eye. "I'm working on it."

"Admit it," he said with a warmth radiating from his growing smile. "You need my help. Please, won't you let me assist you?"

His sincerity comforted me. "We'll see." I offered him a smile. "You should get back in there before he fires you too."

"Doesn't matter. I'm going to be working for you soon, remember?"

The twinkle in his eye powered me with a rising hope.

"Will you let me help you?" he asked.

I went to protest, but the small cry at the end of his words stopped me. He needed closure to my saving him from getting fired. "Fine." I gazed at him, at a loss for the next move. "I've got your cell number from my directory." I tapped my box of belongings. "We'll stay in touch."

"Great." He stood up and shook my hand. "You're going to be better than ever."

"Dean?"

He crossed his arms over his chest as if arming up for a lengthy question.

"Why are you offering to help me this way? It's way beyond repayment."

"Because it's the right thing for me to do." He winked, and in that wink I saw a man's spirit burst to life, as if he needed that shove out the door as much as I probably did. "Have a good day, Ms. Stone." He headed off.

"Dean," I yelled to him.

"Yes, Ms. Stone."

"If you want to repay me, you can start by never calling me Ms. Stone again. That stupid boss set that stupid rule. I am Lia to you now. Understand?"

"Crystal clear." He waved. "I'll be in touch, Lia."

I watched him walk away, dumbfounded by all that had just transpired in a matter of half an hour. One moment I'm in the kitchen heating up a cup of coffee and prepping for a nine o'clock briefing meeting with the senior staff, and the next I'm a jobless woman hanging out on a park bench devising plans to open up a business.

For the next hour, I walked around the park, conjuring up all sorts of ideas for that 'said' business. I could rent a small office in one of those downtown renovated mills, the ones with the tall brick walls and sprawling windows. My staff would have bagels delivered for our weekly team meetings, and meet over drinks for happy hour.

Why not? Why couldn't I open up my own business? Sasha did it. Surely I could too.

I walked onward, past a set of new mothers pushing their baby carts around, and thought about my parents and their potential reaction to my getting fired. I'd do anything not to have to face them with the ugly event of the day. After all they had sacrificed for me in putting me through private school and college, I couldn't disappoint them with my problems. I would get back on track, run a successful business, build up my savings, and help them ease into retirement without a care, as I always planned.

My smile started to fade slightly as I reminded myself I had no job and no way of moving forward in life, only backward. I walked past the bakery on the corner where I ate my breakfast each morning, past the bank that I'd have to visit real soon to inquire about a business loan, and back past the place that, for years, served as my home away from home; the place where I earned a paycheck every two weeks to pay all the bills piling up in my mailbox.

The panic swept in like a bad storm and stole my confidence.

I was fired.

I had no job. No one would be waiting for me to return from lunch that day. I would not have a place to go to the next morning. I would never sit at the head of the conference table and conduct meetings with my staff and interns. No more brainstorming sessions over lunch spreads from Panera. And that vacation Sasha and I wanted to take to the Caribbean in the spring, vanished before my eyes. I would not have any paycheck entering my bank account in two weeks. I would not have money to pay my new apartment rent or my massage chair bill. Christmas was around the corner and I would have no money to buy Sasha that sapphire bracelet she stared at every time we walked by Jarod's at the mall. How could I start my own business without any money to my name? I only had bills.

So, I needed a job, not a business.

Where would I find an employer who would want to hire someone who was fired?

I managed to control my panic until I cleared past the windows of my boss's corner office. I didn't start to cry until I entered Dunkin Donuts, at which point I convulsed right there in line as I ordered a medium coffee with extra cream and extra sugar, to the dismay of a helpless young kid who looked about ready to throw up from sheer fright of what he must've seen in my face. I thanked him profusely, tossed my last five dollar bill on the counter and bolted toward the back table right underneath the Keno machine.

I sat in that booth, drowning myself in extra sweetness when in walked a group of ladies. They powered through those doors like they owned the joint, shoving the donut scented air out of their way with a wide swing to their arms. Confidence traced every inch of their faces. A few minutes later, they sat in a booth adjacent from me sipping on black coffees and flinging their straight, bouncy hair over their toned shoulders.

The blonde one spoke first. Her voice, as smooth as silk and without a trace of an irritating accent, sailed through the space in a pleasing melody.

"I say we get the guys from that furniture store to represent the team. They're perfect."

"They're also expensive," the red head said, curling her eyes up to meet the alpha blonde's.

"It's all in the delivery," the blonde said.

"I agree." The third lady scooted up taller, straightening her blouse's collar. "Let's do it."

They nodded at each other with a devilish grin.

They were so put together and powerful. I liked them. I liked their poise. I liked their confidence. I liked their group think. They fed off each other. The business world answered to them, not the other way around.

Sitting in that booth, staring at a trio of powerful ladies, my strength caught back up with me.

Dean was right. I could be successful. I could take matters into my own hands. I could be my own boss. I could carve my own path. I didn't have to let another human being overpower me. I could create my own destiny.

Life was too short for anything less than that.

A moment later, I called Dean from that booth. "When can we meet?"

"Let me call you back in five minutes. I'm on the other line."

He hung up, and the echo sat with me for those long five minutes.

As promised, he called right on the mark. "Sorry about that. I was just on the phone with Mr. Allen."

"Mr. Allen? The logo Mr. Allen?"

"Yes."

"Did our goofy boss urge you call him and apologize?"

"That goofy boss has no idea I just talked to him or that I've been talking to him regularly about his accounts."

Mr. Allen was one of the biggest clients of the marketing firm. He owned and operated a dozen small businesses from flower shops, to hair salons, to gas stations, you name it. "Are you trying to get fired?"

He inhaled deeply, as if already annoyed with my sarcasm. "I'm trying to build a future."

"By hijacking your boss's client?"

"I didn't mean to change his logo. I just wanted to play around with a concept, and accidentally saved the new logo over the existing. Apparently, Mr. Edwards has territorial issues."

"No," I said. "Mr. Edwards has self-awareness issues. And you managed to step on his big fat ego."

"Well—" He paused. "I sent the revised logo to Mr. Allen just a few minutes ago, and he loved it."

"You are trying to get fired."

"No. Again, I'm trying to build a future. The man obviously understands business. He's willing to mentor you tomorrow morning at his home office if you're up for it?"

"Mr. Allen? Seriously?"

"I told you, I'm resourceful and can get things done."

My heart beat wildly at the prospect of a real meeting with one of the area's leading entrepreneurs. "Where and when?"

"I'll text you the address."

"You're coming too, I hope?" I asked.

"Mr. Allen wouldn't have agreed otherwise."

Of course not.

He hung up and I sat in the booth like a goofball with a grin too large for my face.

# #

When I returned to our apartment later on, Sasha was making herself a shake with peanut butter and almond milk.

"I've got some bad news," I said, reaching out for the peanut butter covered spoon.

"I've got to run and meet a potential client, so can it wait?"

"I got fired today."

She scanned my face, as if looking for the pun.

"I've already got a meeting lined up with a potential mentor to talk with me about opening my own business."

She snapped away from me and continued blending her shake. She poured the thick vanilla cream into her shake tumbler, and finally looked me in the eye. "I'm sure you'll figure it out." She patted my back on her way past me. "There's some rice and tuna in the fridge."

No hug. No kiss. Not even a fight to stir the stagnant emotions a little.

The life had been sucked out of our relationship, and we hadn't even paid our first month's rent yet.

Such a typical cycle. Start out fresh, end stagnant. Happened every time. Why should my experience with Sasha be any different?

That was life for you.

# #

When Sasha returned home at eleven o'clock that night, I pretended to be asleep. She nudged me anyway. "I don't think this is going to work out anymore."

I sat up. "Because I was fired?"

"It dawned on me in the kitchen earlier. We hit our first bump as a couple, and I'm not ready to hit bumps in a relationship yet. I'm not ready for the fun to be done. I'm not ready for real life to hit us and knock us down after only six months together. We used to have fun, remember? But, since we domesticated ourselves, nesting in this new apartment that I don't even like, it feels too serious and real. We're so young, and there's so much I want to explore. I feel trapped. And now with this news of getting fired, I feel the pressure even more. I don't want responsibility. I just want to keep having fun. But I think that's over now that real life caught up to us."

"Life is real. What do you expect?"

"I'm not ready to commit myself to real life yet. I want to date and get silly on wine, wrestle on the living room floor, be spoiled with flowers and chocolate. I'm not ready to say goodbye to a first date. I like change. It keeps me young and fresh in my mind, and right now, I feel kind of old and static. It's too routine."

"Then we'll change things up." I reached out for her, desperate to feel her in my arms again.

She pulled away. "No, I want to walk away." She stared into my eyes. "I'm going to walk away."

"Right now?"

"My sister's waiting outside in my car for me."

"It's that easy for you. Just get some tough news and walk away?"

She shrugged. "We had a fun run. Let's preserve that memory and just move on."

"So I was just temporary fun?"

"Everything's temporary. It's best not to fight it and just enjoy things for what they are, then move on when it's over."

I turned away from her, and she didn't fight to turn me back around. She simply gathered a few items and walked away, letting me know she'd be back in the morning to gather the rest of her things.

#

That next morning, when Mr. Allen ushered us into his beautiful home, I pushed Sasha far into the back of my mind. I would not let her ruin the learning opportunity in front of me.

We toured his gardens, his three living rooms, and his home office. He showed us books filled with accolades for his chemical product patents that he helped produce along with a few other scientists, notable scientists he added. The man, with hair as white as fresh snow and wrinkles deep as worn leather, enjoyed stepping back into his past accomplishments with us. He talked as if in a rush to get out every last thought on the subject of his still fruitful career.

I searched for a way to break in, but couldn't find one in the mix of the rapid-fire energy pooling around us. At one point, he stopped just long enough to cough.

I must have smiled too broadly because he caught onto it and frowned. I immediately wiped that smile off my face and surrendered to listening with a cocked head and arch to my right eyebrow. My listening signal reignited his exuberance, and he dove back into monotone descriptions of his dealings with the U.S. patent office.

Under the veil of his watchful eye, I prayed that Dean would shut this man's motor for a second so I could pee. He offered no break. We had come to learn how to open a business, and he tossed us boasts about chemical patents instead.

I had no idea what half of his words even meant.

Dean sat on the edge of his seat, timing his listening cues with precision, and pretending as if he understood the lingo of brilliant scientists who jumped for joy over atoms mixing with each other.

I kept eyeing the room around us, with its tall, hand-carved, wooden furniture and elaborate tapestries that hung sixteen feet tall, volleying escape ideas back and

41

forth. I could pretend to get an emergency phone call. I could tumble over in pain. I could feign a migraine.

I needed to get out of there and find a job.

I had bills.

I had responsibilities.

I also had a new healthy respect for silence.

I squirmed and tapped Dean's leg.

We exchanged a knowing look.

"Excuse me Mr. Allen," Dean said, interrupting him mid-sentence about a metal's property he discovered, yadda yadda yadda. "My friend wanted to hear your ideas on how to start a business."

I braced for the unknown. Would he point us to the door for interrupting him? Would he continue on his metal rant?

"Well, that's simple Dean," he said with a straight face. "She needs to do what I did."

"What's that exactly?" Dean jockeyed for position like a salesperson with an edge.

Meanwhile, I sat like a third wheel with no business being in the room, as they discussed my future. No wonder Mr. Edwards liked the guy so much.

"Well first things first. She needs to pay off and cut all debt from her life. One never wants to start business in debt. Then, save. Then and only then, open up the business owing nothing to no one."

I laughed.

Mr. Allen ignored my outburst and charged forward. "She also needs to be clear on why it is she wants to be in business."

"What else?" Dean asked.

His lips remained in a straight line. His eyes blazed into Dean's. He stopped talking. He allowed silence to fill the space. I heard a robin chirp. The fan creaked above our heads. The curtains swayed and rustled, kissed by the wind coming in through the screen.

Really? Silence? Now?

I cleared my throat. "Exactly. What else, Mr. Allen?"

Mr. Allen's wrinkles spread as he smiled at me. "You need to have passion. Can you convince me of your passion?"

How? Jump up for joy? Run in circles? Sing a song? The guy was a loony.

Dean tapped my arm. "You heard the man. Tell him."

I had passion. I had passion for things like chocolate, Merlot, and four color ads, CMYK and RGB color palettes, and crop marks. How would a scientist understand that passion?

"Lia?" Dean snapped. "Tell him your passion."

"My passion." I scanned the ceiling and its crown molding, the gaudy rag-rolled orange walls, and then Dean's panicked face for my passion. "It's hard to put to words."

Dean blinked and tightened his lips, begging me to stand up to the moment, the moment he went on a limb to set up for me.

"Tell me what it is you want to do," Mr. Allen said.

I settled on logic. "I want to open up a marketing firm."

"Why?" he asked, crossing his leg over the other in a move much too fluid for someone so stodgy.

What did the man with all the answers to world metals want to hear? "It's profitable."

He shook his head. "A baker doesn't open up a bakery to sell muffins. A baker opens up a bakery to bring a sense of comfort to her customers. That's her passion, you see, bringing others a sense of comfort through her baked goods. It's not the product. It's the emotion her product delivers."

I searched for a better answer in the afghan fibers under my legs; one that wouldn't sound like I just picked it off someone's cover letter.

Dean jumped to my rescue. "She's fantastic at it. She motivates people. She's the reason people rise out of bed in the morning, drive through maddening city traffic, and pay enormous parking fees just to be a part of the energy she creates. When an ad campaign comes together in all the right dynamics, her spirit balloons so wide, the room cannot contain it. She's infectious, and is too talented to not be creating that same environment in her own business. That's why."

My jaw dropped. My back suddenly got too heavy to stay erect, and I collapsed backwards against the oversized pillow. "Really?" I whispered.

Dean ignored me, and focused on Mr. Allen. Failure of any kind was not an option for him, and who was I to get in his way?

Mr. Allen tapped his fingers against his wooden arm chair. He rose to his feet. "Let's drink some tea and talk about your finances."

Talk about my pathetic finances, did we ever. An hour later, embarrassed about my lack of financial responsibility, Dean thanked Mr. Allen for his time and I apologized for wasting it.

We stood in between our cars, fumbling with our sets of keys.

I broke the silence. "So, it's been established that I need to start applying for jobs."

"I wouldn't surrender just yet." He tossed his keys in the air and caught them before opening up his door, sliding in, and driving off.

I watched as he sped down the road, dizzy with how much I just wanted my old job back so I could slide back into that comfortable mode where I knew what sat ahead. If the past two days, filled with all of its political pulls and pushes, represented a typical day of running a business, it would kill me. Why would I ever want to bring that into my life anyway?

I slipped into my truck and realized I hadn't thought of Sasha once since entering Mr. Allen's house. A strength settled into my heart as I sped out of his driveway. Fuck Sasha. I didn't have time to worry about her at that point anyway.

She was right. Everything was fleeting, even my feelings for her.

I had a new mission in life, and I had complete control over how I'd pursue it. I would focus on only what I could control from then on.

Later that afternoon, long after I drove myself home and ate a fattening lunch of pizza and fries with a side of coke, I sat in front of my computer scanning online job portals. Then, Dean called.

"Are you ready for some good news?"

I stopped reading the overly-complicated job posting in front of me. "I could sure use some."

"I've got Mr. Allen on the other line, and he's ready to talk funding."

"With me?"

"He found out you saved me from getting fired. Needless to say, he's all yours now. He'll pad your account with whatever you need."

"Oh my gosh." I jumped up and paced my living room. "I'm not prepared."

"He already knows that."

"Right." I ran my hand through my wild hair. "Send him through." My voice rose up to meet with my joy.

"Oh, by the way," he said. "I hope I'm not being too presumptuous when I tell you that I prefer my own office with a window, and one of those cute little Keurig machines."

"Just pass him through," I said, already taking the liberty of setting the perimeters of a proper working relationship.

Present Day

After Willow dropped us off from the flea market ordeal, Dean knew I'd need some wine. Not more than five minutes off the elevator, we broke out one of the bottles of Merlot we had left over from a benefit dance we helped organize for the local animal shelter. I settled into one of the cushy chairs in the reception area and sipped thoughtfully.

Dean sat down on a heavy sigh. "I'm not going to get much work done on the proposal."

"Screw the proposal."

"The allergy is eating up my mind."

I knew it. I knew he would trip over that prediction. Some things never changed. Even Willow's aunt had the same impact on people, freaking them out with psychic babble. "It's total bullshit."

He sat up tall, combing his hand through his thick hair, nursing a worried look. "How did Willow's aunt know about your truck?"

"Who knows? Maybe she paid a guy to watch people as they entered. It's kind of a creative way to build a loyal client base. Reel people in by scaring them just enough to excite a craving for more information." I sipped again, balancing on the smooth, black cherry flavor.

"I'm going to have nightmares for weeks over this." He sniffed the wine, swirled it, and then sipped it like a wine snob. He winced. "Is it me, or does wine just suck?"

I swallowed a mouthful. "I don't care. It's wine."

We sipped in silence, both presumably tangled up in psychic wonder.

"So," Dean said, lounging back against his chair. "Was it me or did I sense a little chemistry flying around that front seat?" He ran his finger around the tip of the glass, setting up too casual of a question.

"Chemistry?" I laughed. "No, you witnessed pure gratitude for help needed. She didn't have to drive us all the way across the Massachusetts state line to bring us back to Providence the way she did."

"Technically, I suppose she crossed state lines to help us out. But, the drive took us twenty minutes." He arched his eyebrow at me. "So, no, gratitude is not it. The vibe in that car reminded me of an awkward first date when silence is the one obstacle both parties try to avoid at all costs. I could sense the rush to fill it on both of your parts."

I poured myself more wine. "I'd never get involved with a psychic."

46

He chuckled. "Famous last words. I can see it now."

"It's a shame." I twirled my wine around, watching it flirt with the edge of the glass.

"A shame?"

"That she still freaks me out. We'd probably get along great otherwise."

"I suppose it would be rather difficult to engage with someone who can read your mind. Imagine how entertained she'd be in your head."

Some minds were better left unopened. "When she calls, just tell her I'm overbooked and not able to take on new clients. I don't have time to be dabbling in affairs of the occult. That's one door I have no desire to open."

He raised up his glass. "If she calls, you mean?"

I chugged the rest of my wine. "Yeah. Whatever. If. When. Just blow her off."

He watched me with a smirk on his face. I kicked his shin. He kicked mine back. I stuck out my tongue at him. He went a step further and chucked me the bird before sticking his finger in the wine and stirring it. "This would taste so much better with fruit, triple sec and some brandy."

I stood up and took his wine from him. "You shouldn't be drinking anyway. I'm going to need a ride to my parents after we find a new air compressor."

I downed his glass and met his stern gaze.

"Right, because whatsoever else would I be doing with my gorgeous, sunny Saturday afternoon?"

I tapped his shoulder. "Playing Solitaire like you do every Saturday."

He stood up. "Well I'll have you know that I play it online, and I've met some pretty incredible friends on there."

"How exciting for you."

"Well, hey, at least I have a social life."

His honesty stung, even wrapped up in the friendliness of the banter. "I prefer work."

He pointed his finger at me. "That's by your choice. Ever since Sasha walked out of your life, you've been using work as a tool to fill her void."

I shrugged. "Work is a trusted partner. What can I say?"

"That's sad." He nodded and offered me a knowing smile. "You're in love with work."

Work would never hurt me. It would only serve to help me in life. "Enough about me. Let's get hunting."

"Let me go to the bathroom, and after I'll see if I can find an air compressor for dear old dad."

"I'll search on my computer too. We'll compete. First one to find an air compressor gets a week of bagels starting Monday."

"Deal." He charged toward the men's room, and I hung a sharp left to my office.

While Dean was in the bathroom, the phone rang. I let it go to voicemail and began to search EBay for a comparable air compressor. It had to be the same exact one because as far as my father would know, I got it from Ernie that day. Dean flew by my door en route to enter the challenge. Two minutes later, he stood in my door. "You're never going to guess who left us a message."

"Us?"

"I forgot the package of terry cloth napkins in her back seat."

I stopped scrolling. "You did that on purpose."

"Did not."

"Did too." I stood up. "You wanted an excuse for her to call because you wanted another chance to ask her aunt about your allergies."

He stared me down, and then caved. "She saw your truck getting broken into. The lady's onto something that we mere mortals are not. I was just being practical."

"Go call her then. Get your precious terry cloth napkins back from her."

He turned to go, but then stopped. "You're not the least bit curious about her?"

"She's cute, yeah, but she's always been a wacko to me." I shooed him. "Now go, call her and get it over with. We've got an air compressor to find."

48

"I'll wait until later. I don't want her to think we're too anxious. You know?"

"Yeah. We are not anxious at all."

"You said, we." He cupped his fist under his chin and released a giggle.

"Just go before I win the competition."

#

Thirty minutes after Dean first jumped into air compressor competitive mode, he yelled out. "Found one."

I ran over to his office. "Great. Where is it?"

He folded his lips in. "You're not going to like this."

"Can we pick it up and get to my father's party in reasonable amount of time?"

"Not unless you've got a time machine." He twisted his mouth. "It's in Kentucky."

Five minutes later, air compressor ordered and slated for delivery to my father's house two days later, Dean zoomed me off to my father's party empty-handed and heavy-hearted. When he pulled up, I placed my hand on his wrist. "Do you want to come in and enjoy a party with your mean boss and best friend?"

He didn't answer with words. He simply put the car in reverse and backed into a spot between two trucks that looked an awful lot like mine, then turned off the ignition. "Thank you."

"For what?"

"For saving me from another afternoon of Solitaire."

"Well, it is the right thing for me to do," I said on a friendly wink.

Chapter Four

I couldn't sleep that night after Dean dropped me back off from my father's party. My mind kept wandering back to the events of the day. My poor truck. Poor Dean with his new worry. And, Willow. Wow, how she had changed.

I imagined a fairy godmother, propping her up on a pedestal and waving a magic wand around to turn her into an exquisite sight. Gone were those thick eyeglasses, that ugly bowl haircut, and that square, straight body. In their place, a prism of beauty shined its spectacular array of visual appeal.

Still, I couldn't get past that weird side of her I remembered from those campground days. Underneath the polished hair and sparkly blue eyes, that weird girl had to still be alive, peeking up over the edges of her beauty and waiting to pounce out with a prediction when the mood struck her.

She used to freak out Anna, my adopted sister, who even back then would walk around with a set of rosary beads in her pocket. I always got a kick out of how Anna would panic whenever Willow drifted past. She'd say how Willow the Weirdo walked by her with that stealthy look in her eye again, like she honed in on her psychic radar and searched her mind for treasure that didn't belong to her. She warned me to never stare directly at her because her eyes were like weapons that could pull innocent people into her close range so she could snack on their thoughts.

"Psychics should have to walk around with signs that warned people within close proximity that their thoughts were not secure," she had said one night after Willow bumped into her in the refreshments line. "At least people could censor their thoughts."

I'd always imagined Willow snooping around people's minds and reading them like a library catalog. How many books did I have in my head, and how much entertainment did they offer her? How many times had she flipped through my brain catalog, and uncovered something so private, even I didn't want anything to do with it?

My sister used to wear a Red Sox baseball cap to the rec hall just so Willow couldn't access her brain waves. When Willow would gaze at Anna with her laser sharp focused eyes, Anna would run off back to our campsite and to the comfort of the bonfire and s'mores.

Ah, the good ole days.

I chuckled out loud in my empty room, pulling up my blankets and wrapping them tighter.

I would upset my sister greatly if I opened up that wormhole into the past. If I upset Anna, I'd upset my father too. My father, like most people, adored Anna and trusted her sharp instinct.

I should just nix the offer to consult with Willow the Weirdo to keep the peace. Hopefully Dean hadn't called her back yet.

I rolled over and stared up at my shadowed ceiling.

Had she read my mind that day? I thumbed through my thoughts of earlier. Air compressor. Strange lady with clown outfit. Dean being a fool paying fifty dollars for a palm reading. How incredible Willow looked when she walked out from behind that black booth curtain and smiled. Damn, gorgeous and sexy didn't describe her enough. I definitely didn't expect to find such a surprise at the flea market.

Did she sense the flutters in my stomach when she tossed out that subtle flirt to me on the roadside?

I banked on her weirdness to keep me grounded. My tummy might've enjoyed the flutters at that point, but those flutters only lasted as long as the first argument.

Screw that.

I stretched my arms up over my head to work out the kink in my neck. On my exhale, I wondered how one even became a psychic. Was a person born with that knowledge? Did someone teach it to her?

My imagination began to run wild.

Was the person's brain wired differently? Did it run in the family? If Willow had kids, would they too be able to freak people out by telling their past, present and future?

Were Willow and her aunt the devil's helpers or were they just a couple of fakes who simply got lucky with their guesses?

Did the aunt just guess wrong about Dean's allergy or would he really suffer one day out of the blue? Poor guy had already started to bite his nails down to nothing over the imminent allergy attack that steadied itself to launch an assault on his skinny, delicate body. I wouldn't be surprised if he already put a call in to his general practitioner for a full body scan to see if the little allergy critters were already wreaking havoc on his system. I could see the future now. Dean would place his clammy hand in mine as he underwent allergy testing. With each prick, he'd wince a little louder until he'd begin sobbing.

Actually sobbing might be a good thing. Dean confessed to me that he had never cried a tear past infancy. Not one tear. He said he wished he could, but no matter how hard he tried, he couldn't cry.

The guy never lied.

I looked at my trusted analog clock. It just ticked past the eleven thirty mark. God, where had the night gone?

I needed to get Dean and Willow out of my mind. I needed sleep.

I turned over and looked out at the full moon through the slit in my curtains.

How did her aunt know about my truck? Did she see the scene playing out like a movie minus the popcorn, Twizzlers and giant-sized Diet Coke? Did life play out for them both like a movie screen where they could witness the good and the bad, and escape from their lives and into others? If so, did they get mostly horror flicks, or did the occasional warm-hearted story filter through and allow them to deliver happy endings instead of broken steering columns and doomsday allergic reactions?

Now I wondered, could a psychic *really* delve that deep into everyone's brains? Or could they just read snippets from certain people, like luck of the draw. Maybe

53

they could only get signals from people in tune with such nonsense, and those who didn't believe in it, subconsciously blocked them from reading thoughts by masking them with a protective coating.

I rolled over on my other side and stared at the friendship card Dean had sent to me of a little boy kissing the cheek of a little girl as he offered her a bouquet of flowers.

I wondered, what would it be like to kiss a psychic? What if, in some delusional state, I decided to kiss Willow? Would she experience my secret thoughts? Being that connected to the root of her subject like that, I'd imagine she'd have a front row seat to whatever silly, chaotic, and dramatic thoughts I happened to spiel out at the time. If I hated the way she kissed, she'd know it. How horrible. She'd know, and then I wouldn't be able to look her in the eye ever again. I guessed though, having my thoughts read instead of spoken could be advantageous, too. If I wanted her to soften her lips and swirl her tongue a little more, I could just think that and voila, she'd receive the intended message and shape up the kiss. Without a word, we'd solve all issues and continue onward satisfied.

Being in a relationship with a psychic would be pretty cool in that regard. I'd never have to bring up awkward things like I had to with my ex, Sasha. I'd never have to answer dumb questions about whether that outfit added weight to her or argue that her crunching on ice cubes drove me crazy. I'd just sit close, focus on what I wanted to say, turn my head in her direction and think it loud in my mind.

I stared at my clock. So much for a full eight hours of sleep. If I fell asleep right that very second, I'd get six hours and thirty-two minutes.

Alright, I needed to disengage the mind.

I rolled over to my back and stared at the shadowed ceiling again.

I counted the ticks from my clock.

I stretched my legs.

When those two things didn't work, I resorted to counting backwards. I recited one hundred all the way down to twenty five. At that point, I sat up.

How the hell did that lady know about my damn truck? If she didn't scam, it had to be real. If real, how did it work?

My curiosity stole any chance for sleep. I climbed out of bed and decided to do a little research.

I entered my dining room, sat at my laptop and began googling. Thousands of pages popped up. I read through the first page of Google's search findings and exhaled, overwhelmed with the amount of information. I just wanted a simple one-sheeter to tell me how it worked, if it worked, and why it worked.

If anyone could find it, Dean could.

Despite the late eleven o'clock hour, and knowing full well Dean was probably reclining back in his sleep number bed with his Tempurpedic pillow and gelled eye mask, I reached for my cell anyway and called him.

"I need your help," I said.

"It's eleven thirty at night."

"It's important."

"If I'm going to talk to you at this hour, I want lunch at Twin Oaks next week."

"Fine," I said. "Can you find me credible scientific information on psychic ability?"

"Now?"

"I can't sleep, and I won't be able to until I understand how the inner mechanics of the psychic mind works."

"You're freaking out," he said. "Stop freaking out. I'm not going to die of an asthma attack. I already managed to line up an inhaler just in case."

"What? Where? When?"

"I have connections."

"Of course you do." Dean's idea of connections meant the back room of some shady shop in the middle of downtown Providence where old women, with crooked spines, doled out medicinal herbs from tin cans hidden behind a beaded curtain. "I'm not concerned about your death by asthma attack. I see you dying in a far more heroic manner, like saving a dog in a burning building or something like that."

"Dogs hate me. I won't be saving any dogs."

"You fear dogs. That's why they hate you, and that's why I resent you a little. How can I ever adopt a puppy with that silly fear of yours? I'd never be able to take her to work with me, and you'd never come over and visit."

"Again," he said. "It's eleven thirty. Can we get this conversation moving?"

"I can't wrap my brain around how that woman knew about the guy breaking into my truck."

"Well, Willow is coming in on Monday morning at ten o'clock to drop off the terry cloth napkins. No need to do internet research in the middle of the night. You can ask her yourself. She's in your calendar for a meeting."

A jolt shot through me. "You already called her?"

"Yes, and I told her how excited you were to meet with her."

"I should fire you for this."

"Well, could you hurry it up? I have a dream to reenter where I am journeying on the edge of a lush green field, picking—"

"—Good night."

"Wait, Lia." He paused. "She's also excited to meet with you. Her words. Not mine."

"Good night," I said again, feigning a stern tone.

I hung up and sighed, trying to calm the rising nervous tingle in the pit of my stomach; the second nervous tingle of the day.

Screw research. I needed a good long soak in the tub, some Mozart, and chocolate.

# #

I drove to work in a rented Jeep Wrangler that Monday morning, enjoying the fresh air on my face and thinking of the day ahead.

I would meet Willow again.

My stomach knotted.

A few hours into my day, she arrived. When she walked by my glass walled office wearing a red dress and straight, smooth styled hair, a hushed whistle escaped my lips. She walked across the wooden floor, tapping out a tantric beat with her bouncy, confident gait. She looked like a woman in love with life, and ready to tackle the day with the spirit of a tiger; cool, calm and collected.

Part the aisles staff, we've got ourselves a tigress beauty.

I slid off my chair, as though she'd hear me before I could sneak a better peek, and tiptoed to my doorway. Dean greeted her with a flushed face and a bow. She handed him his package of terry cloth napkins, and Dean offered her way too many nods to be good for the tendons in his skinny neck. He transformed into a bobble head, bee bopping his head around like a spring-loaded toy.

She cocked her head, and her hair swayed off to the side, exposing her toned, golden shoulders.

My tummy broke out into that flipping thing all over again as I walked out to greet her.

Dean wore a stupid grin on his face that told me he, although not operating with a single psychic bone in his body, could read my wayward mind in that moment.

"Oh look, here she is now," he said, waving me over.

Willow turned around, and the current she circulated with that tiniest movement, created a windfall of tickles in me. "Thanks again for the drive back here," I said, offering her my hand.

"Oh, my pleasure." Her left eye twitched when her hand landed in mine.

"Shall we?" I waved her toward my office.

She nodded and followed. I only peeked back once, and, in my view, I saw Dean's eyes sparkle with delight in the halo of her blondeness.

Once inside, I opted to sit on the couch. "It's less formal."

She sat, and crossed one long leg over the other.

I never remembered seeing those creamy, long legs under her baggy jean shorts as kids.

"So, you look very nice this morning," I said, smiling.

She smoothed her dress over her exposed leg. "Thanks, I normally go to work in yoga pants, but today is a special day. I get to listen to my son and daughter sing at their recital."

I continued to smile through a peculiar jolt of disappointment. "Oh you have children. How old are they?"

"Eight and six."

"So you got married?"

She curled her eyes up to meet mine. "I did."

"How long have you been married?"

She waved off my question. "Oh, we got divorced a few years back."

A peculiar jolt of relief now washed over me. "Not the right one?"

"Nah. Didn't work out." She rolled her eyes and released a scoff. "At all."

Wouldn't she have known about the eventual divorce? "How did you not see that coming ahead of time?"

She paused, reflecting on my jab. "It doesn't work that way."

I wanted to know how it worked. Did she sense something about me? Could she tell her naked calf teased me? I blocked the question, and focused on the meeting at hand.

I inhaled for rebalance, and she broke in with another question. "Did you get married too?"

I studied her, curious to see a display of psychic recognition spread across her face as the biographical question sat between us. "You don't know the answer to that either?"

"How would I?"

"Don't you have special powers to reach into my mind and pull out those kinds of facts?"

She laughed. "Seriously, it doesn't work that way."

I eased back against the couch. "Well, how does it work? Do you go searching people's minds for information?"

"Of course not."

"Okay, then do the facts just symbiotically seek you out, like a plant's roots searching for water? Are we roots to psychics, searching for someone to help us provide nourishment in the form of predictions?"

"Wow. What an incredible analogy."

I offered a cocky smile. "I am a marketing woman. It's what I do. I fish for information so I can provide proper nourishment to clients. That's what marketers do. And, I would imagine what many psychics do. They start asking random questions, fishing for someone willing to bite the bait."

"I can't speak for others. I personally don't fish. If someone's energy is open, I sometimes get a sense. Thankfully, not with everyone because my mind would be on constant play mode. I'd be kind of crazy, right?"

"So when you shook my hand just a few minutes ago..."

Her eyes flirted with mine, latching onto a piece of my soul again and tugging at it. "You were nervous."

"Oddly, not that time."

She playfully kicked my leg. "So, you do admit to being nervous around me at some point before, then?"

I fidgeted for a better position.

"I knew it," she said, arching her eyebrow. "I always knew you and your sister were afraid of me."

"I don't scare easily. My sister, on the other hand, feared you." I rose to her challenging brow arch. "She didn't like having her thoughts invaded."

"She's an open book."

"Anna?"

She nodded. A tease played in her eyes.

"Did you ever sneak into mine?"

She leaned in and whispered, "I don't sneak into the minds of people I like."

Her delicate whisper dizzied me.

Her eyes remained soft. "In all honesty, I don't read thoughts. I just sense energy."

Could she sense the delightful flutters in my tummy?

Stop it, I silently screamed. *Stop being foolish.* "Okay, then. Some things are better left a mystery, I suppose."

"You've always been a mystery."

I looked away, indicating we were done talking about me. I raised my invisible shield, protecting myself from further banter. "Let's hear about this wellness center."

"It's a long story."

"I've got all day." I relaxed back, draping my arm over the top of the couch, like I really did have all the time in the world to listen to her.

"Right. And I've got a recital to attend. So, I'll condense it for you."

I waved her onward. "Great. Proceed then. What convinced you to enter the wellness industry?" I suddenly felt like my angel investor, Mr. Allen.

"I always loved yoga and dreamed of centering my life around it as a career one day. It took many years for that to happen. I have my aunt to thank for bringing me face-to-face with the opportunity. The means to my yoga career came walking through our flea market booth one day. Yvonne is her name. Yvonne is a licensed acupuncturist and holistic healer, and she captured my aunt's heart the moment she sat down before her to chat about her psychic abilities. Long story short, they hooked up, and Yvonne eventually asked my aunt to join her as a healing guide at her wellness center. She refused. My aunt loves to run her own show at the flea market. Ms. Independent." She chuckled. "Then she told Yvonne that I taught meditative yoga, and I've been the lead yoga instructor there ever since."

"Do you have a say over marketing?"

"She trusts my judgment." She eased into a soft grin. "As well as my reasoning for talking with you today."

"And your reasoning would be?" I asked, carefully opening up the slit to that new world and peeking into its mystery.

"Marketing of course." Her eyes flickered as if trying to convince herself of that.

"Just marketing?" I challenged.

She smirked. "Well, maybe not just marketing." She gazed at me as if trying to figure out how to put a really important point into play. "I just wanted to make sure you're okay."

The hairs on my arms stood tall, suddenly. "Why wouldn't I be?" My pulse quickened, awaiting some scary revelation to come passing out of her lips.

Her chest began to rise and fall quicker. "Well, it's just that I—" She paused and stared deeply into my eyes. "—I sensed an imbalance the other day."

"An imbalance?" I could hear Anna in my mind, counseling me to back away from her while I still had a chance. "You're freaking me out."

She blinked back my harsh tone. "I'm not trying to scare you."

The atmosphere between us changed from a light morning breeze to a thunderous storm. "You should ask permission before you start launching into a reading on someone."

Her face reddened. "I'm very sorry. I'm just warning you so you can be proactive about it."

"Proactive?" The alarm in my brain raged bright red and stole any and all space for clarity. "I'm no longer comfortable." I stood up, blocking her with my open hands, as if that would be enough.

She stood up to meet me. "Please don't say that. I'm not here to make you uncomfortable."

I backed away from her, and grabbed onto the back of one of my chairs. "Yvonne should be the one sitting in this seat, and I should be sitting in mine, and we should be having a conversation about strategies, budget, and marketing outcomes." I rambled, for lack of anything more productive to do with my nerves.

"Okay, look. You're right. Let's forget I brought up the imbalance. I didn't mean to worry you. I shouldn't have said anything."

"You're right. You shouldn't have."

She shrugged like a person itching from a scratchy sweater. "I feel terrible. I should go."

"Yes, you should."

"Listen, if you need help rebalancing, come and see me and Yvonne at the wellness center. We're there to help."

I gripped the back of the chair harder. "Is this some sick way to get people to visit the wellness center and take yoga? Tell them they're out of balance and have them sign up for some special psychic package that includes mud baths, chants, and energy healing with crystals, followed by yoga poses in a hot room?"

She winced. "Of course not."

I walked toward my door and opened it. "Please just leave."

"I didn't come here to scare you. I came because you're a nice person and I wanted to help."

Help me with what? Was I dying? Did I have cancer? Would I live to see the following summer? Who would take over my business? "Please leave," I said, drawing air too shallow to be worth the effort.

"I'm sorry," she whispered.

I crossed my arms over my chest and looked out of my window, wanting her to just disappear.

"Sorry to have bothered you." She turned and walked away, toward the stairwell.

When she disappeared through the door, a strange buzz filled my head and tiny tremors vibrated through me.

"Lia? Are you alright?" Dean asked, taking my hand and leading back to the couch. "You look like you're going to faint."

I sat down in the spot she just rose from. "That woman is not right in the head," I said through clenched teeth. "She's irresponsible tossing predictions around like she does."

Dean sat down beside me, took my hand and squeezed it. "What did she say?"

My heart clenched, tangled up around the new seed she just planted. It hadn't even been two minutes since its induction into my body, yet it grew woody and thick and strangled me from the inside out. "She told me I'm imbalanced and urged me to visit the wellness center."

Dean stretched his eyes wide, and he eased up on the hand squeeze. "She's not right in the head, like you said. Don't pay her any mind."

I pressed my lips together, and leaned back against the couch, staring up at the ceiling tiles, hoping she really was not right in the head.

Dean reciprocated the pose.

We remained recumbent without speaking for several minutes, just being there together. At one point, he reached over and clasped my hand in his. "You do feel okay, don't you?"

"I think so." I swallowed softly, afraid to wreak havoc on my potential fragile system. I pictured synapses in my brain snapping, blood vessels collapsing, bones crumbling, blood turning thick as oil, and cells changing from pink to black as they died off one by one.

"We should ditch work and go play at the beach," he said. "Just forget about everything for a few hours and come back clearheaded. I'll call and reschedule our meeting with the new client. What do you say?"

I squeezed his hand, comforted by his presence. "I say that sounds like a mighty fine plan."

He stood and pulled me up. "First one to the elevator gets to drive?"

"Deal."

Chapter Five
Willow

Yvonne, my aunt's wife, always followed her dreams. I admired that about her.

When she wanted something, she just visualized it, and it appeared in her life. Most people accessorized their homes with artwork or family pictures. Not her. She filled the walls with endless affirmations, stenciled as borders in most every room, sparing only the laundry room and the pool house. Even years after starting that practice, she still sought out white space when a new affirmation inspired her. Aunt Lola and I always got a kick out of seeing her perched on top of a step ladder and singing off-key as she taped plastic letter stencils to the wall. When she dove into creative mode, she climbed up and down that ladder measuring, moving the ladder, re-measuring, and pressing the stencil against the wall with a satisfied grin on her face. Aunt Lola and I always just sat back, sipped wine, and remarked how much we wished we had half as much of her energy.

My aunt always said things like, "I swear she's got an invisible cylinder with endless energy strapped to that back of hers. If she keeps splashing our walls with her personality like that, we're not going to have any more white space."

Yvonne's late husband built her the home they now lived in. Their house far outdid any leading five-star tropical resort. Well, if you could get past all the affirmations, of course. The Queen Ann style house with its round tower, wrap-around porch, and complicated asymmetrical shape showcased its regal qualities. Step inside, though, and comfort coupled up with practical to create a soft, lived-in environment that clicked nicely with Yvonne's earthy, energetic vibe.

According to Aunt Lola, when Yvonne's husband passed away from a massive heart attack only ten years after she had married him, he left behind a jewelry business worth thirty-two million dollars. He also left behind a mistress that crawled out of the ground like a big, fat, slimy earthworm and demanded she get part of the estate, as she had spent the last eight years by his side too.

Apparently, Yvonne decided not to let the woman leave empty-handed. Quick-witted as always, Yvonne placed the key to her late husband's safe-deposit box in her hand and said her share would be there. Of course, her share didn't consist of valuables, but rather sappy sentiments. He had stored all of his precious childhood memories in that box, including coloring books with his scribbles, paper plates with the outline of his hand to serve as a turkey, and empty boxes of his favorite sweets like candy cigarettes, because he always feared the house would burn down and he'd lose those memories forever.

After handing her the key, she asked her to wait a moment as she ran to get something else that might've been of interest to her. She landed back in front of the mistress and handed her a sealed box. "Open it in private. I'm sure he would've wanted it that way."

The mistress accepted the sealed box, which contained his dirty underwear and gym shorts, turned with a satisfied grin, and marched across the wooden porch and down the stairs. When she walked past the stone wall, separating the porch garden area from the driveway, Yvonne turned on the sprinkler system and laughed her ass off as Little Miss Horn Ball sprinted through the green grass to get to her car parked at the far end of the circular driveway.

After that surprise visit, Yvonne decided to go on a self-discovery tour, using all her new money. She went to medical school where she specialized in internal medicine. Hating the system, with all its rules on efficiency over functionality, she ventured away from traditional, and sought a more holistic approach that would allow her time to get down to the root causes of illness and help people find answers that could bring a higher level of quality to their lives.

When Yvonne set her mind to something, she got it. She wanted to learn eastern philosophy medicine from its authentic source, so what did she do? She dug and dug until she got what she wanted – a firsthand introduction to a well-known Indian healer who practiced Ayurveda.

Ayurveda, otherwise known as the Science of Healing, was a 5,000-year-old system of natural healing that began in the Vedic culture of India, and a science that clicked with Yvonne right away.

She had met her calling.

After many years of training under that healer, she decided to return to America and open up The Physical Healing Center, and had managed to turn it into one of the area's premiere Naturopath destinations.

When I started working for her as a yoga instructor, she put me through some rigorous training, not just in her philosophy of yoga, but in all aspects of health, balance, nutrition, and even interpersonal skills. That woman knew how to operate a first-class center.

Aunt Lola wanted nothing to do with that side of her. "I'm the one who gets to bring her back down to the Earth plane at the end of the day," she would joke.

I credited Yvonne for helping me to get over the emotional trauma of my failed marriage. All that chanting and summoning of universal energy that she insisted I do in my early employee training, helped me understand that negativity just bred more negativity and sucked the life out of anything that attempted to be its polar opposite. For years, I used to think I did something wrong to cause my ex-husband, Robbie, to be miserable all the time. Thanks to my new yoga training, I learned a few things. Turned out, he was just a miserable asshole all along!

It still amazed me how much clarity could come from a few focused sessions of sitting on a yoga mat and humming to center myself. In those sessions, reality and truth always arrived and showed me Robbie had been miserable all along because he wanted to be, and no amount of smiling, cajoling, or spoiling him would've ever put a smile on his face.

We disliked each other.

He hated my eccentric side, and I hated all of his sides.

He hadn't smiled since before I got pregnant with Anthony. I found out later on, the only one who got to see his smile after that point in our marriage was Sharon, the woman who supposedly got to see more than his smile.

When Yvonne taught me her methods of yoga and meditation, the anger disappeared, just as she told me it would. It allowed me to forgive him. I no longer went around referring to him as an asshole or a conniving, two-timing bastard, even though that used to perk me right up. I now could even smile at his straight face when he dropped off and picked up the kids on his weekends. I've even offered him a soda from time to time.

Sharon made him happy, and ultimately handed me a ticket to freedom.

Win-win for both of us.

I loved being free. I got to do things I loved, and without having to justify why. If I wanted to spend three hours in the living room repeating my sun salutations, I could damned well do that. Try explaining yoga to a man who thought a chakra was a form of voodoo.

I no longer had to pretend I enjoyed things with him, like sex, sleeping in on Sunday mornings and having to listen to his snoring, or sharing the porch with him as he stunk up the air with his cigars that he started smoking when he found out I was pregnant with Charlotte.

My aunt warned me about him, after I first introduced them. Stubborn me though, I ignored her advice to flee. No one before him had treated me to Saturday nights at the Dance Harbor or challenged me to games of pool at Sunday night Football events. In my naïve view, I had struck gold. Turned out I struck a dark dead end; I couldn't see the writing on the wall in front of me.

"Life always works out to everyone's advantage," Aunt Lola loved to remind me. "It's just a matter of which reference point you're looking at life from on any given day."

I struggled believing her. Even now.

Life hadn't exactly worked out to my advantage. Specifically with Lia Stone. She kicked me out of her office like I was a no-good troublemaker. That same fear from the campground sat on her face like a mask. I only wanted to help her, not freak her out.

I couldn't erase the memory of her tense look from earlier that morning.

So, I ventured to my aunt's house to get away from that sinking feeling.

I sat on a lounge chair under the large umbrella and sipped on some iced tea. Aunt Lola walked toward me carrying a bowl of tortilla chips and salsa. She wore her big straw sunhat, the one with a bow on its side and a floppy rim. She wore a flowery one piece with a skirt, and with every stride she took, her skirt flipped up in the air.

We all dressed for July, yet April had barely started. We had a heated pool plus higher than normal temps to thank for that.

My aunt handed me the chips and yelled for Anthony and Charlotte to come get some. They climbed their water-logged bodies out of the deep end of the pool and shivered all the way over to us, dripping and carrying on about how the slate burned their feet.

"It's hot out here, but not that hot," I said.

Anthony hovered his drenched, skinny body right over the bowl and dripped all over them.

I nudged him backwards. "Honestly? Did I raise you to be a chip destroyer?"

He flipped his hair and wrinkled his nose, digging in. "Yup. I love soggy chips." He broke into a clumsy dance wiggling his butt and arms out of sync and singing how he loved them soggy chips, *loved them real good.*

Charlotte scanned the bowl like her brother had poisoned the chips. "He ruined them."

I closed my eyes. One afternoon. That's all I wanted. Just one peaceful afternoon without bickering and whining.

"Charlotte, sweetheart," Aunt Lola pulled her into her arms. "I've got some fresh ones in the pool house. What do you say we go get them and hide them from him?"

I shot her a warning look. "Aunt Lola, stop. You're spoiling her."

"I can't help it. It's what Auntie does, right?" She squeezed Charlotte. "We'll be right back."

Charlotte took her hand and skipped by her side, forgetting all about that hot slated patio and how it burned her feet only moments ago.

I laid back against the chair, closing my eyes while Anthony inspected the nearby spring grass for insects. In the black space between my closed eyes and lids, I saw Lia's flabbergasted face again. "I'm such an idiot," I whispered.

"What did I tell you about talking to yourself like that?" Yvonne snuck up behind me and tossed a towel at my face.

I groaned.

"Why would you lie around saying that kind of trash to yourself?"

"Because I messed up," I whined.

"Your aunt already told me about the train wreck." Yvonne straddled the chair next to me. "Eh, it happens. We cause a pile up and we move on." She squirted me with her water bottle. "Right?"

"I should've just minded my own business."

"You're damn right you should've." She leaned back and took a good long inhale, raking her hands through her sun-bleached cropped hair. "I'll tell you what you should've done. You should've approached her a little less like you were trying to sell her an annual membership to our facility. We're not Bally Total Fitness." She cupped her hand over her eyes and stared at me as if waiting on me to agree.

"I wish I would've had the hindsight."

"Hindsight would've told you that you could've just invited her to an open house and let me talk her into a complimentary package deal that included full body scans." She twisted her mouth to drive home the point that I acted way out of the responsible lines.

"That would've been the obvious strategic move."

70

She cupped her hand on my shoulder. "Well, you and I both know that if we sat across from each other with a chess board between us, it's likely you're not going to win," she talked through her laughter.

I broke a chip in half and chomped down on it. "I hate chess anyway."

She looked up to the spotless blue sky. "You know the rules, sweetheart. We can't go forcing ourselves on potential patients. They come to us when the universe tells them they should."

"I just wanted to help her."

She cupped her hand back over her eyes again. "Help her what? Avoid the regular stresses of life?"

"I got a vision of her talking to a doctor."

She stretched her eyes. "I'd say that's pretty darned clear, then. Roll out the casket, get the organ tuned up, and order the funeral flowers."

"I didn't say she was going to die," I said, raising my voice.

"What did you sense exactly?"

"She was pacing and upset."

"Maybe she was getting a boob enhancement consultation and he told her she couldn't get a double D because her back couldn't support it." She cupped her boobs in her hands. "These suckers do hurt the back. Look at them. They're like gigantic floating devices. Who needs a lifejacket out in the middle of the ocean when you've got a set of these attached?"

I laughed. "You're a nut."

"I have to be, to keep up with you and your aunt. You two will always be a mystery to me." She sat up tall. "I prefer keeping it that way. Whenever I try too hard to understand you both, my brain gets all twisted up like a sailor's knot."

I stretched my legs out in front of me. "We're not that difficult."

She shot me a sardonic smile.

"All I know is that I acted out of a sheer desire to help her," I said. "I wasn't trying to drum up business."

"I love you to pieces for being so sweet," she said, putting her finger on the trigger of that squirt bottle. "But, that's not how we operate. Capisci?

I eyed her trigger happy finger. "Yes," I said.

She removed her finger and looked over at Anthony crawling around the grass on his knees.

I sighed and leaned back again, closing my eyes and enjoying the light breeze. The cicadas, early to arrive that year in New England, chirped in full force, waving high and low with their song. The pool filter gurgled. Someone mowed grass in an adjacent yard. I slid into that sweet springtime pocket of relaxation. Then, Yvonne squirted me again.

My eyes shot open and landed on her standing above me with her trigger finger depressed. "What do you say we just drown out this bad vibe here, and teach your son how to do a cannon ball jump?"

I wiped the water from my face and pulled my knees up to my chest. "I don't know how to do a cannon ball jump."

"Oh," she said, staring down at me. "I guess I have to do everything around here. She took off her sandals and her beach dress, and ran toward the diving board, giggling like a kid jacked up on sugary candy, waving her arms in the air, and yelling over to Anthony to watch and learn.

He ran over to the pool, yanking his bathing trunks up higher, and arrived just in time to catch a glimpse of the most clumsy single flip cannon ball jump known to mankind. Water splashed everywhere, and soon the top of Yvonne's short cropped hair bobbed up and down along side of the waves she created. "Ah, that was amazing," she screamed, whipping her head around and flinging more water at anything within a ten foot radius.

Aunt Lola and Charlotte walked out of the pool house door, took one look at the sea of wavy bubbles and turned to head back into the safety of the pool house with their fresh bowl of chips.

Yvonne laughed at them, then swam to the side. "Well come on," she said to me. "We don't have all day to get that sourpuss off your face. Get on over to the diving board and have a go at it."

For anyone else, I'd close my eyes again. For Yvonne, I'd do anything she instructed. That lady knew her stuff. I certainly could've used some of her magic that afternoon. So, dutifully as ever, I climbed off the lounger, removed my t-shirt and headed over to the diving board where I proceeded to refresh myself in a good old-fashioned cannon ball jump.

Chapter Six
Lia

Dean drove us back and forth to the beach. He didn't once bring up Willow, and I didn't either. We spent the day goofing off on one of Rhode Island's big tourist destinations, the Cliff Walk in Newport, and then later pigging out on hand-churned ice cream in Brick Market Place. I enjoyed slipping into tourist mode, wearing my big shades and pretending like Willow's visit that morning didn't affect me in the least bit. Then Dean asked, "Have you ever considered scuba diving?"

That question poked at me, reminding me how little I had lived in my short thirty years. I hadn't done anything remotely close to that type of thrill and adventure.

I just shrugged, clinging to my comfort zone.

"We'd have a blast. Look at that water. The world is comprised of seventy-one percent of it. The vast amount to be discovered boggles my mind." He propped his foot up on a stone and sniffed the air.

"I'm a fan of the twenty-nine percent land."

"Oh come on. Picture scuba diving in the Caribbean and getting right up close to a school of tropical fish. Picture how exciting it would be to swim alongside a large sea turtle." His eyes grew large. "I'd be in heaven down there." He leaned against the fence separating us from a large twenty foot drop down to the rocky shoreline. "I heard they have these vacation packages where you live onboard a ship for a week or two, they call them liveaboards, and you can dive right in the middle of the ocean. You jump off and descend sixty to a hundred or so feet and hang out with the sea creatures. Then, when you ascend and get back on the boat, the crew feeds like you are a king."

"Sounds like someone's been doing his research. How did I not know you were this much into scuba diving?"

"I've dreamed of it since the first week I landed in America when I saw a video of a scuba diver holding hands with a grey seal. The seal gripped the diver's hand and affectionately cradled it to his chest," he said, animating his voice. "Whenever the diver stopped moving his hand, the seal wiggled his flippers until the diver touched him again. I'd never seen anything quite so brilliant. I instantly wanted to take up scuba diving."

"Well do it then."

"I need a dive buddy."

I backed away. "Don't look at me. That's not on my bucket list, nor will it ever be." *Bucket list*. I didn't even have a bucket list. *I really should have a bucket list.*

"Which is why I never asked you. You're not very adventurous."

"I'm adventurous."

"Climbing the rock wall at Bass Pro Shop is hardly adventurous." He smirked and began walking back up the walkway.

"That rock wall was extremely tall, and I slipped. If that's not adventurous then what is?" I followed him.

"Not that."

"I could've killed myself dangling from the ropes. And you had the nerve to laugh at me. You stood below me, my buddy, looking up at me while munching on Moose Crunch popcorn. Meanwhile I dangled all the way down until I hit the ground."

"No. You slipped and the safety harness and rope eased you down."

"Same thing."

"It's not the same thing."

We bickered like that through the rest of the walk, through eating ice cream, and through our drive home. I loved every bicker that he launched because it kept my mind off my morning with Willow.

Later on that night, I brewed a cup of tea, sat down with it on my couch, and contemplated my lack of a bucket list.

I didn't have grandiose dreams to hold hands with a grey seal, ride around a race track going a hundred miles an hour, complete a marathon, backpack through Europe, or write a book like other people did. I just wanted to expand my business.

I probably should've had grandiose dreams. Everyone did, right?

What would I want to accomplish if I knew I would die soon?

I stared at my tea, dunking the tea bag in and out of it as if that would release a world of adventurous ideas.

I already accomplished my dream. I wanted to open up a business, and I did so. What now?

I sipped my tea and closed my eyes.

My life consisted of getting up, working out, drinking a cup of coffee, showering, driving to work, slaving over work, getting dinner, watching the news, and going back to bed. I left myself no time to dream of doing anything outrageous and fun. I wired my world so tight, that nothing else could cram into it.

I couldn't just take off for ten days and sail the blue ocean, jump in and catch my dinner, and resurface to enjoy the sunset. I couldn't just tell my clients that I had more important things to do like hike the Appalachian Trail from Georgia to Maine, climb a mountain range, go kayaking around Bar Harbor, or fly over a volcano in Hawaii.

Even if I listed those things on a bucket list, what the heck would I do with it? Pin it to the wall and pray by some sheer miracle that suddenly my days lengthened from twenty four hours to thirty?

I sipped my tea again.

When did I become such a dud?

Even Dean had grandiose dreams.

When I was younger I wanted to become an archeologist so I could explore cool caves in search of primitive pans, dishes, and silverware used by ancient civilizations. I would spend my summers down on my hands and knees, digging the rocky soil for special rocks, imagining the discolored ones were really precious gems. I would pretend I led an expedition with a team of archeologists, where we dug in the hot sun,

77

using specially designed instruments that NASA astronauts used when digging in the lunar soil on the moon. I imagined I was a famous archeologist who landed on the pages of National Geographic, lifting up clay baskets with my team right by my side, smiling just as wide as me. I also imagined the look on my parents face when they saw me on the cover, and again when they read the full spread and looked at all the photos with captions like "Lia Stone does it again." I would picture them sitting on their front porch bench, holding hands and admiring the work of their daughter.

That childhood dream faded as I entered high school. Turned out, I liked marketing a hell of a lot more than I liked digging in the dirt.

I enjoyed a good life.

I fulfilled a lot of goals. I graduated college. I opened up my own business. I turned it into a success. I owned a cute place. I drove a nice truck. My furniture was top-of-the-line, soft Italian leather, solid maple, and designer showcase quality. I even owned a star.

I did alright for myself.

I wasn't a dud. I was a hard worker, and I was happy in that role. Not everyone needed to climb Mt. Everest or scuba dive in paradise to die a happy person. That kind of stuff just set people up for disappointment anyway. Scuba dives would end. Climbs would stop at the top of the mountain. And then what?

I stood up and headed to my bedroom. "I am happy with my life," I said out loud to my naked condo.

I fell asleep that night affirming that fact.

As the days of the work week piled on top of each other, I continued to affirm the fact that I was a happy-go-lucky woman. As I woke up, worked out, showered, drove to work, worked, ate dinner, and returned to bed each evening, I reminded myself, "Yes, I am happy."

When I doubted myself on that, I'd go through my laundry list of things I had to be happy about: my business, my rental car, my soon-to-be repaired truck, my flowing bank account, my comfy home, my new patio set and my wardrobe.

What more could I ask for?

Well, I'd love to get rid of the bad taste I left behind with Willow. I hadn't been able to focus since I kicked her out of my office. I just kept seeing the shock settle into her eyes as I insulted her.

I had overreacted kicking her out of my office, and quite frankly, wanted to kick myself for being so foolish. What if she really did just want to help me?

What if she saw something more than just an imbalance, but feared to tell me the truth?

Imbalance could mean anything. I could have a cold virus hanging out in the back of my throat, waiting for the right moment to attack me. Maybe that's what Willow saw. Or maybe the imbalance referred to my tight hamstring muscles that I failed to stretch after my workouts. I didn't have the time to lounge around the gym stretching my hands to my toes. I had a business to run.

Imbalance. What an elusive word.

To me an imbalance meant something snapped and became misaligned, fighting my system, and rendering me helpless to becoming needless suffering's next victim.

My imagination rolled.

I got a vision of my cells rallying a meeting in the pit of my stomach. *How do you want to attack this body boss? Should we do an all-out assault or just leak a few dormant cells and pull the trigger on them once they enter the bloodstream? Or, if you prefer, we could place markers in all of the cells present at today's meeting, let them hunker down as they gain strength out in the live system, and at a predetermined date, we signal for them to release their toxins and see what kind of chaos they can emit.*

I needed to get in touch with Willow.

Stat.

I somehow drove myself home on autopilot from dinner with my parents. I pulled into my parking space, and with my engine still idling, I called Dean. "I know it's late."

"For the love of God, you'd better be calling to tell me you just found a million dollars and need to unload it on me."

In no mood to banter, I cut to the chase. "I need Willow's number."

"Willow?" he asked. "As in, I never want to talk to that woman again, Willow?"

"I want to hear the whole story from her."

"No you don't."

"Give it to me. That's a direct order."

"This isn't the military," he said. "You can't issue me a direct order."

"Please," I begged. "My mind is jumbled up and getting more tangled by the second."

"It's not a good idea. You're messing with the natural order of things."

An unreasonable jolt of panic flew through me. "She told you something, didn't she?"

"Good God woman. When did she have time to tell me anything? She stood before me for a mere five seconds before you pounced out of your office door and over to her personal space, which by the way, you need to work on that. You invade people's personal space."

"I do that on purpose."

"You do not."

"I do too," I said. "Her number, please."

"What if she tells you something terrible? You're going to freak out, and then I'm going to freak out. It's just not a good combination."

"If something is ever wrong with me, you don't get to freak out. You're going to let me freak out, and then you're going to calm me down."

"I can't guarantee that," he said. "You know I stress over watching Titanic, and I've seen it twenty times already."

"Well, at least I don't usually get stressed."

"No, you get weepy-eyed."

"Well, at least I *get* weepy-eyed, which is more than you can say Mr. I've-Never-Cried-Once-in-My-Adult-Life."

"I can't help that my eyes don't cry."

"Enough about your eyes," I said. "I just want to talk with her. I promise whatever she tells me, I'll spare you any ugly details and just proffer the rosy version."

"You can't do that. See now, when you call me back and tell me everything's fine, I'm not going to believe you."

What if everything wasn't fine? Panic gripped me again. "I'm a little scared."

"Lia," he paused. "Nothing can happen to you. Understand?"

His sincerity pinched at my heart. "As long as you understand the same goes for you."

We sat in comfortable silence for a few long seconds. Then Dean broke it, "I'll text you her number."

"And I'll tell you the complete truth."

We allowed the comfortable silence to swaddle us for a few more seconds, then, "You know," he said. "We should devise a promise right now, before we hear anything from her, that we will create a bucket list together and start checking items off of it."

"I don't know what the hell I would put on it."

"Maybe we could start off with something easy like roller skating."

"Rollerblading, you mean?" I asked.

"Don't be a grammar guru at a time like this," he said.

"When am I going to fit in rollerblading?" I asked. "You've got me so overbooked, I'm not going to have time to eat lunch, let alone skate down a path and break my neck."

"Scratch the rollerblading, then," he said.

"Yeah, I suppose you're right. I've got too much going on right now."

"I'm not talking about your overbooked schedule. I just want to keep your neck on straight and your body in one piece."

"What if that turns out to be the least of my concern?" I asked, swallowing past the instant lump in my throat.

"You're freaking out way more than is necessary."

"Okay, Mr. Already-Bought-an-Inhaler."

"I'm hanging up now."

After I heard the click, I just sat still with the engine running, contemplating my life with no filter. If I only had three hundred sixty five days left to live, would I care if my carpets were white, soft and luxurious rather than beige, practical Berber carpeting? Would the fact that my floors were honest-to-goodness real wood and not Pergo really matter in the grand scheme of life?

Things enriched my life. When did I become such a wealth seeker? Did I spoil into that trait before or after my father beamed with pride over purchasing his first brand new vehicle or when my parents were able to move us out of that three bedroom, third floor apartment and move us to the town of Lincoln where politicians and business owners lived? I loved the rush of my parents buzz and wanted to experience it for myself. I didn't want to end up living life in a dilapidated apartment on the third floor of an old, broken-down building with horsehair plaster for walls and frosted windows in my shower stall.

'Things' were nice. Even though they could be stolen or burned, they were easier to replace than the loss of wasted time, effort, or energy.

Acquiring things brought me comfort, admittedly.

If I died, and Dean wrote my obituary, what would he say? *She acquired many great items in life. That convector oven of hers was her pride and joy. She honored the things in her life by polishing them up to perfection so they shined brighter than anyone else's. Lia Stone knew what to buy and how to buy it. We will miss her greatly.*

I suddenly wanted to dismantle that comfort zone I created.

Imagine a eulogy? I left nothing worthy for Dean to highlight. He'd have to stutter his way through my life's accomplishments and stumble over the fact that I had yet to experience black Hawaiian sand between my toes, a cross-country drive in an RV, a vigorous climb to the top of Mount Everest, an afternoon sailing in the ocean, a vacation in The Alps, or the power of flying an airplane.

I would've died a person who failed to achieve any of those things.

My heart started to beat erratically.

Could Willow see my death?

Would I have to endure a long, messy drawn-out saga one day?

I wished I could choose the way I would die, like ordering takeout from a Chinese restaurant. *For an appetizer, I'd like an extra-large order of healthy blood platelets, some badass immune protectors, oh and can you also toss in some of those brain chemicals that ease pain naturally? And for my main death entrée, I'd like to order menu item A-1, Fall-asleep-and-never-wake-up. And can you delay that until I reach ninety-two? That should fund me with plenty of time to get through a few things before the order goes through, no?*

Hell. Why did she have to plant such nonsense in my mind?

I needed to understand the imbalance.

#

I poured myself a vodka and cranberry drink with a splash of lime, then sat down on my couch with my cell phone. I kicked up my feet and placed them on the coffee table. I leaned back against my soft Italian leather, sinking into its comfort.

Just one quick phone call to ask her one quick question. Then, with her answer, I could get on with my life. I could stop obsessing over the details of an imbalance I probably didn't even have. In and out. Just like going to the dentist. Go in, open up the mouth, get the teeth scraped, and get out. No big deal.

I stared at my cell, darting my eyes around the numbers I would enter on the keypad. *Just seven quick taps, press send, and you'll be on your way to clearing the path back to your sanity.*

I sipped more of my drink, waiting on its courage to take up root in me. My hands trembled around the glass. My tummy did those flips again.

Just do it. Just jump in there, get wet, and get back out. Worry about drying off later on, once the sting of the water on your prickly skin fades.

I tapped out her number and pressed send, then tensed. My chest pounded and my teeth chattered.

Her voice message picked up. I exhaled, temporarily relieved. I sat tall, exhaled sharply again and left a message. "Hi Willow, it's Lia. Lia Stone. Could you please call me back when you have a chance? My number is 555-345-5698."

I hung up, steadied my erratic heart, and laughed at myself for being such a nervous geek. What would she tell me that would change my life? *I see a future where you have some health issues.* Well didn't we all have some issues? I survived many health scares over the years. I've had my appendix burst in me, a mole removed from my back, and countless flus and colds. And, hey, I was still alive.

"Imbalances are part of the human experience," I reminded myself as I passed by my full length mirror. "Get over yourself. You're going to be fine."

I marched into the kitchen still laughing at myself, swallowed the rest of my drink, and washed the glass. Then, I popped some microwave popcorn, salted it, and gobbled that down while watching *Wipeout.* I laughed my butt off at some dude who flung himself against a buoy so hard, I nearly peed my pants watching him.

By the time I showered, read the newspaper, and turned out the lights, my senses were back in check and I decided I'd just ignore her callback. I didn't need to know any more than I already did. I was alive right now. That's all life guaranteed.

I turned over, hugged the comforter tightly around myself and closed my eyes, ready to embark on some good dreaming.

Before long, I drifted into a field of wildflowers, tore off my sandals, opened up my arms nice and wide, and ran into the wind, inhaling its life force and sweet flavors. I closed in on a big maple tree when my phone rang.

I opened up my eyes in a flash and stared at the red vibrating light. My heart began to buck, and all the insecurities from hours ago poured right back inside me, filling my veins with a bitter coldness.

Who was I trying to fool, pretending wildflowers and maple trees were going to defend me against the madness of my ravished imagination?

I flung the blankets off and jumped up to get the call.

I needed answers.

Chapter Seven

"Thanks for calling me back," I said.

"I'd be lying if I said your call didn't surprise me," Willow said. "I've never been kicked out of someone's office before."

"Well, I've never been personally visited by a psychic at work before, either." I tried to match her sweetness without success.

"I'm sorry if I scared you. You probably think I'm some kind of weirdo now."

Now? "Unique is a better word. Don't you think?"

"Sure," she laughed. "Let's go with that."

We both paused.

"Did I scare you?"

I would never admit that she did. "You scared my assistant, Dean. He's been begging me to call you back and apologize."

"So, are you?"

"Am I what?"

"Apologizing." A laugh trailed her pretty voice.

"I acted kind of rude, I suppose. You sort of caught me off guard."

"I tend to do that to people."

"Hmm." I fiddled with my bed sheet trying to figure out a way to break into the conversation without appearing panicky. "So, apparently, the suspense of my future is killing Dean. Care to enlighten me so I can put his mind at rest?"

"Killing *him*?" she asked, exaggerating the pronoun. "Remember, I'm a psychic. You can't lie to me."

Are any of my personal thoughts sacred in her presence? "Fine. I might be a little curious too."

She rolled out a soft chuckle. "I'm sorry I showed up at your office. I'm usually not that unprofessional."

"Does a professional protocol for psychics exist?" I asked.

"Well, it's not like we follow a written code of ethics. Though I suppose if such a thing existed, a lot of people might be living in ignorant bliss right now. I'm not so sure that's such a great idea. Do you think it is?"

"Don't be tossing this back at me," I said, sounding flirtier than I wanted. "I don't buy into all the psychic hoopla, so you're asking the wrong person."

"Well, in your defense, a lot of fake ones take up space only trying to steal a quick buck or gain attention."

"Oh, like your aunt."

"My aunt is not a fake. She may not be clear in her premonitions, many of us aren't, but she doesn't pull things out of the air to pay her bills. She's got plenty of money. She doesn't do it for the money at all. She does it because it brings her purpose."

"So, what you're saying is that Dean really is going to suffer an allergy attack?"

"If she says so, I don't doubt it. It could simply mean that he's going to wake up one day and have to take an allergy pill to clear his sinuses."

"Dean totally thinks he's going to die of an allergy attack, and now he thinks I'm going to die of some terrible disease."

"Oh, that's ridiculous."

"He's even begged me to write out a bucket list. You have the guy thinking I'm dying. Please give me something I can tell him so I can calm him down. I can't get anything done around the office. He's like a chicken pecking around me, searching for the seeds of this imbalance you've planted."

"I didn't plant any such imbalance. I'm just the messenger." She paused. "You're going to be fine. I just sensed that you need to take better care of yourself."

"How exactly does this sense come through to you? Is it like a movie? Like a fantasy movie or a dramatic one?" I spoke way too fast and erratically.

"You're panicking. Please don't panic."

"I'm not panicking," I said too loudly. "I just want to understand."

"Sometimes I get a clear picture, like I'm right there observing real life. Other times, it's like a bad acid trip where things blur over and make no sense at all."

I pictured her as a hippy with loose braids hanging down to her breasts, swaying to sexy music, and sporting wildflowers in her hair. "So was mine an acid trip?"

"This is hard to explain over the phone. Would you be interested in meeting up with me for a cup of coffee tomorrow morning?"

I suddenly wanted to be right there, sitting in front of her and having her explain it all to me. "I guess Dean can wait another day."

"Can you?" she teased.

"I'm sure I'll survive," I said softly. God, I loved sharing those flirty innuendos with her way too much.

"Hmm. I'm sure you will too."

"Can I get at least one hint that I can pass along to Dean tonight?"

"Tell him he's going to have to attend your birthday parties for the next six decades. At least."

I squeezed my eyes in delight. "He'll be most grateful. Don't be surprised if you get a fruit basket delivered to the flea market this weekend."

"Tell him I love pineapples." She giggled, sounding just like a girl skipping over puddles and delighting in the splashes she created.

"You'll get twenty of them, if I do that."

"Then, I'll share them with you."

I pictured us sitting on a beach feeding each other pineapples and wiping the juices from each other's faces. I snapped away from that vision. "Okay, so tomorrow. You're not by chance an early riser, are you?"

"How early?"

"Eight?"

"I've got two kiddos, remember? I haven't slept past six in eight years now."

A vision of her lounging in bed with her hair loose and wavy, legs long and sleek, one dangling over the other, crept into my mind. I shook off that vision too.

"Great. Eight it is. How does Cassie's Café downtown sound to you?"

"It sounds yummy," she said, softly.

Her voice comforted me. I worried for nothing.

# #

The next morning, I walked into Cassie's Café and spotted Willow sitting at a table at the far end. She was sipping coffee and smiling at the two blonde children sitting with her coloring.

"Hey," I said, slightly apprehensive to break into their peaceful moment.

"Hey," she said, easing back against the wicker chair.

"Mommy look," the little girl said. "I stayed in the lines."

"You did not," the young boy said, pointing to one of her many spillages over the outline of a teddy bear.

The little girl's eyes sank and her chin followed the same trajectory.

"But look," I said, jumping in to rescue her. "Those squiggly marks outside the lines look like the teddy bear grew wings." I pointed my eyes to the girl. "I've never seen such beautiful wings on a teddy bear before."

Her smile returned, and her cheeks turned rosy.

The boy analyzed her teddy bear wings. "Whatever." He shrugged and continued coloring a fire truck.

"I think you've just made yourself a fan," Willow said to me. A look of awe swam in her eyes that tickled my ego in all the right places.

"I'm the fan. They're both super-talented artists."

The boy relaxed his face on that compliment, even breaking into a small smile and shy blink.

Willow stood up and waved me to a chair next to hers. "Have a seat." She grabbed her pocketbook. "I'll get you a cup of coffee."

I blocked her. "I'll get it."

"No, I insist." She wiggled around me and walked toward the counter. "Hot coffee?" she asked me over her shoulder.

"Sure."

She walked with a bounce in her step, swinging her hips to a happy beat.

The little girl bit into her donut and white powder blew down her chin and landed all over her pink shirt. She watched me with her big, blue eyes. "My daddy has a shirt like yours."

I looked down at my Old Navy long sleeved crew neck, suddenly self-conscious of my choice.

The boy gulped his milk, then asked me, "Who are you?"

I sat down and folded my hands under my chin. "I'm your mother's friend."

"My mother doesn't have friends," he said.

"Everyone has friends."

"I don't," the little girl said. Powder covered the entire lower part of her face.

"You have your brother here, don't you?"

She crinkled her nose. "He's not my friend."

He gulped his milk again, undeterred by her rejection.

Willow walked toward us with a steaming mug of coffee. "I hope you like hazelnut." She placed it in front of me, and caressed my shoulder with her warm hand. "It's the most delicious coffee I've ever tasted."

I sipped the nutty flavor as she sank into her seat. "It's delicious, thank you."

She looked over my shoulder and panic stretched across her face. "Hang on a minute." She climbed off her chair and her skirt lifted and refused to go back down as she rushed over to a man sitting at the counter. She confronted him with her hands on her hips. Her skirt stuck in on itself, showcasing a pair of white undies with pastel hearts.

She had absolutely no clue.

I should've told her, but I liked the entertainment factor.

She wagged her finger at the older man, and he stood up in quiet surrender. He spoke slowly, and backed away from her. She stood confident, tall, like a wrecking ball waiting to swing her mighty force on him should he not continue on his backward descent from the café.

"Your order is ready, sir," The guy behind the counter yelled out to him as he approached the door. He turned and rushed out of the café, tipping his hat to Willow before heading down Broadway.

Willow plucked up the tray from the guy behind the counter, tossed him a few bills and walked back over to our table with a serene smile on her face.

I'd never seen anyone look quite so devilishly beautiful before.

She sat down and offered me the plate. "Pancakes?"

I laughed. "What just happened?"

She tilted her head, examining me for a few long seconds. "That man has followed me for days now."

I dug a fork into the pancake pile. "Yet, you're so calm about it all."

"He's a reporter."

I stopped chewing. "What does a reporter want with you?"

"To prove I'm the real deal, I suppose."

"Or a hoax?" I countered.

"That wouldn't cook up a great story, now would it?" She winked one of her pretty blue eyes at me.

My tummy flipped again. "What did you say to him to get him to leave so amicably?"

"She told him she has a gun," the boy said.

"Anthony." She tapped the table in front of him. "What did I tell you?"

"Not to say the word gun," he said in a rehearsed voice.

"It works, mommy," the little girl said matter-of-factly. "You said it yourself to Aunt Lola. When someone bothers you, you tell him you have a gun."

Willow dug her fork into the pile of pancakes too. "Sometimes they have no filter," she whispered.

"They're adorable," I said, smiling over at them.

We each ate another bite. "So, do you really have a gun?"

She licked her fork with her rosy red tongue. "Maybe." Her plump lips closed in around the fork as she gazed at me.

I blushed.

"So," I said, trying to take the attention off of my red face. "I'm trying to understand this. How do you know he's a reporter? Did he tell you?"

"He interviewed me. Then, he had the nerve to ask if I could demonstrate on a stranger." She batted her eyes. "It's not like I can go up to random people and peek into their brains. It doesn't happen that way. It's random."

"And he's hoping to catch a random glimpse?"

"Exactly," she said, continuing to eat another piece.

"Fascinating." I sat mesmerized watching her lick her fork again. Her tongue swept up and down its shiny surface, curling at the tip with each ascent. "It's like the paparazzi of the psychic world."

"He's wasting his time."

"How so?" I asked, staring at her lips and waiting for her tongue to unfurl against that metal again.

"It's not like I go into some rabid trance when it happens. I don't know what he expects to see."

"You do twitch."

"Did I do that with you," she asked, mid-swallow.

"Yeah. And at the campground you twitched all the time." She didn't really, but I enjoyed watching her skin turn red now.

She bowed her head, fiddling with the pancake. "I don't twitch."

"You totally twitch."

"Okay, maybe I do twitch. But, not during a psychic reading," she teased.

We stared at each other, fighting off knowing smiles.

She looked away first and at her two children who were devouring their breakfast while continuing to color. The boy's crayon kept inching off the paper and onto the table. "Gosh, I hope that's washable crayon."

I chuckled, before looking down at my oversized watch.

"Oh God, I'm probably blocking you from getting to work on time," she said. "So, I should probably stop eating pancakes and tell you a little bit about what I sensed, huh?"

"For Dean's sake."

"Yeah." She broke out into an easy smile. "For Dean's sake."

"So, what am I going to go back and tell him?"

"Well, for starters, you're going to go back and tell him that you're not dying." She pointed her fork at me.

"So, you mean, he should cancel the life insurance policy that he had drafted?"

"Most definitely." She crossed her leg and it dangled by my side. "You should warn him that the bucket list is going to get pretty long, as you have many years ahead of you to tackle it."

I moved in a bit closer and my jeans brushed up against her bare leg. I left it there. "You mean I can push some of the big items to the end of that list, seeing as I have a lifetime to get to them?"

"Is skydiving one of them?" she asked, increasing the touch of her leg against mine.

My inner thighs quivered. "Of course he's trying to sneak that one on my list. That'll be the last item I check off."

"Do you want to be sky diving at ninety-two?" She inched up closer to me, resting her wrist under her chin and staring dangerously deeper into my eyes.

All the anxiety of the night before disappeared. "I'm going to live until ninety-two?" The little hairs on my arms poked up again.

"If you take care of yourself. Sure. Why not?" She broke our gaze and dug in for another piece of pancake.

"So, you don't know?" I asked, dueling for the same piece with my fork.

She tapped my fork with hers. "I'm a psychic, not God."

I pushed her fork away and reclaimed the piece. "I'm glad we've ironed out that detail."

"I'm sure you are." She surrendered the piece to me, dropped her fork, and wrapped her hand around my wrist. She twitched again.

"You just got another reading off me, didn't you?"

She contemplated my question with a blink. She looked to her quiet children coloring.

I pulled her hand to gain her attention. "Look at me, please."

She pointed her eyes to me. "Fine. Yes. I just sensed something."

"What?" Panic rose again, sobering me.

"It's confusing."

"Well try me. What did you see?"

She swallowed and squirmed in her seat. "You and Dean. You were in a hospital."

"Why are we in the hospital?"

"I don't know." She looked about ready to cry.

My heart began to race.

"Mommy, look at what I drew. It's my very own teddy bear," the little girl screamed.

"One minute, Charlotte," she said with authority as she kept looking straight into my eyes.

"Mommy, it's a green teddy bear," her voice screeched.

My nerves were on full alert. "What are we doing in the hospital? Are we injured? Are we being operated on?"

"I don't know why you're there."

95

My mind reeled out of control. "Think."

"Relax," she said, cradling my wrist again.

I waited for another twitch.

"You're in the room, and you're calm. Actually Dean is flirting with the doctor."

"That is a total crock. Dean doesn't flirt."

"He flirts." She laughed. "He's totally flirting."

"What else?"

"I just sensed that you were stressed. Maybe work stuff? Maybe life balance? It's all workable stuff. That much I can sense."

"Mommy can you look now?"

She flashed me an apology, before turning her attention to her kids. "That's beautiful, honey. Can you color me a red one too?"

"Sure," she screeched.

We sat in comfortable chaos, staring at the colorful table and listening to Anthony slurp milk out of his straw.

"How do I work it out?" I asked.

"Come to the wellness center. We're having an open house this weekend. Bring Dean with you. We're going to have speakers and food, and you'll get to meet Yvonne. She'll tell you how to get rid of the stressors in life."

I nodded, wishing I could see what she saw. "Maybe we should."

She picked up a crayon and began doodling. "Yes, you should."

I eyed the magenta crayon, grabbed it, and then began drawing my own version of a teddy bear.

# #

That night I dreamed of Willow. The sun was setting on the horizon, and we sat on a lifeguard chair at Sand Hill Cove Beach. We swung our legs and talked about things like whether man really did walk on the moon back in nineteen sixty-nine, and about how long it would take to walk from Rhode Island to San Diego.

The sky radiated a stunning blue, highlighted with a few brush strokes of wispy white. Not a soul could be seen from where we sat all the way to Galilee. The ocean and beachfront belonged only to us. She leaned over at one point and rested her head on my shoulder. I ran my fingers through her soft, blonde hair and enjoyed the sound of her relaxed breaths. "I wish this moment would last forever," I said.

She looked up at me, her moist lips a mere inch away, and whispered, "It's our vision, and we can prolong it as long as we want to stay in it."

I stared into her blue eyes, and in them I saw a beauty that went deeper than words could describe. The deeper I ventured, the warmer and more secure I felt. "Why do we get so much time?"

"Because, in a vision, time doesn't have any bearings. Are you ready to see what I see?"

"I'm ready."

"Close your eyes and relax."

Her breath teased me. I closed my eyes and relaxed into her softness and into the subtle curve of her lips. The darkness in front of my closed lids turned into a rainbow of trees, flowers, and ground cover. I clung to Willow's back as she flew up above the tree canopy and gifted us with an aerial view of a dense forest bursting with life, song, and wild, earthy scents. She giggled and dipped back down into the forest, gliding alongside birds and butterflies. Her hair flowed behind her and tickled my face.

We landed on a thick branch of a tree that stood taller than a high-rise building. She eased me down, then curled up beside me, nuzzling me with her nose. She kissed my neck with soft, feathery strokes, warming me to the core. I caved into her affection, seeking her touch with more hunger. She kissed my neck harder, suckling on it, offering me her sweet desire. I reached out for her lips, hungry to quench the thirst taking over my heart, my mind, my control. We breathed as one, connecting to the root of everything healthy and sacred in our private forest. Our bodies shared the same pulse, the same energy, the same life source.

A distant bell chimed, calling out to us. She attempted to pull away, but I wouldn't let her. I gripped her as she tried to pry her lips away from me. "Please don't go. I'm not ready for this to be over."

"We're ready. We saw everything we needed to see."

The bell chimed louder. "You said we had all the time we wanted."

"I did. That's all the time I should share for now." She pulled away and dangled her long, sinewy legs from the branch.

The bell pierced my ears.

"How do we get down from here?" I asked.

"I don't have all the answers. I'm sorry. I just don't. I don't know how it ends." She flew off, leaving me to hang by myself.

The bell's chime grew louder until I couldn't take it anymore. I covered my ears and cried out. Then, just like that, the branch turned soft under me. I opened my eyes, and I sat alone in my bedroom. My alarm chimed. My feet touched the soft carpet. The sun peeked through the blinds.

I was safe. I was home. I was okay.

Chapter Eight
Willow

I put together the open house event in record time. Typically, those events took at least a month to organize and get the word out. I did it in five days. I arranged the food, the giveaways, and the guest speakers. I spent two whole days on the phone calling nearly every person in our client database, inviting them and a friend to come and listen to Dr. Rhonda and Dr. Viola speak about *10 Ways to Live a Healthier Life* and *Five Things Every Kitchen Should Have in It.*

I needed the event to look like something that had been planned for months and not something I just pulled out of my butt five days prior. I wanted to see Lia again, and an event about health and nutrition seemed like a comfortable recipe.

I set up a tray of fruit, nuts, and seeds and placed them on the table next to the organic herbal tea. Next I arranged the giveaways in a semi-circle. I spent an entire night labeling and stuffing small baggies with organic bath salts. I even managed to find time that morning, in between running the kids to Aunt Lola's and listening to her lecture me on threatening a strange man in a public café, to run to Trader Joe's and pick up a few bouquets of tropical flowers to display around the reception area. Phew, task complete.

I stepped back and took it all in. Not bad for short notice.

Now I just hoped Lia would show up.

I walked back to the treatment rooms and tidied them up. I lit the beeswax candles, filled the diffusers with essential oils, and smoothed the white blankets on each treatment table. Next, I walked into the aquatic center and inhaled the calming salt air. The pool was our grandest asset of all. Yvonne taught exercise classes every day. I taught a yoga fitness class a few times a week. And we had open lane swimming for fitness enthusiasts. The pool raked in profits, and drew in peripheral crowds that ultimately always veered to other treatments once they learned more about the center's offerings. A lot of the local athletes enjoyed the tests Yvonne performed on them to examine their oxygen levels, metabolic rates, and other vital measurements to assess their overall health, deficiencies, and strengths.

As I stood admiring the room, I noticed something move on the wall next to me. A huge spider crawled on the thermostat, wiggling one of its legs on the plastic.

I shivered.

I hated spiders ever since my cousin tossed one in between my bed sheets. I'd never quite gotten over the panic from that night or the huge welt it left on my leg from its bite.

I knew they served a purpose in the great scheme of life, but why did they have to hang out with us? Couldn't they just live in the woods or under a pile of rocks like creatures should? Wouldn't their food source be more plentiful that way? They'd have a better chance of meeting their mates and having spider babies, wouldn't they? How would a spider get pregnant hanging out on a thermostat in an aquatic center? Surely some programming in evolution went wrong along the way.

Dumb spider.

I stared at it, contemplating my options.

I couldn't just leave it there. What if it disappeared before someone could catch it?

I looked around and spotted a swim fin.

Grasping it, I tiptoed over to the spider with it. I stood at arm's length from it, staring at its black skin and creepy hair.

The room sat silent between us, except for the hum of the air vents.

I moved in closer, waiting for the perfect moment.

It wiggled again.

Now or never. I closed my eyes, wound up my arm, and smacked the wall with the fin, creating a loud crashing thud.

I screamed and ran to the door.

Slowly, I turned around, with my hands over my eyes, and peeked through my fingers. The thermostat's faceplate hung, and wires dangled from it. The spider sat on the floor up against the wall.

I inched closer to see if it was dead. It began to wiggle again and fled across the floor at me.

I screamed and ran. I ran as fast as my feet would carry me out of that room, slamming the door shut.

I stood in the hallway for a good half hour contemplating my next move, staring at the frosted French doors.

I couldn't go back in there.

So, I left the frosted doors closed and walked out to the reception area to straighten up the semi-circle of my giveaways one more time. About twenty minutes later, Yvonne walked in.

"Hey," I said.

"Hey." Yvonne took in the front room scene, and nodded her approval. "This deserves more than just a 'hey.' This looks great, kid."

I shook off a residual shiver. "Now I just hope everyone shows up."

She headed over to the front desk, carrying her tote bag full of her nutritional goodies, most likely flaxseeds, chia seeds, egg beaters, watermelon, pineapple, and some form of lentil dish. "You're nervous. Don't be."

I walked over to her and took her tote bag from her. "I'm not nervous."

She nodded her head, then flipped through the schedule book. "You're wearing heels. You're nervous."

"Only because my work shoes are being washed."

"Save it." She turned to me and grabbed a hold of my shoulders. "You're also wearing your push-up bra. Can I just say? I am very jealous of your perky boobs."

I laughed. "Yvonne!"

"Enjoy them while they're still flying high. That's all I'm saying."

I punched her arm. "So you like the setup?"

101

"It looks great. Honestly, it does." She looked toward the hallway. "I want to check on the rooms and freshen them up a bit."

"I already did."

"You know me. I'm a perfectionist." She shimmied out from behind the receptionist desk.

I swallowed, trying to figure out how to break the news to her that I broke her thermostat. "Oh, hey, did you see the kids this morning?"

"No. But, I sure heard them," she said. "They were sliding down the stairs on their rumps. Sounded like an earthquake."

"They love your stairs."

"Well, I don't like earthquakes."

I latched onto her from behind and hugged her. "You can act tough all you want, but I can see right through it. You're a softy just like the rest of us. Thank you for putting up with us the way you do."

She pulled out of my arms and headed for the display table. "I don't like the way these are falling all over each other. You can't tell what they are." She began rearranging the giveaways. "You know, those kids are doomed with a bunch of softies like us as role models."

My heart sank when she joked with me about things like that. I hoped she was wrong. They were spoiled beyond belief. I couldn't stand to ruin their fun or shovel more hurt into their lives than their father already did. The man promised to pick them up on weekends and only did so once a month. Yet, he flaunted how great his stepchildren were, and how great a stepdad he was to them. My kids never got to see Disney World or go camping in the Shenandoah Mountains the way his stepchildren did. His stepchildren walked around with the latest technological gadgets, meanwhile he supplied his own kids their leftovers. He even dropped off three bags of their used clothes, telling Charlotte and Anthony they were for them now. He noted that they were "designer clothes." Like that meant something to a six and an eight year old.

"There. That's better." She swiped her hands, then walked toward the hallway.

"Seriously, I already straightened out the back rooms. Let's have some tea instead."

"Your idea of straightening up and mine are on different spectrums, honey." She bee-lined for the hallway.

My mouth dried up. Everything sped along so perfectly until I ran into that stupid spider. "Yvonne."

She turned. "Yeah, honey?"

My cell phone rang. It was Lia. "Hang on, let me get this. Don't go anywhere. I need to tell you something before you head back there."

I picked up. "Hello."

"Hey, good morning. It's Lia," she said with a happy beat.

"Hey, happy Saturday," I said with way too sexy a tone.

"I'm heading there now. I just wanted to check in beforehand to see if you need anything for the open house. Donuts? Cookies? Bacon? Any other artery clogging substances I'm overlooking?"

I loved her sense of humor. "Green tea maybe?"

Silence.

"I'm kidding."

She laughed. "I would've hunted it down."

"I don't doubt it," I said. "Just bring yourself."

"Oh Fuck," Yvonne yelled. "Willow, what have you done?"

I gritted my teeth. "Shit."

"What's happening?" Lia asked.

"You don't happen to have a tool belt you can bring with you, do you?"

"Are you serious?"

"Willow?" Yvonne yelled again.

"I have to go." I hung up and braced for my verbal lashing.

I ran toward the door and down the hall. My heels clacked against the ceramic tile. With each step, my toes jammed against the unforgiving leather. I passed by the two Reiki rooms and through the open consultation area with its magnanimous wall hangings of a Shaman and wolves. Then, I passed through the frosted French doors to the aquatic room and met up with a wave of heat.

"I'm sorry," I said, bending over at the knees to take in whatever left over coolness remained in the lower extremes of the room.

She stared at the loose wires. "What did you do? Take a baseball bat to it?"

"Not a baseball bat."

"It's broke. I can't turn the thermostat down. It's all the way up to ninety-five degrees."

"Can't you just turn off the machine?"

She turned around. "The machine?" She threw her head back and groaned.

I clasped my hands over my face. "I'm sorry."

"I've got my mother's group from the senior center coming in later this afternoon for their first aquatic fitness class. I've been trying to get her to agree to come here for months. I even arranged a senior shuttle. They'll be stepping off that shuttle wearing their skirted bathing suits and bathing caps, clutching their canes and heading into the water to relieve them of pain that's been building for years. This cannot be broken today, of all days."

"What can I do?"

"We need to fix this."

She stared at me like I carried a tool belt around my waist. "Can't we call a repairman?"

"On a Saturday?"

I squirmed my toes around in my heels, trying to find an area in them that wouldn't chafe, as I attempted to comfort the onset of a blister. "I'm in a dress." I looked down at it, showcasing it like a sheath of rare jewels instead of the thirty-nine ninety-nine special I'd found on the clearance rack at the outlet stores.

"Like that matters." She swallowed back her disappointment. "We don't have any tools in here anyway." She looked around the room as if we stood in the center

104

of The Home Depot, and wrenches, hammers and screws should've been stacked up along the finely-painted walls. Crossing her arms over her chest, she exhaled. "I'll just deal with it." She kicked the fin I had used in my attempt to smash the spider. "Somehow."

"I'm so sorry."

"Why did you break it?"

I dropped my arms and cleared my throat. "I um, broke it when I tried to fix something."

"Fix something?"

I cleared my throat again this time with more force. "I saw a spider."

"A spider. Of course. Destroy the world to get rid of a spider." She looked around the floor. "Where is it?"

My face turned blotchy. "It got away." My voice turned into a wisp of air.

"Well thank God for the spider's sake." She walked past me and pushed through the glass doors. "I have to rebalance. I'm going to meditate for a few minutes."

Lia had called almost an hour ago, and still hadn't arrived.

Dr. Rhonda walked over to the projected image on the wall and pointed to a flowchart. "Ninety-five percent. That's how many Americans will be overweight or obese in two decades if they keep filling their fridges and cupboards with empty calories of junk."

The thirty people who showed up nodded and mumbled words like 'wow' and 'crazy' and 'unacceptable' as she paced the floor.

Just then, Lia and Dean opened the door. Her face turned bright red. "I'm so sorry we're late." They hurried past Dr. Rhonda and down the aisle between the two rows of chairs I set up. She spotted me leaning up against the receptionist desk and shuffled over to me, mouthing an apology.

She wore her hair gelled and tousled, and smelled earthy and fresh like she'd just walked through a pine forest. She dropped her backpack on the ground and unzipped

105

it. "See," she whispered. "I stopped by my father's for his tool belt." She smiled, and in that smile radiated a warmth that evaporated all traces of my earlier stress.

"So anyway, as a country we have a real dilemma," Dr. Rhonda continued.

Lia straightened up and listened to the speaker, but not first without offering me a guilty shrug.

I adored her innocence and quiet confidence. My smile threatened to overtake my entire face.

"The problem with people is that they want miracles and a quick fix," Dr. Rhonda said, pausing on point with her sharp inflection. "They want to pop a pill and continue on as normal without changing anything else in their lives. They don't realize that they could save lots of money on visits to medical specialists if they just cut out junk food and got their digestive tracts in better shape. The truth is, people are unwilling."

Lia crossed her arms over her chest and nodded, taken in by Dr. Rhonda's information. I sensed her mental wheels cranking, allowing the information to seep in and revolutionize her thinking on health and wellness. A curiosity swam in her dark eyes as if experiencing a delightful ah-ha moment. Her eyes zeroed in on the speaker, as a recognition seemed to play out in her mysterious mind. The tight folds of uncertainty that always accompanied her loosened and released a new level of clandestine intelligence.

She intrigued me.

The speaker presented fascinating information on the digestive system and how it affected the entire human body system if out of alignment. Meanwhile, in between her pregnant pauses my stomach gurgled as if on cue. Every time it did, Lia would nudge me with her elbow while smiling and looking straight ahead. I'd catch her peeking at me out of the corner of her eyes, probably trying to see if I flinched or not.

No flinching or sensing happened the entire two hours we listened to both speakers present their information. After the presentations, Yvonne thanked everyone for coming and welcomed them to stay and ask questions.

A group gathered around. Lia's friend, Dean, stood right next to her.

Lia picked up her backpack. "I hope you have patience, because Dean is going to become your resident client now that he has heard everything laid out for him. He's going to drive me nuts. I just know he is."

"What about you? What did you think?"

She tossed her backpack over her shoulder. "The second speaker lost me at gluten-free. I can't imagine abandoning whole wheat pasta and bread."

"Ah, you like the brain fog, then."

"It protects me from all the stupid people in the world." She chided herself. "It's my protective barrier, my shield, my safe place."

"Well, Ms. Foggy, how about I show you my mess from this morning and see if one of those tools will help us put it back together again. By then, Yvonne should be free."

"With Dean asking questions, Yvonne will never be free."

"Come on," I reached out for her hand and led her down the hallway.

We walked past the candle lit rooms and the consultation room, and straight ahead to the aquatic center's doors. "Prep yourself. It's going to get hot."

"Oh?"

I opened the doors and heat smacked us in the face.

"You weren't kidding."

Steam limited our view. I scanned the immediate floor for the spider, and when I didn't see it, I led Lia to the thermostat. "I kind of got a little crazy this morning."

She laughed and moved in closer to examine it.

I moved in and examined it with her. Our breaths swam together in the sea of steam before us.

"I'm not even going to ask how you did this."

"It's best to leave that up to your imagination."

"My imagination tends to run pretty wild," she said.

"Even better," I said, daring closer to her. "Much more exciting than if I told you the real reason was a spider."

She turned to me, and chuckled. "That's adorable," she whispered, her breath mixing with mine. "I'll just need you to turn off the circuit breaker for this room."

"You talk like you've gotten your hands dirty in this type of thing before."

A cocky smile crept onto her face. "I've gotten my hands dirty quite a few times over the years."

Our chests rose and fell in unison. "It's hot in here."

Her lips brushed the air next to mine. "You don't say."

My pulse quickened. Her heart beat just as wildly as mine. I boldly reached for her hands, and caressed them in mine.

She followed my brave move with one of her own. She traced my lips with the tip of her finger and stared deep into my eyes, then took my hand in hers.

I wanted to kiss her.

She traveled to my cheek, sweeping it with gentle strokes.

I closed my eyes to savor the intimacy, leaning in closer to catch the warmth of her on my face. She placed her moist lips on my cheek. They trembled against my skin, causing my heart to twirl. She traveled down to the corner of my lips, and nibbled ever so gently on that sensitive spot.

Her tongue unfurled, as if indulging in the taste of me.

I needed to kiss her.

She lingered on the corner of my lip as if waiting for the perfect moment to dare further. Time stood still as we embraced that present moment when nothing else in the world mattered, just the two of us caught up in a hot and steamy prelude to a kiss.

Her lips softened on mine, tender and delicate. I responded with a gentle moan. Our lips fit perfectly together, dancing in harmony as they feathered against each other in a slow, seductive passion that ignited my core. I let myself go, surrendering as she parted my lips with her tongue and twirled it with mine.

She sought me out with more intensity. I closed my eyes and embraced her soft, sweet touch, caving into that moment I'd only ever dreamed about. My body drifted alongside of hers, carefree and at home in the arms of a woman. A hunger to taste all of her sweetness drove me. Her lips heated against mine and she tasted fresh and minty. She ushered me into a heated tango, teasing me with her playful elegance. I loved the warmth of her lips on mine and the gentleness of her breath on my skin as we delved into the lustful swirl of our tantric first kiss.

My breath became her breath.

In a state of nirvana, I subconsciously floated, rising up into the vapors of the steam surrounding us. My body ached for her, wanting more. Her lips cradled against my tender skin, sending ripples through me. I entered a dreamlike state where the rest of the world vanished and allowed us the space and freedom to indulge in each other's sensual dance.

She slowed our kiss down, then traced her finger down my cheek and jaw line. "Did you feel anything?" she asked.

I struggled to find my voice. "Oh, I'd say so."

"Tell me what you saw this time."

I pulled back. "This time?"

She swept over my lips again. "Did you get another vision?"

Vision? She wanted a vision? I pushed off of her. "Really?" I fought to regain my senses. "Is that why you kissed me? To get a better vision?"

Her eyebrows furrowed. "I didn't mean it like that."

My heart sank. The air tightened in my lungs, pressing against my chest walls. I chastised myself for being such a fool to believe she enjoyed the kiss as much as I did and for believing that, for the first time ever, someone so beautiful could view me as someone more than a freak of nature. "I'm not some kind of an instrument you can tune into like a radio."

Lia stared at me with concern. "I don't think of you as a radio."

I blinked away the embarrassment. "I should get back out to Yvonne and the rest of the group."

She placed her hand on my arm. "I didn't mean to upset you. I enjoyed the kiss. Really, I did."

I didn't have to be a psychic to see the truth in that lie. "I'll switch off that circuit breaker for you." I walked away from her and headed out of the pool room, poised despite the hurt.

Chapter Nine
Lia

I stood in the dark, trying to recapture my senses. I could still taste Willow on my lips and smell her light fragrance in the steam. I had hurt her, and hated myself for it.

I never should have kissed her in the first place. *Why did I kiss her?*

My goal was not to fall into her arms like some lovesick puppy. I wanted answers. But, the steamy heat, the closeness of her face with mine, and her innocence to her mishap wove together and formed an intimacy that I couldn't deny myself. I folded into the moment, and savored it. My knees had buckled, and every fiber of my being had capsized in the wake of her touch. In that moment when our lips touched and my heart spun erratically, I had panicked.

I don't think of you as a radio?

"Argh." I cringed and bent over at the knees. I could've gone with something a little more prolific and less demeaning.

Just then, the door opened and Willow walked back in.

"Are you alright?" she asked.

I stood up and the heat smacked me like a hammer in the head. "Yeah. I'm good."

"I just wanted to check that I clicked the right circuit breaker." Her voice rose up in an animated tone.

"Seems so." I smiled at her silhouette.

"You don't have to do this," she said, coming over and checking out my tool kit.

She was right. I could've just walked away from the whole mess right then. Just packed up the tool kit, walked through the frosted doors, grabbed Dean and got out of that place, leaving behind the memory of the kiss and the anxiety of a silly psychic vision.

"You're hesitating," she said. "I'm sensing you're not comfortable with any of this."

"By any of this, you mean the thermostat?"

"What else would I mean?" she laughed.

"Nothing, I suppose. Listen, I'm going to fix this." I bent down again, and reached into the tool kit for a screwdriver.

"No," she said, picking up my father's rusty hammer and examining it in the glow of my flashlight, like it was an ancient tool picked out of an archaeological site. "Don't trouble yourself over that. Come back out to the front and talk with Yvonne."

"I can talk to her after." I reached out for the hammer. "I want to fix it."

She raised her hands in surrender. "Fine. I'm not going to argue." She began to back away. "Can I at least get you a cup of tea?"

I placed the hammer back down in the tool box and studied her. "You do believe me when I tell you our kiss meant something, right?"

She chuckled, stretching her eyes up in a playful dance. "It was just a kiss. Not a big deal."

My heart took a nosedive.

She had moaned during our kiss. She had caved. She had sunk against me. "I don't believe you."

She crossed her arms over her chest. "How can you state that so confidently without having any psychic ability?"

Were we teasing? "I don't need to be a psychic to know that you are lying."

"You're being too serious about this," she said, waving me off. "It was just a silly kiss."

My heart halted. "A moment ago you walked away upset with me."

She placed her hand on the door frame. "You like to flatter yourself, I see." She shook her head and smiled.

I stuttered over a comeback, but none matched hers. "Maybe I misread."

112

"Sure your timing to ask me about a vision was horrible, but eh, who cares? You're curious. I get it. You figured my lips would tune you into a clearer channel setting. It's not the first time, and won't be the last time." She turned and walked out of the room, leaving a trail of mystery behind.

Just a kiss? Not a big deal?

I bounced the light around the wall in a chaotic frenzy, trying to digest the past few minutes.

I should've just left. I should've just escaped through the emergency door and called Dean to have him meet me around the backside of the center. I could go back to my life and pretend Willow never appeared. I could refocus on my work, take better care of myself, and never ever step foot in that flea market or wellness center again.

Walk! Just get the hell out of harm's way. Go!

I didn't do any such thing. Instead, I stood in the dark reliving her kiss, feeling faint with desire over how much I still wanted to taste her, put my lips on her soft cheeks, and enjoy her freshness again. I wanted her to lean into me and whisper how she loved being so close to me. I wanted to hook onto that sense of freedom enjoyed moments ago when she responded to my touch with a deep and meaningful sigh.

I wanted that moment back, and all the moments that preceded it.

In a comfortable kind of way, I enjoyed volleying Willow around in my mind. She kept me company without even knowing. She kept me company when I woke and when I went to sleep. Her voice traveled in and kept me company during long client meetings and long into the night when I sat alone in my condo watching late night television. I didn't want to shut off her light just yet. I enjoyed its warmth, and its undetermined direction. I liked not knowing what to expect on the other side of the curve. She interested me in a brand new way. She wasn't a textbook personality with refined features that spelled out exactly how she would act in any given circumstance. I never knew what would escape from her mouth, and I enjoyed that unpredictability.

She sprinkled fresh air into the staleness that had become my life. She managed to find her way through the locked windows and doors, curling her energy and personality up into hidden cracks and showering me in the unexpected. The air around her moved freely, and when I walked in that air, I glided, like gravity no longer weighed me down.

I was sure she reciprocated those feelings.

So, like hell she was over it. Granted, I effed up comparing her to an inanimate object. What woman wouldn't protect herself with a nonchalant front after such an attack?

I would smooth over my stupid remark by fixing the thermostat and hopefully proving that kiss meant more than just an investigative study into my future.

"Okay," I said, swiping my hands together like I knew what the hell to do with the thermostat. I stared at the loose wires and the bent casing.

I had no freaking clue how to fix it.

So, standing in the dark, I decided to call my father and ask for his help.

"Are the wires ripped and smashed too?" he asked.

I examined them, switching over to Bluetooth to free my hands for the flashlight. "They look intact." *At least something still was.*

My father talked me through the mechanics of how to fix that thermostat.

I took it apart, found the loose wire culprit, rewired it, straightened the casing box out with a rubber mallet and put it all back together again as my father remained patient on the other end.

"I couldn't have done this without you, Dad."

"Eh, it's a piece of cake."

"Yeah, I guess you're right." I stepped back and admired the remounting. "I should turn on the circuit breaker to see if it works."

"Remember, your circuit panel is a little tricky. I labeled each room on a spreadsheet."

"Oh, I'm not at my place. This is for a wellness center I'm visiting. As a matter of fact, do you remember that girl Willow that Anna feared from the campground?"

"How can any of us forget?"

I laughed recalling Anna's extreme praying to ensure Willow didn't read her mind.

"Well, she works here, and the thermostat broke, so..."

"Are you friends with her?" His tone changed from concern to judging.

"Sort of." I feared pushing the button too hard, not wanting to hear that tone.

"I know I don't have to warn you about her."

I gritted my teeth, bracing for a wave of disappointment that my father, my sweet father, could be judgmental. "I'm a big girl now, Dad."

"You're also naïve."

I jumped into defense mode. "Naïve?"

"Naïve in a sweet, endearing way, Lia." He cleared his throat. "That girl was never right. She even scared Father Richard."

"She's a nice person, Dad."

"Easy does it kiddo. I'm not trying to start an argument. I just want you to use your head."

I heard enough. "Thanks for the tip. I can handle it from here."

"I know you can. Now listen, I'll wait on the phone while you turn on the circuit breaker."

"I've got it from here. Thanks for your help. I have to go." Bitterness sat on my tongue, burning a hole through it.

I hung up on my father before he could say goodbye.

# #

I walked back into the receptionist area, and Willow was talking to a skinny guy with a bald head. He leaned in close to her and talked too loud for the small area.

"The guy was ready to charge me five hundred dollars to replace the engine in the lawn mower. I was like, hey man, I'm going to be dead next summer. I'm not going to pay you five hundred dollars."

"What did he say?" Willow asked.

"Well, his jaw hit the floor," the guy laughed obnoxiously. "And after he picked his fat jaw off the scummy floor, you should have seen him. He stuttered all over the freaking place." His laughter grew even more obnoxious.

"Did he discount it for you, at least?" she asked.

"The guy did it for free."

"For free?"

"What can I say? Having cancer has some perks," he said, backing away and raising his hands up in the air like he just scored a touchdown. "Hey, doll, I'll catch you later. Don't forget to call me when my probiotics arrive. I'll have the wifey stop by and pick them up for me."

"Sure thing, Pat. Tell her and your daughter I said hi."

He walked past Yvonne. "Bye beautiful." He bent down to kiss her cheek. "Thanks again for letting me use the hot tub. Legs were extra tight today. I'm as pliable as Gumby now." He released one more obnoxious laugh before heading out of the door.

"That guy," Yvonne said, "is nuts. Certifiably nuts. I couldn't love him more."

Dean stared out the window at him, as he dashed across the busy street.

"He's got cancer," she said. "He's done a couple of talks here for us. He's hysterical, and helps put life into perspective for people."

"What kind of cancer?" Dean asked.

"Liver cancer. The guy ran a marathon and experienced a stabbing pain as he crossed the finish line. He thought he suffered a muscle spasm. Turned out he had not one but three baseball sized tumors sitting on his liver."

Dean bowed his head. "How's he still laughing?"

Yvonne shrugged.

116

I turned to Willow to get away from the conversation. She typed a document, focusing on it like she was decoding critical information that could save humanity.

I tapped the desk. "I fixed it."

She turned her head on a snap. "Awesome. Thank you." She went back to typing.

Desperate to keep the lines of talk open with her, I decided to play her words back. "It was no big deal."

She never looked up at my smile. "So what do we owe you for that?" she asked, typing with renewed gusto.

I proceeded forward, tiptoeing on that line of vulnerability. "How about dinner at The Coastguard House?"

She looked up at me with a smirk. "Oh, I can't do that."

Turn around and walk out. Just bow your head, cut your losses, and save yourself from additional embarrassment. I ignored myself, tracing my finger along the edge of the desk. "Sure you can."

"I'm afraid not. Toss me a dollar figure."

My ego fell flat at my feet. "Fine. Five hundred ought to do it."

"I'll cut you a check in just a minute after I finish what I'm doing here." She picked up the phone, dialed, then, "Hey, Mrs. Friedman, I hoped I'd catch you." She looked up at me and placed her hand over the receiver, whispering, "Go introduce yourself to Yvonne. She's dying to meet you." She looked back at her computer as if I was nothing more than another patient in the center. "Yes, I'm preparing the documents now and am wondering if I should include last year's figures too or just the bottom line balance."

I waited for her call to finish. Each time she blinked in my direction, my blood turned colder. I effed up, big time.

"Very good, Mrs. Friedman. I'll send them over as soon as I'm done."

She hung up, and wrote something down.

"I was joking about the five hundred."

"But not about the dinner?" A tease played out in her eyes.

117

I had no idea how to play the game. So, I opted for an innocent shrug.

"We're not going for dinner. We're not looking for a handout. What's fair is fair. You fixed it. We owe you." Her eyes bore into mine.

"You sound like you're about to shake my hand and ask for my W-9 form." I laughed.

She didn't. She continued to stare me down.

"I'm not taking money."

"Well," she said, hitting the printer icon. "We do have some valuable holistic insights to share. Will that do?"

I didn't dare refuse. "I'm open to hearing it."

She laughed, and in her eyes I saw a flirt. "Let's see what we can do." She walked away from the desk and toward Yvonne and Dean.

"Okay." I followed her.

She swung her hips and walked with a new lift of confidence under her feet, swinging her arms and commanding the floor. "Yvonne, have you met Lia?"

Yvonne, a solid, strong woman with short, highlighted hair, folded her hands out in front of her. "You were my other late arrival." She extended her hand. "Please, let's have a seat over by the window."

Dean lifted up a small baggie of purple colored salt crystals to me. "Get some of these. They're supposed to relieve stress. Just plop some in the bath water and voila."

"You're such a good student," I said, gripping his upper arm and pinching it.

He yelped, then sat down on the edge of the couch.

A young woman wearing an apron with the center's logo on it brushed into the room to clear the tables of literature.

"April, can you get us some tea," Willow asked, placing a clipboard on her lap. "The herbal infused with ginger, please."

The woman cocked her head as if surprised by Willow's order, looked at Yvonne who nodded curtly at her, then shuffled toward the cart with the tea and treats.

"So Yvonne, Lia is here today because I invited her. I sensed an imbalance and just wanted to pass along information on how she can be proactive to gain balance back. I wanted to have her talk with you about a few techniques to get her started and maybe have you introduce her to some of the holistic services we offer."

Willow spoke with such sexy authority. Why couldn't she be a bitch or an airhead?

Yvonne tilted her head, examining Willow with amusement. "Of course." She then turned back to me. "Willow is my right hand person. She's perceptive and a gifted healer through yoga."

"Yoga is a phenomenal practice," Willow said all business-like. "Through it, a person can improve her flexibility, reverse the negative effects of cell oxidation, decrease inflammation, and help a person look and feel younger."

The woman wearing the apron handed me a tea cup.

"I assumed it had great benefits," I said to Willow.

"Of course it works best if a person is open to it. I get people in here all the time who balk at it and disrupt the flow of the energy in the room."

"I might be one of those," I said half-joking. "I once took a meditation class and had to walk out because I couldn't stop laughing. The teacher forced us to hum, and some people got a little crazy with theirs. I had to leave the room. I almost peed my pants."

"She would never survive yoga," Dean said, sipping his tea like a gentleman.

"That happens." Willow jotted something down on her clipboard. "You'd have to gain a lot of self-control before you enter a yoga studio."

"You say that like I don't have any now."

She squinted at me. "Okay, we'll just let that one rest."

I mirrored her squint, and flushed under her powerful eyes.

"She won't be practicing yoga any time soon." Dean bit into a cookie. "She's got zero self-control when it comes to laughing. She once laughed at a funeral. I'm not talking a little giggle. I'm talking laugh out loud, tears flowing, convulsing at the

119

shoulders laughing." He picked a crumb from his shirt and put it in his mouth. "No self-control. Not an ounce."

"Well, it's not meant for everyone." Willow crossed her legs and wrote some more.

I peeked at her clipboard but couldn't read it. "I'm sure I can handle it."

"Yoga isn't something to handle," Willow said with heavy command. "It's a well-respected practice."

Yvonne put her tea cup down without taking a sip. "Okay, so, we've established Lia is a laugher and yoga is supreme. Let's now get the conversation rolling over to why you're really here. You're looking for some answers, and I want to provide you with some." She folded her hands in front of her like a steeple.

"She's been driving me nuts," Dean said. "We need solutions to this imbalance." He grabbed another cookie from the tray on the table in front of him. "But, before we get to that, I'm curious about something. That guy that just left—you can't cure him with natural healing?"

"Odds are low," Yvonne said. "He came to us with advanced cancer."

"How successful is natural healing?" Crumbs dropped down to his lap.

"Depends how you measure success and what constitutes a need for healing."

"Aside from that guy, if someone comes to you with a death sentence over his head, do you typically cure him?" he asked.

"I'm not going to sit here and blow smoke up your ass, dear." She smiled as if she just offered us a plate of cookies and tall glasses of ice cold milk.

"I love this lady," Dean said.

I dug her too. I liked that she wasn't some pretentious doctor who couldn't crack a smile.

She smiled and winked at Dean. "First of all, our focus here is always on improving the quality of life, rather than engaging in a fight for survival. Embrace the enemy, and the enemy weakens." She winked.

"Oh, good one," Dean said.

120

"Also, a person has to believe in what we're doing here for it to work on a deep level. A lot of my patients are people who favor a proactive approach to their health. In other words, many come to me before issues arise so they can learn to heal themselves on a continual basis and not just in the darkness of an illness."

I jumped in. "So, kind of like washing one's hands before touching her face to prevent illness?"

She pointed her finger at me and offered me a wink. "Exactly."

Willow smiled, focusing her eyes on her paperwork as she curled her fingers around the ballpoint pen.

"We all need healing," Yvonne continued. "The world is cruel and can suck the life out of you. Just walking out that door and standing on the street corner can raise your blood pressure. Getting a call from a pain in the ass friend demanding your time can too. Returning a library book one day late can be a bitch. And traffic, don't even get me started." She sipped again. "That's why we all need healing."

Dean stared at her in awe. "Remarkable."

"That kind of stuff doesn't bother me," I said.

"Like hell," Dean said, before turning back to Yvonne. "Lia is the queen of road rage."

"I do not have road rage," I said to Yvonne.

"Of course not," she said with a motherly smile. "I can sense you're cool as a cucumber and healthy as a newborn baby," she added with a nod.

Willow shifted in her chair and continued jotting words down.

"I do feel great," I said. "I'm focused. I'm energetic. I don't have any aches or pains." I looked over to see if Willow noted that too. She sure did. "So, just playing devil's advocate here, what do you do with a healthy person like me who walks in?"

"Well, let's start with those who come to us with chronic illnesses like mood disorder, depression, anxiety, sleep disturbances, fibromyalgia and fatigue. We run a series of tests to find out if they're lacking any nutrients, how their body's PH levels are, or if they have any food sensitivities or not. We also recommend a comprehensive test that provides them with a fifteen page print out of everything and anything they've ever wanted to know about their bodily functions, including the Creb cycle."

"Thankfully, I don't have any of those disorders," I said on the end of a chuckle.

"I'd like to differ," Dean said. "Precisely on the mood disorder." He spoke to Yvonne. "If she doesn't get her bagel in the morning, then watch out world."

I looked over at Willow who had lost interest in taking notes on me.

"Yvonne," Willow said. "Maybe you can just list out a few home practices she can do to rebalance?"

I shrank on that couch. Willow's professional confidence outgrew the space between us and overinflated into the far recesses of the room. I morphed into a crumb in her way, an item on her to-do list that she could now check off and not look back on, a moral obligation completed.

"We should go," I said to Dean, trying to pull him up off the couch with me, but to no avail. He sat like a stubborn mule.

Yvonne charged forward with her advice. "Here's what I recommend to people like yourself who come to us already healthy. Be proactive with your health so you don't get to a point where you need to run expensive tests and visit every specialist up the east coast to find answers to any future plaguing issues."

Dean crossed his legs, and pumped the air in a nervous frenzy. "How does one go about doing that?"

"Start meditating, daily," she said, speaking to him instead of me. "Soak your feet in Epsom salt each night for magnesium. Start your day off with sun salutations to get your blood flowing and your body balanced. Take a probiotic to regulate your digestion. And eat a balanced diet."

The entire couch began shaking under Dean's foot pumping. I shot him a look.

He stopped. "So, you heard her. Next week we schedule for all such activities."

"Do you even know what a sun salutation is?" I asked him.

"I'm from India. I know a sun salutation when I see one."

"It's on YouTube, just in case you need a refresher." Yvonne winked.

"Who doesn't need a refresher from time to time?" he asked.

"I recommend a good refresher." Yvonne stood up. "So, that's it. I'm not going to poke and prod you with needles and gadgets just yet." She winked again, bending over to shake my hand. "But, if you so insist, I am here. We offer many proactive services like acupuncture, reiki, and yoga to keep you focused on a healthy lifestyle. We even have a pool in the back to do yoga and laps."

"Yes," I said. "I saw the pool. I fixed your broken thermostat."

Yvonne blinked. "I assumed you were just being rude disappearing during my lecture."

"She fixed it, and refuses to take any money," Willow said.

"Well," Yvonne said, wrapping her arm around my shoulder. "You just earned yourself a free acupuncture session."

"I don't think so. I'm not a needle person."

"Can I come in her place?" Dean asked.

Yvonne pinched his cheek. "You, my friend, are welcome here any time. I wish for a hundred patients just like you."

His dimples grew deeper in the wake of her compliment.

"You really fixed my thermostat?" she asked as she walked us toward the front door.

"Yes. It was simple."

"Well, I don't care what anyone else says. You're a keeper." She hugged us both, thanked me again, and opened the door.

Willow clutched the clipboard. "Thanks again." She ripped off the paper and handed it to me. "Payment for your help today. Transcript of today's session along with Yvonne's invaluable suggestions. Do these and you'll be rebalanced in no time."

I looked down at her handwriting. It was awful. "If I can't read your writing?"

"Call Yvonne. She'll remember everything you both talked about."

"Of course." I folded the paper and stuck it on my tool kit.

"Good luck with everything," she said with riveting calmness.

123

"Thanks." I nodded and closed the door, carrying the heavy loss of possibility with each step I took away from her.

I hated loss more than I hated needles, and perhaps even more than Willow hated spiders.

Chapter Ten

Just as I had feared. Willow became that unattainable challenge who sat out in front of me like an elusive dream, taunting me every morning, afternoon, and evening.

For the entire month following my visit to the center, I hadn't been very successful with my focus. I needed her out of my mind, and so I poured every last bit of my energy into my business.

As another month passed, I began to regain my business footing. I called old clients and rekindled working relationships with them. I strategized new campaigns in place of tired old ones. I designed new concepts to replace outdated ones. I even landed a few clients on the evening news by arranging a media party that included lobster, fresh out of the ocean, thanks to a client of mine who was in the lobster industry.

Business was great, and I began to regain my stride.

Then, Dean and I decided to take a drive to Newport to scope out a few local businesses in need of a marketing revamp. At least, we aimed to do that. Instead, we got sidetracked by all the shopping and sites. We acted like a couple of tourists, just like we did every time we hit Newport. "You need to talk me out of business trips here," I said, licking my Pistachio ice cream.

He spooned a heap of Chocolate Chip ice cream into his mouth. "Never."

We walked back to my car in the parking garage, loaded up on ice cream and empty on new clients. I tossed my shopping bags in the bin of my truck and hopped in the front seat.

Not until we drove up to the garage's exit, did I realize I had tossed my pocketbook in with the shopping bags. "I need some money," I said to Dean.

"I don't have any. I left my wallet at the office."

"Seriously?"

He nodded. "Afraid so."

I climbed out of my truck to get my pocketbook and already three cars pulled up behind me, headlights on, ready to charge. I rushed to get my pocketbook. Back in the driver's seat, I thumbed through to find a few dollars and pulled up to pay the clerk.

"Where's the person who's always here?" I asked Dean.

"This world no longer needs people to run. Machines do a far more efficient job. Hope you have a credit card."

I pulled out my credit card and it fell to my truck's floor. "Shit." I bent down to get it and pushed it too far out of my reach. "What the hell." I climbed out of my door, reached under the seat, and grabbed around for it.

The horns started beeping. "Come on lady. Get your act together."

I reached further, pulling out a coffee cup, a candy bar wrapper, and a package of crackers. Finally, I found the credit card.

The horns beeped louder. Now six cars piled up behind us.

Suddenly Dean started screaming and batting his hands around his face. "Argh, A wasp. It's a wasp." He banged his shoulder up against the door. "Get me out. Argh it's attacking me." He swatted himself and pushed against the door again.

"Just open the door handle," I said to him.

He glazed over in panic. The wasp buzzed around, toying with him. Dean's arms flailed, and he managed to grab the handle and fall out of the door and onto the pavement below. The wasp followed him. He swatted some more. The horns beeped some more. The man yelled some more. And before I knew it, Dean screamed bloody murder. "It's stinging me." He crawled to his feet and ran around in circles beating up the wasp while grabbing his neck.

I ignored the beeps and yells and ran to his aid. His face turned beet red, and panic rested on every square inch of the poor guy's face.

"Let's get you back in the truck." I put my arm around him and walked him to his door.

I sat back in my seat, armed with my credit card. "You're going to be fine. It was just a little wasp. We'll have a good laugh about this in a few minutes once I get out of this effing parking garage." I swept my credit card in the machine and waited for the arm to lift up and set us free.

I pulled out and began driving down the road, then looked over at Dean. He grabbed his neck, and his face turned white. He struggled to breathe. "Dean," I shook him.

He turned to me and mouthed. "I can't breathe."

"You're fine," I shook his arm. "You're just panicking. Stop panicking." Meanwhile my heart raced. I swept my eyes from him to the road, and I decided to just pull over. "You are fine, aren't you?"

He shook his head. "My tongue is swelling."

I opened his mouth and his tongue had doubled in size. "Shit."

I pulled out my cell phone and called 911, yelling at the operator to get us help STAT.

She kept me on the phone, reassuring me help was on the way.

Dean broke out in hives all over his face, neck, and arms. He began to wheeze, and looked over at me. "It's happening."

I shook him. "What is? What's happening?"

"My allergy," he whispered. Then, he collapsed onto me.

#

I drove behind the ambulance, praying Dean's shot of epinephrine continued to work until we got to the safety of the hospital and were surrounded by instruments, miracle medicines, and doctors who could keep him alive.

When we arrived, a security officer told me I couldn't park at the entrance. I screamed at him, tossed my keys at him, and told him to either move it himself or tow it. I followed the paramedics as they wheeled Dean into the emergency room. A team of nurses waited on his arrival and carted him off to a private curtained corner. They placed a new oxygen mask on his face, stuck him with an IV, and took his vitals, all

127

while he stared at me with huge eyes, as if daring me to disagree that psychics were real.

Then, the doctor on call walked in wearing a smile and joked saying, "The best way to get out of a day of work is to piss off a wasp."

By then, even Dean cracked a smile.

The doctor walked over to the hand sanitizer dispenser and rubbed his hands together, then pulled off Dean's mask. "Take a nice deep breath."

Dean did as instructed, not taking his eye off the handsome blonde doctor. "Oh, that's much better," Dean said, with a flirt to his voice.

My God, Dean flirted with a doctor in a hospital. The hairs on my arms stood up tall.

The doctor picked up Dean's wrist and took his pulse.

I waited for drool to start leaking down his chin.

Yeah. He was going to be just fine. I relaxed in a nearby chair.

"Nice," he said. "Pulse is perfect." He checked Dean's IV, then listened to his lungs. "You're going to live."

Dean inhaled. "So does this mean I get to carry around one of those nifty epi pens?"

"I'll see what I can do about hooking you up with one." He examined his face. "You've got a few hives still enjoying a bit of a party on your cheeks here. They'll go away with the IV meds. We'll have you stay here for a little while longer with it." He looked at the side of Dean's neck. "You have a small bump right below your ear. How long has this been there?"

Dean shrugged. "I didn't know it took up refuge on me." He smiled, clearly proud of his playback on humor.

The doctor's brows furrowed as he examined it. "It could just be a swollen gland. Have you been sick with a cold lately?"

"Nope." His face grew concerned. "Should I be worried?"

128

"It's probably nothing more than your body fighting against a virus or upcoming cold. Just to be sure, I would recommend that you follow up with your primary care doctor."

"Okay," he said, swallowing heavily.

I could see the questions racing around his brain already. His night would consist of reading the entire site of WebMD. I would get numerous calls after midnight with prognoses that delved into the warped category. He would most likely believe by sunrise that he was dying and needed to write a will before having to undergo surgeries and treatments for some weird disease he contracted somewhere between India, America, and our ride down to Newport that afternoon.

"Okay, my job here is done," he said. "Once the IV is done dripping, the nurse will remove it, issue you an epi pen, and you'll be on your way." He shook Dean's hand. "Be sure to get that bump on your neck checked out. Better to be safe than sorry, right?"

"Right." He eyed the doctor carefully.

Poor Dean was in for a rough night.

When he walked out, I expected a full launch into panic mode, consisting of sweats, chest pain, and dramatic pleas to God to save him during that trying period.

Instead, he sat calm, folding his hands in his lap. He picked up the remote and clicked on the television, settling on *The Ellen DeGeneres Show*. A smile spread across his face as he watched her dance through the aisles of her studio, shaking her hips and shimmying against happy fans who eagerly shimmied back. "I love this woman," he said, shaking his head, not taking his eyes off the screen.

I opened my mouth to say something in follow-up to the doctor's concern, but closed it when I saw his eyes sparkling as he watched a few hundred people having a good time. I pulled my chair up next to him, embracing the peace in that moment; the moment when the world stood still and allowed my good friend Dean to laugh without a knowing care in the world.

# #

In the two weeks that followed, Dean slacked off at work. Typically he arrived well before I did, oftentimes working through lunch to stay ahead of the crazy schedule he kept for us both. Not that week. He kept taking 'walk' breaks where he'd plug in his earphones and walk up and down four flights of stairs for fifteen minutes at a time. Several times, I walked in on him lying on a yoga mat in his office, earphones plugged in, head and knees propped up with sweaters that were usually hanging off his chair, and eyes closed. "I'm balancing my chakras," he would say.

I'd just walk out, close the door, and pretend not to be concerned that my former hard-working assistant had turned into an office slacker.

A few times in those weeks, he'd let my phone go to voicemail. I'd peek into his office to see why, and I'd find him watching funny videos on YouTube, cracking himself up.

Then, one morning, almost three weeks into his slacker journey, he didn't show up for an important day of work. I had to face a set of high-end clients without any of the usual prep he painstakingly went through. He hadn't created folders, cheat sheets, or conducted preliminary research. I sat at the head of the office conference table, staring into the eyes of clients who had been recommended to me, waiting on my words of wisdom. Without Dean's help, I stumbled and stuttered like a fool.

I was lost without him.

So, when he came back in the office sucking on a Dunkin Donuts iced-coffee, I called him in. "What the eff is going on here? Do you realize the clients now see me as a fool? I had nothing. You can't just leave like you did without any warning. I've got a business to run."

He stopped sucking on his straw and looked at me point-blankly. "And, I've got a life to live."

"What?" I tore into him. "Have you lost your mind?"

"Quite the contrary, Lia." He smiled at me with a smugness that he reserved for I-told-you-so moments, inhaling like we sat in a garden of roses. "My mind has never been clearer."

I stood up, walked over to the edge of my desk in front of him, and crossed my arms. "What's going on?"

He met my stern gaze. "If you must know," he said, pointing his finger. "Though, I am under no legal obligation to tell you, seeing as you are my boss and can pull the rug out from under me very easily shall you not like what you hear."

"Just tell me."

He drew another sip. "I met with an oncologist this morning."

The blood drained from my face. I fumbled to keep my balance on the edge of the desk. "An oncologist? Why an oncologist?"

His face sobered. "My primary care advised me to after he saw "suspicious artifacts" in my CAT scan. So, he referred me to the oncologist who had me get an MRI. I meet back with him in two days to go over the results. So, I'm going to need that day off. He's all the way up in Boston."

CAT scan? MRI? Oncologist? Boston? I squeezed the desk until my fingers tingled. "What is he looking for exactly?"

He tilted his head up at me. "Cancer I would presume."

I swallowed hard. "Why didn't you tell me sooner than this?"

He nodded, and smiled. "Some things in life are better dealt with alone."

Hurt blazed through me. I dragged him to a wellness center because of an irrational fear over a cute psychic's vision. The man faced possible cancer and he didn't need me?

I just wanted to hug him.

When I did, he patted my back as if to relieve me of my stress. I squeezed my eyes shut to stop the tears, but it was no use. They leaked like I'd turned on a faucet, rolling down my cheeks and onto his shirt. He just continued patting my back, nurturing me.

"We should get ready for your next client," he said.

I pulled away, wiping my face. "What do you say we get out of here for a few hours instead? Drive back to the beach and just hang out?"

He bounced his leg up and down, contemplating my proposition. "Your day is chocked full. You can't afford to."

I couldn't afford not to. "First one to grab their keys and get to the elevator drives?"

"I should have strange bumps pop up on my neck more often." His eyes twinkled. "Alright, then. You've got yourself a deal."

I bolted to my desk to get my keys, and he bolted to his office to get his. When I ran out of my office door and saw the grand smile on his face as he dipped his hand into his desk drawer for his set, I pretended to still be searching for mine in my light sweater hanging off the back of my door.

A minute later, he held the elevator for us. As I passed him by, he grabbed my arm. "You drive."

"Why? You won."

"Noble gesture." He nudged me onto the elevator. "But, I refuse to turn into your charity case just yet."

I playfully nudged him back, adding a forced giggle.

He just pushed the button, and off we went.

# #

Dean and I sat on the rocks overlooking Galilee. The air smelled like fried fish and salt. A steady breeze came in off the water and blew our hair, swelling it so we now looked like frizzy, cotton heads.

"I have to confess something to you," Dean said.

I couldn't take any more bad news. "Fess up." I tore off a piece of clam cake and tossed it to a seagull.

He stared out over the water, his eyes closed at half-mast. "I've never once in my life built a sandcastle."

"That's your confession?"

"What were you expecting, exactly?"

132

I bit into the clam cake. "Oh, I don't know, maybe something like, I'm a virgin or I've never tried pot. But, I've never built a sandcastle?"

"I have too tried pot."

I nudged him, accepting his confession and ignoring the one he failed to address. "So, you want to build a sandcastle?" I asked.

He looked at me like a child begging for candy. "Can we?"

"We can." I stood up and reached out for his hand. "We're going to use our chowder containers to do so, too."

He leaped to his feet. "Let's do it."

Within a few minutes, cups and containers gathered, we headed to the shore and began construction on our first ever sandcastle.

We spent two hours filling our cups with water and sand, building our dream castle.

Dean handed me a cup of water to fill the lake I created under the bridge. "I really did have something to confess earlier. It had nothing to do with sand and castles."

"It didn't?"

He shook his head. "I fibbed about that because I wasn't sure how to confess this."

My heart sank. "Is it bad?"

He tossed sand at me. "Only if you're not a fan of the idea of me indulging in some kickass yoga instruction from a beautiful yoga instructor."

I tossed sand back at him. "You went to see Willow without telling me?"

A cocky grin blossomed on his face. "Not yet."

"Yet?"

"I scheduled an appointment for acupuncture with Yvonne, and then a yoga class with Willow following it."

I carved a window into the tower, using a pen I found in my tote bag. "Go for it."

"You won't mind?"

"Who am I to stop you?" I carved too hard, and the window crumbled. "It's your money."

"Will you come with me?"

I stopped saving my broken window. "You know that would be awkward."

"I know. Forget I asked." He poured more water into our lake under the bridge.

"You're willing to go to an oncologist solo, but you want me to be there to do yoga poses?"

He shrugged. "A visit to an oncologist is not life affirming. Yoga is."

"You're saying my life needs affirming?" I stabbed the front lawn of the castle with my pen.

He arched his eyebrow at me. "I won't satisfy that question with an answer."

We continued to play in the sand. "I've been doing a lot of reading up on Yvonne's center," he said. "Everything they do there is in line with proactive health. I want to take all the right measures, just in case."

"Don't say that."

He formed a doorway using his chowder spoon. "Shall I just not talk about it, then?"

I cradled his wrist. "Let's just admire our castle and worry about everything else another time."

He sat back, taking in the full view of our four-tiered sandcastle, complete with a bridge, road, and grand entrance. "It is a beautiful structure."

I crawled up to his side and leaned against him. "It sure is."

We sat there for the next half hour, taking in the sea air, the seagulls, the kids running past us, and the water lapping up against the shoreline. Then, high tide rolled in reclaiming its rightful use over the land.

We stood up, and watched the sea swallow our bridge, our lake, and our beautiful sandcastle.

I looked up at Dean. A pensive look surfaced on the fine lines around his eyes, as if he willed tears to come. As usual, they remained stubborn and caused him to suffer in stoic silence.

I looked away, reaching for some strength from the sea to be the kind of friend he deserved. I put my arm around him and hugged him.

"There will be other sandcastles," I said, wiping away my downpour of tears.

"None ever as poignant as this one, though." He fought against his shaky voice. "I realize that sandcastles are temporary. Trying to build them into permanent structures is an impossible dream. They fall down quickly, with little warning. They crumble and fall back into the sea and become the foundation for something else in the waiting."

I slipped my arm around his waist and we stared out at the sea. "So profound."

"I certainly can be."

"Yes," I said, comforted by his lack of modesty. "You certainly can be, my friend."

We stood wading in the sea, clinging to the only certainty we had in that moment, which was each other.

#

That night, long after Dean and I had built a sandcastle and watched the tide sweep it away, I sat alone in my dark condo and analyzed Dean's confession. He wouldn't have gone to his appointment at the wellness center, an appointment he decidedly needed to go to, if I had asked him not to.

He cared more about me than himself.

I wanted to be by Dean's side through the ordeal. I had to find a way to touch base with Willow so I could walk into the center without causing more stress. For Dean's sake.

So, I called her.

She sounded sleepy when she answered. "Lia?"

"Can we talk?"

135

"Of course," she whispered.

I hesitated, not sure where to begin other than in the obvious place. "I'm sorry I called your aunt a fake."

"Okay. That was a long time ago. But I accept." She laughed. "Why are you calling me now and saying this?"

"It came true."

"What came true, Lia?"

"Your aunt forecasted Dean's allergy correctly. He landed in the hospital a few weeks ago after suffering a severe allergic reaction to a wasp."

She sighed. "She thought he would suffer a food allergy."

"She did?"

"She and I are not always right-on with things."

"The ER doc found a lump near a gland in his neck. He's seeing an oncologist to go over MRI results in a few days."

"I'm so sorry," she said in a soothing tone. "Are you alright? Is he alright?"

"I was hoping you could tell me."

She paused. "I wish I could. My visions aren't accurate. I see bits and pieces of scenes."

"Well, you visualized me in a hospital room pretty darn accurately. And Dean flirted with his doctor too."

"I wish I wasn't accurate."

I would hate to have her skill. "He's going in to see you for yoga soon."

"I know," she whispered. "I saw his name in the appointment book."

"I know you'll take care of him."

"He's going to be okay," she said with quiet confidence.

I balanced on that statement. "I believe you."

We paused.

"Lia? Can I be honest?"

My heart stopped. I needed hope, not more dread. "What is it?"

136

"I'm happy you called me."

My body warmed to the sound of that, sliding into its comfort head first. "I'm happy knowing that."

"I hope you'll consider coming with Dean."

Surrendering to her friendly welcome, I lowered all defenses. "I definitely will, now."

"I hope so. I won't even kick you out of yoga if you laugh."

"It's a date then," I said without hesitation.

"Great," she said softly. "It's a date."

We hung up and I just sat staring at my phone, embracing the warm sensations trickling through me. Hearing her voice comforted me, folding me into a temporary warm pocket that erased any trace of loneliness in that moment. I rested back against my bed, closed my eyes, and continued to enjoy the warmth she placed within me.

I dreamed of her again. This time, I imagined myself walking in a dark forest and down a cold and dreary path. I came across a well sitting in the middle of a clearing. I innocently opened up the lid to that well, climbed inside and began descending down a set of spiral steps. The deeper I got, the darker and colder the cave became. My curiosity fueled my desire to continue down to the bottom. So, further and further I descended into the cold, dark, recesses of Mother Earth, landing on a dirt floor. I looked to my right and noticed a doorway lit up. Unable to resist the temptation, I opened the door and discovered a raging river under a beautiful, pristine, blue summer sky. I escaped the dark cave in awe of the beauty, and found complete bliss in the refreshing splashes of tepid water from the raging river.

I scanned the landscape, and across the river I saw Willow. She wore a white, silky dress, and her hair hung down past her shoulders in adorable waves. She hoisted an umbrella and giggled as she looked up into its bright vortex. She danced around the edge of the river without a care of falling into it. With one graceful leap after another, she twirled and laughed her way to a swinging bench. Her smile radiated as she leaped onto it with her bare feet, cradling the long chains that secured it in place with one hand and the pink umbrella with the other. She leaned her head back, away from her umbrella and opened her mouth. Sticking out her tongue, she lapped up the fresh rain that began to drizzle down onto her red, rosy soft lips.

Just then, a rabbit scurried by her, and she called out to it. She leaped off the bench and onto the rocky ground, bending down to its level. She picked it up, and nuzzled its neck. It closed its eyes, obviously comforted by her sweet and innocent soul. The entire forest beamed to life with her presence. The green leaves danced in the wind, waving their beauty and offering her a light breeze to once again dance with. The ground smelled fresher. The air lightened. The sky looked bluer above the canopy of trees.

Willow twirled the rabbit with her, kissing its nose and humming a melody to it.

I wanted to dance with her like that. I wanted her soft lips to tickle my skin. I wanted her to spin me around in wide, wonderful circles as she tilted that umbrella at just the right angle to award us a splash of freshness without getting pummeled by the bigger drops. No distractions. No disease. No worry of psychic snippets slipping in to steal the moment. Just me and Willow, dancing to our own song, in our own forest, in the valley of greens, violets, yellows and pinks.

Mesmerized, I inched closer to the water's edge. Suddenly, the ground moved, pulling me away from her. It swept me so far away that she turned into a speck amongst the colorful backdrop, still twirling her pretty umbrella. Then, like a star in its final state, a small light flickered and grew into a great big light, too bright to look at. I peeked through my fingers, but the light blinded me.

Then, the ground stopped moving, and the light vanished.

I once again found myself in the bottom of that well staring up at the small light at the top of that long stairwell. I began to climb, and with each step I took, the heavy loss knocked me to my knees. I climbed those steep stairs on my knees, reaching up for the next step, desperate to get out of the damp darkness and back into the warm, healthy, healing light of Willow.

138

I reached the top and climbed out, staring in awe of the now gorgeous landscape in front of me. Wildflowers bloomed at my ankles as far as my eyes could see. I peered up at the sun. It beamed high in the sky. Its warmth trickled inside of me, protecting and loving, and reminded me that no matter where in the world I stood, I only had to peer up at the sky and know an energy existed on a universal level that would always work in my favor if I chose to invite it into my heart. I closed my eyes and fell to my knees in gratitude. I feared nothing. I controlled nothing. I wanted for nothing. In those brief moments down below, Willow had shown me life's true colors in the form of her love and admiration for life.

The air smelled so crisp, fresher than the ripest cucumber and nectarine and the most mature sprig of the garden. I dizzied myself on it, trying to capture as much of it as I could. I was ravenous and greedy and wanted to stockpile it until it overflowed, seeping into every single morsel of my being. I wanted to trap it inside of me and save it for those days when the skies opened up to torrential rain and when I sat alone in my condo playing Solitaire to pass the time. Yet, I knew better than to harbor such an incongruous dream. I couldn't trap something that offered so much freedom.

So, I enjoyed the moment, curling myself right up into it until I could stay there no longer.

Chapter Eleven

Dean and I sat in the oncologist's office in silence. He flipped through a magazine, and I watched as his chest heaved up and down. We'd already waited forty-eight minutes for the doctor, and if I had to wait another twenty seconds my heart might implode.

Finally, the door opened and in walked a middle-aged man with short gray hair and a clean-shaven face.

We all exchanged the usual niceties about the beautiful weather and the smooth traffic flow before he got down to business and put Dean's MRI up on the light box.

He examined it, moving in close to the series of thumbnail-sized images of Dean's head and neck.

He closed in on one of the images, cupping his hand to his chin. "It's unremarkable, at best."

Dean and I exchanged panicked faces.

The doctor walked towards Dean. "That's a good thing. You never want a mass to be considered remarkable."

Was he cracking a joke?

"So what do you think it is?" Dean asked.

The doctor examined the lump. He craned his neck and closed his eyes as he circled it. "It feels innocuous."

I needed a freaking thesaurus to understand the doctor.

The doctor tore off his gloves. "We've got two choices for next steps."

Dean swallowed hard.

"We can do a needle biopsy and see if it's cancer. Or we can just forgo the biopsy and remove it surgically, then test it in the lab. If it's not cancer, you'll be on your merry way. If it is, then, we'll deal with prognosis and treatment options at that point."

141

"The needle biopsy sounds like a no-brainer," I said.

"I'm with her," Dean agreed.

The doctor cocked his head. "Here's why I don't recommend the biopsy." He folded his hands under his chin. "Regardless of the results, I'm still going to recommend we surgically remove the mass. Leaving any kind of mass on a gland would be highly irresponsible."

Dean stretched his eyes. "So, I have to have surgery?"

"I advise it, yes."

"So is it considered minor surgery?" I asked. "You just create a small incision, take it out, sew it back up and call it a day, right?"

"No. It's sitting on the parotid gland, which means I have to go over some risks with you."

Dean labored to remain still, gripping the edge of the table. "What's a parotid gland?"

"The parotid salivary gland is the largest of three and contributes to about twenty-five percent of our total salivary secretion. It releases saliva that contains an enzyme, which helps in digestion by breaking down starch into maltose."

"Am I in serious health trouble here?" Dean asked.

The doctor wore no expression. "The majority of parotid gland tumors are benign, however twenty percent of parotid tumors are found to be malignant. A parotidectomy is an inpatient procedure, which means you'll stay in the hospital anywhere from one to three days depending on how you are healing. Typically, when I perform a parotidectomy I cut a small incision near the crease of the ear, just like in a facelift, and continue behind the ear. I'm careful not to distort the anatomy of the ear. I create a small flap on the surface of the parotid gland to help expose the gland and tissue that I'll be removing."

Dean shuddered.

"Once I've successfully removed the parotid tissue, I'll test the facial nerves for correct function and then I begin the reconstruction. The procedure usually takes about two to five hours. Now, some risks involve nerve dysfunction, Frey's syndrome, which is an uncharacteristic sweating near the glands, numbness, facial asymmetry, necrosis, which is death of skin near incision, and tumor reappearance."

Dean trembled now.

I gripped my chair, on the verge of fainting.

"You have a twenty-five to fifty percent risk of facial weakness directly after the surgery and a one to two percent risk of permanent weakness. Frey's syndrome may occur in up to ninety percent of patients."

"My God, that sounds horrible," I said, unable to hide my shock.

Dean's jaw hung. He fought for control over his quivering chin. "You're saying I have to have this surgery? I have no alternative?"

"We need to remove it. We can't leave it there."

Dean flicked his eyes. "How soon do I need to have the surgery?"

"It's not a fast moving cancer if it turns out to be that. So, a month would be fine, if you want to look at your schedule and clear your plate."

"How about three months?"

"Dean, just get it over with." I rose. "You have a tumor growing in your neck. It's not going to just disappear with a few prayers."

"If it goes away, I don't need surgery. I don't have to risk facial paralysis and sweating on my cheeks for the rest of my life."

That freaked me out more than anything. My poor Dean may never be able to eat a plate of calamari or a bowl of salad drenched in Italian dressing again without wiping the sweat from his cheek.

"I've seen patients cure themselves through prayer and meditation." The doctor scribbled notes on his clipboard. "I wouldn't recommend waiting three months, though."

"I want a chance to take care of this on my own first. If the bump is still there in three months, then I come to the hospital and you remove it. I just want a chance to heal it using holistic techniques."

I ground my teeth, frustrated with his innocence. What did he think? Yvonne would wave a sage brush over his neck and it would magically disappear? Or he'd light some incense, say a few prayers, and wake up to find the tumor vanished? Since when did he become a natural-born healer?

"We'll go with that plan, but if you see the mass growing, you need to call us and schedule it earlier." The doctor extended his hand. "I'll have our coordinator set up a date."

"Fantastic." Dean shook his hand. "I look forward to not showing up."

# #

On the drive home from the doctor's office, Dean asked me if he could have the rest of the week off to plan his next steps. Dean hadn't taken a vacation since the Tuesday following Labor Day one year ago, and then for a two day span when his brother visited Washington, D.C. from India.

My central nervous system went into deep panic mode, already fishing for ways I would be able to get through the next week without him. Of course, no bait in the world would produce the answers I needed.

Nothing that day had turned out as I expected. I expected that we'd walk in there, have a good laugh with the doctor over how Dean's primary care had been too quick to act, out of fear of litigious backlash, and be on our way to some backstreet dive that served dollar beers and all the onion rings we could eat. Instead, we drove hunkered down with a heaviness that turned the beautiful summer day into a noxious nightmare where all the brilliant colors of summertime turned gray.

Once we got back to the office, Dean decided not to come up. "I'll call you and let you know when I'm going to the wellness center."

"Yeah, sure."

He stared at me as if waiting on something from me.

"Okay, then. We'll be in touch."

He nodded. "Yes, boss."

I watched him walk to his car with slumped shoulders. "Hey," I called out.

He turned, and a new defeat sat on his face.

"You're going to be fine."

He offered me a wry smile. "I'll try to get my head back in the game quickly."

I sighed and shrugged. "Please do. I already miss you."

A few minutes later, I sat at my desk and cried.

Bitterness boiled up inside of me, coursing through me like a raging inferno, burning up all sense of peace and reason. I opened up my file cabinet and tossed file after file against my door, cursing God for punishing a man who knew nothing about being mean, greedy, insincere, or cruel.

"Why?" I yelled to my empty room. "Why do you take innocent people and trash their lives?"

I dropped to the floor and bowed my head. I cried for his loss of peace in the coming months, for his potential cancer, for his potential loss of vitality and spirit, for the loss of his laughter, and the pain I might see lining his face.

I cried like a blubbering baby, dull to the vast emptiness of the office without him in there to poke fun at me and challenge me with this quirky factoids and debatable issues.

I remained curled up in that ball pose until the sobs subsided. Then, I looked up to the back of my door and sobered to the fact that not one of my staff members had even knocked to check on me while I yelled and cried.

About half an hour later I summoned up the energy and desire to pull myself up off the floor, walk over to my desk, and face a pile of needs assessments for three large organizations who sought us out to bid on a marketing consultant contract. Landing those accounts had been my goal, my main focal point, and my reason for getting up in the morning lately.

I threw those papers too, not caring about any of it anymore. None of it meant anything without Dean there to cheer me on and share a toast once we acquired their accounts.

I counted on Dean. He kept me in line. His brain worked in mysterious ways as if powered by some outrageous force foreign to the planet. He could come up with new angles on every client, every time we wrote proposals. Clients sought us out because of Dean's creative ingenuity.

My chest tightened, imagining the future of Stone Advertising without him. What if his condition landed him in that twenty percent dismal zone? He'd need so much time off to get treatment. How much time? More than a month for sure. Maybe six months. What if he needed chemo? What if he wanted to go home to his family in India to heal? What if he decided he no longer wanted to work as a marketing assistant at Stone Advertising because it no longer fit in with his life plan? What if he wanted to teach kids, build houses, go back to college, or become a holistic healer?

Everything was temporary, especially life itself.

I stood up and paced my office.

What if, when he evaluated his life over the next week, he actually decided he no longer gained happiness from hanging out with me, and would rather seek solitude to heal himself? My God, what if *I* no longer fit into his plan?

# #

For three days, I hadn't heard a peep from him. Then, on the fourth day, he called to tell me we had appointments at the wellness center for that next morning.

"Tomorrow I've got a meeting with Mr. Allen to go over his campaign."

"Right. Okay, I'll just go alone." His voice sounded so fragile.

"No," I said. "I'll see if I can reschedule."

"It's no big deal. I can go alone."

The disappointment sat on the edge of his words like a fog horn.

"I'll be at your place by eight."

"Okay," he said, weakly.

Annoyed with his drama so early in the journey, I sighed too loudly.

"Am I troubling you?" he asked.

"No. Of course not. We'll figure everything out. We're going to get through this."

146

# #

On the way over to Dean's, I stopped at the pharmacy. As I stood in line to purchase a bottle of vitamin D pills, Anna called. "Dad came over to fix my DVD hookup last night, and we got to talking about that day that he helped you with the thermostat at the wellness center where Willow works. He told me you're taking on Willow as a client? Is that true?"

I stepped out of line and stood in front of a display of Doritos and Coke, hurt that my father would talk to her about that. "What did he say, exactly?"

"He's worried that opening yourself up to someone like Willow is a terrible mistake and he wanted me to talk to you about it."

My blood boiled. Suddenly, I was a teenager again, falling into her shadow. "Dad has nothing to worry about. Willow has turned out to be a nice person."

"Just be careful. People are good at faking it."

Anna, the all-knowing savior, emerges to save the day. "I have to go."

"Be sure to come by soon. The kids miss you."

"Sure."

"Bye, sis."

"Bye." I clicked off the call and attempted to cool myself as I stood in front of the display and focused on the bags. Of course that only reminded me of the days at the campground a year or two after my parents had flown to Korea to bring Anna home and into our family.

Back then, Anna and I would plow through a bag of Doritos and a large, two liter bottle of Coke while huddled up in one of the pull-out couches in the back of my parents' trailer. We'd sit in the shadows formed by a small television and munch until our fingers turned orange, gossiping about everyone at the campground, including more times than anyone, Willow.

Anna carried herself with an air of sophistication that few people had. From the first moment we met, I admired her. She was beautiful like a doll, laughed as if joy bubbled over inside of her, and was super smart about things that one could only learn

147

from intelligent books. I felt smarter in her presence, and never wanted to upset that sweet spot.

I first learned about Anna's crush on her now husband Jeff over a bag of Doritos. Anna loved when we talked about boys, and so we bonded over that. She wanted to hear every last detail about my kissing experiences with them. Well, I didn't have any. So, I made them up. She wanted to hear all about how he smelled and tasted. How his tongue swirled around my mouth. How he caressed me when we kissed. Apparently, she had not kissed Jeff at that point, but rather, hid behind trees or any other large object she could find and dreamed about a life where she did kiss him.

I described my kisses in such detail that her eyes would nearly pop out of her head. Her heart even beat faster than normal, and her cheeks flushed.

I should've grown up to be a storyteller the way I weaved fictitious lies. I even started to believe them myself.

During our late-night talks, Anna would confide in me about how the campground kids wished I would be friendlier. I sensed no one liked me and that they only tolerated me because I was Anna's sidekick sister. Eventually, she stopped asking me to hang out with them at the rec hall. Her popularity grew, and apparently, I tossed a wrench into that equation. She started to draft excuses as to why I couldn't hang with her anymore, saying things like the kids asked her to be part of a planning group for game night and only so many of them could be a part of it.

When she started to date Jeff, she warmed back up to me and included me in playing card games in the trailer with them and hanging out by the bonfire at night.

Jeff adored her and did everything for her. She could do no wrong in his eyes. Now at thirty-five years old, she lived an altruistic life. Shortly after marrying, the two of them entered the Peace Corps where they traveled to foreign countries and taught English to teenaged children. When they returned, they became assistant professors at Rhode Island College and have been there ever since. My father bragged about her success to anyone willing to listen.

I wondered if he ever spoke about my business with the same pride.

Not only was Anna his pride and joy, but now she turned into his confidant.

As I inched back in line, I continued to stare at those Doritos and sodas. An anger sizzled through me that I couldn't extinguish. My father could've just talked to me about Willow if my talking to her again bothered him so much.

Would I ever *not* disappoint him?

#

I called Dean on my way to pick him up. "I'll drive today."

"No," he said. "I earned this drive."

"How can I argue with that?"

A few minutes later, Dean drove us to the wellness center. I jumped right into work stuff. "I'm stumped on the proposals."

He flew through a yellow light without answering me.

"Do you have any ideas?" I asked.

"My mind isn't there right now."

"I could use your help in brainstorming. I'm freaking out about it a little."

"Over a client? Of course. Stop the madness, world," he said waving his arm. "You're stressing out Lia Stone."

"I'm just trying to get your mind off everything."

He sped up. "Just arrange a brainstorming meeting with the other staff members."

The other staff members sat like bumps on a log with me at the helm. "I could be lying in a pool of blood at their feet, and they wouldn't call 911. They hate me."

"Forgive me for being so blunt here, but, Lia, that's because you never take their ideas seriously."

"You're supposed to defend me here, Dean."

He gripped the steering wheel tighter. "Defending you is hard sometimes. If I'm being honest, sometimes you act like you're way above everyone. You intimidate them."

His words slammed against me, knocking the wind out of my chest. "That hurts."

149

"Isn't it better to face the truth? At least you know what you're up against that way. You can deal with it. You can find a solution. Otherwise you're just going blindly into the night without a flashlight, without a compass, and you risk getting lost in some backstreet alleyway littered with rats and empty soda cans. Is that what you want?"

"What gives?"

"I'm just trying to save you from a potential month or two of backlash from them."

I sat back and reflected on the criticism. "I need an example of how I act high and mighty."

"You do it with me all the time."

"How so?"

"You still refer to me as your assistant."

"Well you are."

"Funny, I would've thought by now I might've graduated to more of a friend title."

I stared at his forehead wrinkles, trying to interpret his statement. His poor fingers were whiter than snow with their grip around the steering wheel. "You're going to cut off circulation there, *my friend*."

He tightened even more. "You're patronizing me."

I scoffed. "Patronizing? I'm sitting here, putting my life at risk with your reckless driving, en route to get poked with needles to show my support, and you have the nerve to call me patronizing?"

"How big of you."

"You're acting like a complete ass."

"Me?" He scoffed. "I'm going to say something, and you're not going to like it. I need to get it off my chest."

"Well go on. Tell me."

"Sometimes you act selfishly."

I tossed my hands in the air and contemplated opening the door and jumping out. Surely the road would've been less painful than taking on that sudden assault. "Selfish? I pay you double what an assistant normally earns. I set you up in a corner office with not just one computer, but two, and a tablet. You get a clothing allowance. Who does that? Me? Does a selfish person do that? I don't think so."

"You're yelling at me because you know what I'm saying is true," he said softly. "I presume it's striking a bit of a nerve."

I stared at him, searching his face for evidence that my loyal Dean still existed under that judging frown. "Why are you being so mean to me?"

"I'm being honest. That's entirely different. Right now, you're more worried about running your business without me than anything else that's transpiring."

"That is not true."

"I don't believe you."

I gripped the door handle, turning my fingers their own shade of white now. "I can't talk to you right now."

He drove us on in silence.

I battled with his hurtful words all the way down route ninety-five as we headed to Narragansett. I searched for a viable reason why he lashed out at me. Was I really selfish? Had I been patronizing?

The hurt swelled up inside of me, overtaking my body. I stared out of the window, protecting myself against anger, sadness, and the ugly truth that I did harbor those traits. What right did I have being so bitter with life when I had everything going for me? What more did I want? "I'm sorry if I hurt you," I said gruffly. "I never meant to."

He clenched his jaw.

I cradled my hand around his wrist. "You are my friend."

He squeezed his hand into a fist.

I hated that he viewed me as selfish. "I do care about what's happening to you."

His whole body eased in one exhale. Suddenly, the wrinkles from his frown disappeared. His smooth, friendly face resurfaced. "Thank you. I needed to hear that."

I patted his wrist. "Life's just taking a weird turn. It'll all straighten out quickly."

He squinted, sinking into focus. "You know, we're put on other people's paths for a reason."

"I agree."

"Life is a series of pathways, and we crisscross with each other along the way."

"Absolutely."

"When our paths intersect, we take a break, have a snack, a cool drink, catch our bearings, learn a lesson or two and then break time is over. Time to move on to the next intersection, carrying everything we learned with us. We might still need the same people with us through many of those winding paths and intersections, and then one day, we realize we need to go in different directions because I've got something to learn in the west and you've got something to learn in the east."

The air stopped moving between us and a hollowness took over. "Please don't say that. I can't imagine this journey without you in it with me."

"I hope so." His eyes softened, and in that softness I caught a glimpse of a man struggling with how to move forward on his new scary path, trusting someone who put herself first.

I leaned my head against his shoulder as he continued to drive us. I watched the rain droplets dance across his windshield, carefree and reckless, wishing I could join in their simple journey. A few miles down the road, I asked him. "Are you going to be okay with everything?"

He shrugged. "Honestly, now that I've had a few days to let it sink in, I've never felt more alive." He relaxed his grip on the steering wheel. "It's like life took on a whole new power source. I'm fired up, like I have all of this extra drive to seek out new things. I'm finding I don't care about the petty things like if my pants have the proper crease down the front or if the deli guy accidentally puts regular cream cheese on my bagel instead of light. I spoke with my parents over Skype last night, and I told my mother to stop digging for information about my love life. She's asked me about a girlfriend for the past four years, and every time she did, I would bow my head in embarrassment and tell her I was working on it. Well, last night, I told her, with utmost respect of course, that she had no right to ask me that anymore. She bowed her head instead and accepted my statement with reverence. I simply care less about formality and more about honesty suddenly."

Hence his attack on my lack of selflessness.

He pulled into the parking lot of the wellness center and parked a few spaces from the front door.

"I know you're worried about the office," he said. "It's who you are. I don't blame you. Just let me have these few weeks to get my head back in the game."

"Will that help to keep your mind off of it?"

"I can't afford to have my mind off of it."

I nodded.

A new panic settled in me. I saw myself standing in a room full of staff members who would rather have their toenails torn off than deal with me. How would I run my business without his diplomatic personality acting as intermediary? What if they all walked away, leaving me alone to fend for myself? How would I get through those proposals? What about our friendship?

"I'm scared."

He stared at me with a new strength. "You do understand I need this, don't you?"

No, I don't understand, my self-centered side inwardly screamed. "Of course," I said as selflessly as I could before bowing my head and grabbing the handle.

He reached out for my hand. "Everything's going to work out as it should. I'm not afraid. Neither should you be."

My heart tightened. "I hope you're right."

"I promise. Everything's going to be alright. We're going to walk into that wellness center and have ourselves a little needle therapy, and then we're going to go have a nice tall adult beverage and forget this nonsense," he said, taking back the role of caregiver and nurturer.

I rested on the comfort of that plan as I opened the door. "That sounds perfect."

"Lia," he said, squeezing my wrist before I could get out. "I'm happy you're here with me."

"I'm happy to be here with you too, my friend."

"And you're a liar." He laughed and tickled my waist. "Add that to the list of traits."

"A liar?" I punched his arm like old times.

"If I know you well enough, which I do, your insides are tumbling like clothes in a dryer because you're about to come face-to-face with Willow again. Correct me if I'm wrong."

"I don't know what you're talking about." I climbed out of the car, trying to settle the flips in my tummy.

Chapter Twelve

I opened the door to the wellness center, and the bell chimed. Dean walked in behind me.

The smell of sweet honeysuckle drifted in the air. The lights were dim, casting golden shadows on the brown leather couches and chairs.

Willow walked through the hallway door, and her face lit up when she saw us. A healthy glow radiated from her like she'd just taken a light jog. Her hair sat tousled up in a messy bun, and bits of wispy pieces hung down around her cheeks and jaw. "Good morning," she said, walking up to me and extending her hand.

I eyed it and opened my arms instead. "I'm a hugger."

She laughed and cocked her head shyly before slipping into my arms and hugging me. She smelled like spring rain.

She stepped back. "I'm glad you both came." She extended her hand to Dean, and he gladly accepted.

"Can I get you both some tea?"

"We're alright," I said.

The three of us stood staring at each other awkwardly.

Then, Charlotte and Anthony charged into the reception area, flying past us, blowing airplane noises with their chubby lips.

"No flying right now," Willow said with a calm reserve. She walked up to the television console in the far corner and picked up a DVD. "You're going to sit quietly and watch this movie until Aunt Lola comes to get you. Just as promised, right?" She spoke to them as they circled her, still flying as airplanes.

Those kids knew how to have fun, and I suspected that I could learn a thing or two from them.

I peeked over at Dean, and he stared at the kids like they were odd creatures from a different planet. "They're just kids having fun," I whispered.

He rolled his eyes. "If I had ever acted like that as a kid, I would've been imprisoned to my study and fed jasmine rice with water for a week."

"Well then, forgive me for saying," I whispered, imitating his Indian accent. "But your childhood must have been pretty crappy."

He crossed his arms over his chest and continued to stare at the kids as they performed karate moves on each other right next to the delicate display of essential oils. "How are we to relax?"

"Watch this. I'm about to perform a selfless act for you."

I rushed up to Willow, who was wrestling with the DVD player, and grabbed the DVD box from her. "I've always wanted to see *Frozen*. Who's going to watch it with me?"

"Me. I am," Charlotte screamed.

"No you're not. I am." Anthony shoved her out of the way.

"Don't push me." Charlotte pushed him back.

"Why can't the three of us watch it together?" I asked, looking over at Dean who now stretched his eyes far beyond natural means.

Charlotte's little heart beat fast. She opened her mouth several times to answer, but lost her words. She ended on a shrug and dropped down to the floor.

"You've never seen *Frozen*?" Anthony asked.

"Nope." I plopped the DVD in the player and sat down next to Charlotte. "First time for everything."

Anthony plopped down next to me. "Do you have any popcorn?"

I stuck my hand in my pockets and pulled them out. "Nope. No popcorn in them I'm afraid."

Charlotte giggled and threw herself backwards. "You're not supposed to put popcorn in your pockets." Her high-pitch shrill traveled up and beyond.

I laughed and looked up at Willow. "If you want to get started with Dean for his yoga, I can watch them."

"I'll just wait for my aunt to come. She should've been here by now. She's always running late."

"Look at Dean. He's foaming at the mouth to get started. Keep him waiting too long and you're going to see him panting and pacing like a bored tiger in captivity."

She laughed. "Are you sure?"

I clicked the movie. "It's *Frozen*. I'd be mad not to."

"She just wants to get out of needles," Dean said.

"Don't be crazy. I can't wait to get poked. Now, go ahead." I shooed them away. "We've got a movie to watch."

"My aunt should definitely be here any minute. Yvonne is just finishing up with a patient. She should be ready for you shortly."

"I assure you, I'm in no rush."

"Right," she winked at me.

My heart skipped.

She led Dean to the hallway, and motioned for him to walk ahead of her. This granted me a full on view of her backside. Her hair hung over her shoulders and flirted with her fitted yoga outfit, sending my heart into a spin. "Third door on the right," she said to him before looking back at me over her shoulder and mouthing a thank you.

I mouthed *you're welcome* back to her.

We exchanged sweet smiles before she turned away and focused on her task at hand, to take care of my friend, Dean, while trusting me to take good care of her children.

Charlotte sat staring at the television with giant eyes.

"Have you seen this before?" I asked.

"Shh," she said, pointing her little finger at me. "This is the best part."

"It's a preview," Anthony yelled.

"So?" she yelled back.

"Do you two ever not yell at each other?"

Anthony contemplated that question with great pause. "Only when Brandy is sleeping. Then we just stay quiet."

"Who's Brandy?"

"She's me and Mommy's friend, and she doesn't like Anthony," Charlotte said.

"She's my friend too," Anthony growled back at her.

I pictured a beautiful woman with a sweet spot for romance, hugging Willow from behind as they admired the children at play. "Is she nice?" I asked, hugging my knees to my chest to stave off an instant jealous twinge.

"She's very nice," Charlotte said, sighing before looking back at her movie. "I love her."

Her high-pitched answer splintered through me.

A few minutes later, Willow's aunt walked in the front door. The kids went nuts again, flying in circles with their airplane arms. She wore a colorful dress just as she did the first day I met her at the flea market. Her hair fell in a wild mess at her shoulders, tamed only by the sun hat she wore. "Lia Stone." She opened up her arms as if we were long-lost friends. I laughed uncomfortably.

"Willow told me you were going to be here today."

"She did?"

"After she told me you didn't think I was a fake anymore." She smiled and tipped her hat to me. "I'm officially humbled by that."

I half expected her to pull out a bouquet of flowers from her sleeve and offer them to me on a bow.

She bent down to offer hugs to the kids. "Your auntie has a surprise for you."

"Is it a boat?" Anthony asked.

"No. It's not a boat. Though it does go in water."

"A turtle," Charlotte screamed.

"No. Not a turtle. But it does like to hang out in the pool all day."

Charlotte jumped up and down. "Tell us. Tell us."

"You're just going to have to wait and see. Come on gather your things."

They ran around gathering their coloring books, snacks and sneakers. Meanwhile my curiosity ran wild. "What did you get them?"

She leaned in and whispered. "A remote control vacuum cleaner for the pool that's shaped like a fish. They're going to love it."

Just what every child wanted. "I'm sure they will." I could see Anthony standing on it, trying to ride it like a skateboard.

"Come on," she said gathering them up in her arms. "Time's a wasting." She tilted her head at me. "Is Willow in the back?"

"Yes, she's in a yoga session with my friend, Dean."

She circled up to the front desk. "I'll just leave her a little note to let her know me and the kids are going to the mall." She scribbled a note, and asked, "Is your friend doing better since the allergy attack?"

"Much better." I'd let Dean tackle that question with more detail on his own. God knew he'd be back to her table in the flea market before surgery.

"Good to hear." She pushed the note toward the computer and walked back to us. "He's in good hands with Willow and Yvonne." She opened up her arms to the children. "Come on now. Let's get out of here and leave this kind woman with some peace."

"Bye kids." I patted them on their heads.

"Enjoy the peace now." She opened up the door, and the kids bolted like dogs breaking loose of their leashes. She smiled pleasantly at me before strolling after them.

As soon as they walked out, silence invaded the space. It sounded foreign in the trail of the kids' laughter and fighting. It also opened up too much space for me to think about that Brandy friend. Why wouldn't she have a girlfriend? Though, she might've just been nothing more than a friend.

159

I sat down and took in the room. My eyes followed the crown molding, then the suede window treatments, dangling elegantly from a curved, golden rod with intricate carvings. Next, I landed on the first of many oil paintings, a lone wolf howling at a bright orange, full moon. The brush strokes created deep grooves, the haunting kind that stood out from the rest of the painting as cold and isolating.

God, I hoped Brandy was just a friend.

# #

About ten minutes after Willow's aunt left with the kids, the bald guy with liver cancer emerged from a treatment room. Yvonne followed him out.

"Vanilla latte from Starbucks?" He pointed his finger at Yvonne while heading toward the door.

"That stuff is no good for you." She shot him a stern look.

He looked at me. "I'm dying. I can eat whatever I want. It's freaking awesome!" He tapped his chest and laughed.

I laughed too, for lack of a better response.

"I'm getting you a vanilla latte," he said to Yvonne. Then he turned back to me. "You look like you could use some fattening up. So, I'm getting you one too."

He walked out the door on a giant stride before I could even open my mouth to answer.

"He's awfully excited about dying." I watched him stop traffic as he did the last time I was there.

"Either that or he's on some good drugs." Yvonne lingered her gaze on him as a car narrowly missed him. He slapped the hood telling the person to have a fucking lovely day.

"He's really dying?"

"I'm afraid so." She clicked her tongue. "I'm just managing his pain at this point."

"He looks like he could get through an Insanity workout without breaking a sweat."

"Pat's great at hiding his pain." She cocked her head and walked over to the front desk. "It's a shame. He tells me he used to be a real asshole before getting diagnosed."

I arched my eyebrow. "Used to be?"

She smirked. "He's got no filter. But he's harmless."

"Knowing you're going to die has to suck."

"Sometimes a death sentence brings people closer to life." She grinned. "He does these talks for us, like I told Dean, where he speaks about regrets, you know, typical things like wanting to be a better husband and father, wishing he took better care of his business, hating that his roof needs replacing and his yard is too big to tend to, being too stubborn to repair broken friendships, and the one big one is not taking care of his health when he had it. It breaks my heart every time he says these things, even though when he presents it, he's hysterical. He's got the whole audience roaring. He just has that way about him. It's fantastic." She looked whimsically out the window. "Absolutely fantastic."

The same girl from the open house entered the reception area and invited me to follow her into a treatment room. "I'll see you in there," I said over my shoulder.

The treatment room, with its soothing buttercream-colored walls, only reminded me how totally out of my element I was. I did not want acupuncture.

"Here's a gown to dress into. You can keep your under garments on, but be sure to remove your socks." She handed me a blue cotton robe wrapped in plastic. "Yvonne will be with you shortly." She bowed out of the room, leaving me to contemplate whether I should jump out the window and run like hell away from the needles, cream-colored walls, and honeysuckle fragrance.

I slipped out of my shoes, first, then my socks. I wiggled my toes against the soft carpeting. I had committed myself.

So, I climbed out of my clothes, one selfless move at a time, for Dean's sake, and eventually slipped into the gown. My nerves gained full control at that point, rendering me incapable of drawing a relaxed breath.

Moments later, Yvonne knocked and entered. "I had bet Willow twenty dollars that you'd take me up on my free acupuncture offer eventually. Looks like my doggy gets steak for dinner tonight."

"What kind of dog do you have?"

"A cute little mutt I adopted from the shelter a few years ago. If the state board of health didn't exist, she'd be here with me every day. But, they frown upon them, even though they are natural healers and good for a person's spirit. Even better than that honeysuckle you smell."

"I'd love to adopt a dog, but Dean fears them. I'd never be able to bring her to the office with me, so the idea is moot. I work twelve to fifteen hour days typically."

She sat down. "I'm sure your office, like any other office, could use a friendly mascot to clear up some of the staleness those cube farms can create. Acupuncture, as well as some behavioral therapy, can help him with that anxiety."

"That'll never happen."

"Want to bet?" Her eyes sparkled.

I waited for her to tell me she was joking. "Seriously?"

A playful smile blossomed. "Fifty dollars he will be walking around the office with a rescue dog trailing happily behind him within a month."

I extended my hand. "Earning fifty bucks has never been so easy."

"You've got so little faith in the system."

"I'm not a believer." I rolled my eyes before offering her an apologetic grin. "I'm only here for moral support."

She leaned back in her chair. "What are you expecting will happen in today's session?"

"Pain."

"Ha." She slapped her leg. "This is going to be fun."

"How about we just pretend we did a session and not?"

"Not on your life, sweetheart. I don't lie. Ever."

"Ever?"

"Ever." She pointed her eyes at me.

I sat in the chair and bounced my feet up and down, releasing the sudden rise of adrenaline.

"So how are you, really, Lia?"

I exhaled and my chest tightened. "I'm fine. Really I am."

"You're lying." She eyed my legs. "I've spent two minutes with those children and needed Reiki just to calm me down."

I placed my hands on my knees to stop the bounce. "They're actually a nice distraction."

She smiled warmly. "Distractions are always welcome, aren't they?"

"Yes indeed."

"Dean told me about the doc's visit over the phone. So, yes, I imagine taunting and yelling are a welcome distraction. Kids have a way of adding pizzazz to life, don't they?"

I laughed to ease the building of tension in between my shoulder blades. "Yeah. They do." I removed my hands from my knees, trusting in my bodily control again. "Dean said something to me today about how he's sprung to life more since finding out about the tumor in his neck."

She just stared at me, letting my sentence marinate between us.

"Hmm. Just like with Pat, it humbled him with the gift of pause," she stated. "Life has suddenly become critical. The red alarm has blared. His central nervous system has fired up for the first time in years perhaps. Adrenaline has spiked. Synapses have reconnected. Nerves are tingling. A deadline has appeared, and he has woken up to the fact that life is fragile."

"I'm discovering just how fragile it is."

"Disease happens. No one is immune. We all come more alive in the face of adversity. You, in particular, strike me as a natural fighter who would come to battle and face any threat with her fists raised and her best attitude. You'd choose to face the threat head on at first, then, just as many do, you'd take a more Zen approach and

163

search for an alternative way around the new obstacle. You might choose to go around it, dig under it, or even fly over it. Either way, you wouldn't let it stop you."

"Damn. My mind sounds so much better than real life when you talk about it, like it's the next summer blockbuster fantasy movie."

"Threats can bring us back to life because they cause us to reflect. Everyone should live as though she were dying. Imagine the things a person would do with her time? I can guarantee, you wouldn't be sitting in front of a television set for four to five hours a night like the average American does right now. Staring at reality is a good thing."

I arched my eyebrow at her, not sure I bought into that line of reasoning.

"Don't be sad for Dean. Be happy that he has the opportunity to discover living again."

I reflected on that for a moment. "That man doesn't need a disease to show him how to appreciate life."

"Neither do you. You've got the power right up here," she tapped her temple. "In your noggin. We manifest everything in the mind. Good and bad, it all starts there. So any lifelessness you're experiencing right now, if you are, you're choosing it. You're creating your own reality with each and every thought."

I studied her soft eyes, and in them I found peace and safety. "That sounds dangerous," I joked.

She grasped my hands in hers and spoke to me. "It's powerful."

The room closed in around us, blocking out everything but her voice and her warm spirit. "Within all of us lies an energy source that, when turned on, can produce extraordinary results. It has a pulse all its own. It lies dormant within our bodies, waiting on that perfect moment when it's given free-range to spread its light and release its power. Its sole purpose is to bring peace and balance to the body it protects. When activated, it becomes like a star, radiating light and healing energy throughout the blood vessels, organs, and cells. The body becomes engorged with its nutritious, life-affirming juice. Every fiber of our being starts to dance to an energizing beat, spreading the light even further into the darkest, most hidden areas of our bodies. Light seeps everywhere, and every cell starts to expand and reach out toward the light, just like a flower turning to the sun and blooming with a brilliance brought on by the refreshing nutrients of Mother Earth. When every cell in your body is at that kind of grateful attention, opened up in full bloom, it becomes a vessel of hope, tranquility, balance, and beautiful health."

She tapped her chest lightly. "We all carry that source within. It wants to be activated. Once it is, it can never be turned off. It becomes our guiding light through every step we take, every interaction, every crisis we meet. It protects us and even allows us to share this with others who haven't learned to turn theirs on yet, or are in a weakened state and unable to flip that switch."

I sat trancelike, listening to Yvonne's words. A lump formed in my throat, desperate to discover that peace for myself. "I'm not capable."

"Sure you are." She squeezed my hands. "Acupuncture can help everyone who is open to it by relieving stress, impurities, and imbalances. Many people experience a heightened state of bliss with it, opening them up to see things more clearly and helping them answer plaguing questions with pinpoint clarity, by unblocking pathways to help get over obstacles so the light can shine through without conflict."

"I want to believe you. I do. It all seems too quirky, though."

"Quirky is one way to put it, I suppose." She laughed. "Quirky or not, it's one of the best ways I know of to tweak energy to our advantage. We all require tweaking. Things build up in us, and we're human, so we require interaction to help us unblock. We're no different in respect to a clogged drainpipe or gutter. Just because they're clogged doesn't mean the gutter and pipe aren't able to see the light of day again. It just means, there's some junk that got in, and it needs some nudging to release it so the rain and the light can penetrate it once again."

She painted a clear analogy. "Dean's going to love this."

"I've never had a patient walk away dissatisfied. It's a unique experience for everyone. I once had a novelist come in, plagued by writer's block. She was a stress

165

ball, tight on a deadline and panicking because she had no story. Stress blocked her creativity. So, we put a needle in it, and after her session, when I entered the room, she begged me to grab a notebook and pen so she could write down the stream of consciousness that came to her. In those fifteen minutes, she wrote down the plotline to her novel, and it's become a bestseller on the New York Times Bestseller List. Another person, an artist, came to me plagued by negative reviews of her paintings. She thought her career had been destroyed. Then, we put a needle in it, and when she came out of that session, she had created a process for dealing with rejection that to this day has helped her critically evaluate the criticism in a way that has helped her grow into an award-winning painter whose work now hangs in the Baltimore Museum of Art."

I wanted what she sold. "I could use some extra creativity, for sure."

"Let's put a needle in it, then." She rose and led me over to the treatment table.

I followed her, and to my surprise, all the apprehension from before had vanished. I walked with a bounce, excited to see what would happen. I wanted that treatment. I wanted that experience. I wanted her to prove me wrong and turn me into a believer.

I climbed onto the table and rested back against the soft blanket. I stared at a painting of a blue sky with white puffy clouds that hung on the ceiling directly above me. "A flat screen television would be an even more awesome idea."

"You'll have your own movie playing in your head in a few minutes."

She began to examine my feet and fingers.

I eased against the table, sinking into the experience.

"I'm looking for reactive areas to determine which points to use," she said.

"Are the needles thick?"

"They are hair-thin." She circled around to my legs. "They're sterile, pre-packaged, and disposable." She picked up a package of them to show me. "I'm going to place the needles at various depths, ranging from a fraction of an inch to two inches."

I wanted to faint.

"I'm also going to use different combinations of points to help stimulate sources of healing in your body."

The room began to spin, as I imagined a thick needle plunging into my skin and squirting blood.

She stood at the bottom of the table near my feet. The needle pricked me like a mosquito bite as she inserted the first one into my foot.

"Is my foot supposed to tingle?"

"Yes. That means it's working. This is called Deqi."

She continued to place needles strategically along my body. With each needle insertion, the pricking lessened and heavy tingling increased. At one point, my foot began to tremble and vibrate. "Is it normal to have my foot jumping like that?"

"That's your body responding favorably. You had quite a blockage in that meridian."

She stood back. "Okay, so now, we leave these in for twenty minutes. I want you to close your eyes, let your mind relax, and focus on your inner peace. Slow, steady, deep breaths. Some people find it helpful to count backwards to keep their mind clear. With each breath, imagine you are inhaling clean energy full of light and power, and allow it to pass through your entire body. Then, when you exhale, imagine you are filtering out the waste and keeping the nutrients."

I closed my eyes and began to visualize as she instructed.

She exited the room.

I counted backwards from one hundred. By ninety, I eased into relaxation.

Before long, I pictured me and Dean at the beach again, building another sandcastle.

We built it up, higher and mightier than before, and that time we laughed and talked more and sank into that moment as though it was the most precious moment in our lives. I didn't want to miss a nanosecond of it. I wanted Dean to focus intently on the fun of it all. That was his moment, and I wanted to help him enjoy it to its fullest.

I wanted every spec of sand to massage his worries away, as it poured out of the creases in between his fingers, and landed like dust at his knees before the sea breeze picked it up and whisked it away.

His shoulders eased down and a peace rested in the spokes of his eyes. He seemed to relax into the smell of the sea, the taste of the salt on the cusp of each breeze, the wetness of the sand between his toes and fingers, and the majestic visual appeal of our shimmery sandcastle as it grew to the largest, most grand that either one of us had ever seen.

I wanted to drop a protective coating on it to save it, so we could always remember that day at the beach when life stood still and all that mattered was the building of that castle and the quiet folds of time and space that blanketed us in safety.

As its walls remained strong and its beauty still very much a part of our existence, we stood back and admired the product of our shared time and effort. And even as that tide rolled back in, just as it did the other day, and washed our memory into the sea, a happy lightness lifted us, knowing that no amount of force could destroy that which we now unpackaged in our hearts, our treasured time together building temporary sandcastles that stood and fell to remind us that life was temporary and so it should be experienced without limits, regrets or unfulfilled dreams.

I closed my eyes in that scene and enjoyed the light mist of sea water on my face. With every inhale, and its respective exhale, the mist cleared up any confusion as to my purpose standing on that beach; to remember that I was, and always would be, just as intricate a part of the universe as the mist, sand, shells, and wind were.

I opened my eyes and stared up at the picture of the blue sky and wispy clouds. I was back in the acupuncture room.

I inhaled the soothing scent of honeysuckle, and a tingle coursed through my entire being. A sense of extreme comfort swam in me. I viewed the buttercream-colored walls with a whole new set of eyes.

I stretched lightly, and a peace overcame me.

168

Then, Yvonne knocked and entered, walking over to me with a smile. "How do you feel?"

I inhaled the honeysuckle deeper into my lungs. "I feel like I ate some pretty awesome mushrooms."

She laughed, and began removing the needles. "Talk to me. What happened?"

"Let's just say, you've turned me into a believer."

She walked over to the receptacle and dumped the used needles in there. "Well, then, let me be the first to welcome you to the land of open chakras, harmony, and balance."

Chapter Thirteen
Willow

The first time I commanded a yoga session, I walked into that room full of yoga enthusiasts and wanted to serve them an experience that would have their mouths watering for more. I wanted their cells to come alive, bursting with a new awareness of energy they never knew existed until that moment when I helped them find their inner healer. I wanted them to devour the good vibes the way I did when I first dove into a downward dog pose. Unfortunately, that first time as a yoga instructor singed me with a hurtful disappointment because I screwed up royally. I didn't know my toe from my pinky because nerves took hold. Talk about a wild mess; a yoga instructor who couldn't take a long deep breath. I couldn't remember the moves. I had blanked out.

But, I kept seeing my future self as someone who taught yoga. So, I turned to my Aunt Lola. She helped center me by reminding me that I didn't have to be an expert to be effective. I just had to be humble. So, humble me stood before my second yoga class and confessed my nerves to a group of people who looked back at me with a connective love that carried me through the first breath to the final relaxed and grateful one. I was open to their feedback, and thus received their welcome.

I wanted Lia to jump right over that newbie hurdle and enjoy her first acupuncture session. I didn't want her to have to deal with the similar apprehensions most people suffer when their fearful minds are blocked off from something new and mysterious. I didn't want her to close herself off from its possibilities the way I sensed she did with a lot of things in her life. I wanted her to love it, and for that experience to serve as the first of many on her travels down new paths that would open her mind to things beyond most people's comprehension.

So, when Lia walked out to the reception area after her treatment with Yvonne and she was glowing, it took all the reserve power I had to control my joy.

I sat innocently on the couch next to Dean, showing him a yoga app for his cell phone, when she strolled up to us, walking with a new air of peace. In the moments between handing Dean his phone back and performing the basic function of breathing, my heart ascended too fast, leaving me disoriented. Within ten seconds, I was that person clinging to the hope that the emotions of that moment would not drop out from under my feet and stop the ride I just mounted.

When she got closer, my face flushed. Within minutes, we'd be alone in my yoga room stretching our long torsos in front of each other, lying on the ground in sensual poses that would set my mind on a giddy strike against any thought professional in nature.

Her eyes bore into mine, causing the room to spin.

"You've got to see how easy this is," Dean said to her.

Lia broke her gaze as Dean handed his phone to her. "Check out this app. Every morning, it guides you through fifteen minutes of morning yoga to get the day started off on the right foot."

Lia turned back to me, ignoring Dean now. "The kiddos are safe with your aunt."

"Thank you," I whispered.

She looked at me with that same sexy smile from earlier when I left her alone with my kids.

"Are you ready for your yoga lesson?" I asked, reluctant to flirt back out of fear I might somehow be misreading her signals. Then, her eyes flickered with an intensity that sped up my heart again. Compelled to keep up with its tantric beat, I reciprocated her sexy smile and reached out for her hand; my subtle approach to a playful invitation.

My hand relaxed in hers. Her face shined with pure tranquility, along with the smooth contours of her jaw and cheeks beneath the soft glow of the center's light. At that moment, a raw beauty stirred in me, a beauty I'd only ever enjoyed once before, the day she leaned in to kiss me in the mist of the pool room.

Just then, my cell phone rang. It was my aunt. I reluctantly let go of Lia's hand to answer. "Hey Aunt Lola."

"Don't freak out," she said. "It's not a big deal. My car has two flat tires."

"Where are you?"

Lia arched her eyebrow.

"We're at the Providence Place Mall. I bought the kids an ice cream cone when it happened. Sure enough, someone got upset with me because I took up an extra spot. I only did that because the spaces are too small. I can't fit in them."

"You've got a Prius. It'll fit."

"Anyway, I'm waiting on the tow truck. Unless you want your little ones being trucked away in some smelly cab of a tow truck, you may want to come and get us."

"Of course. I'll be right there."

"We're near Dave and Buster's."

"I'll be there in about thirty minutes. I'm leaving now."

I hung up.

"Trouble?" Yvonne asked, walking out from the treatment room.

"Your wife has no idea how to drive, let alone park," I joked. "I don't know why I trust my children with her." I turned to Lia. "I'm sorry, but I have to run and pick them up. Can we reschedule your yoga?"

"I'll come with you," she said without hesitation.

My heart leaped. We'd spend an afternoon intimately confined together in the front seat of my car. "Really?"

"Of course," she said without question.

"Does your aunt live near here or closer to the mall?" Dean asked.

"We live about ten miles from the mall," Yvonne said.

"Why don't you go there, and I'll pick you up later, after I'm done with my acupuncture?" Dean asked.

"Are you sure?" I asked him.

"He's sure," Lia said.

"Great. Let me just grab my keys." I skipped off to the desk and grabbed them. As I passed by Lia en route to the front door, she placed her hand on the small of my back, guiding me.

I felt safe, and happy; two emotions I'd been craving for a long time.

# #

On the drive to get my aunt and kids, Lia and I talked about Dean and how he coped so great with his health scare. I told Lia that my gut told me he'd be just fine.

"He believes he can magically erase the mass before surgery," she said.

I refused to rock that boat and tell her I did see him getting the surgery. I wasn't always right. "Even if he needs surgery, I get the good sense that he's going to have it removed and get on with is life, tucking that whole ordeal behind him for the rest of his healthy life."

Lia settled into that news like I'd just flung her a life jacket in the middle of a raging ocean.

An hour later, with my aunt and two wired kids in the car, we drove to her house, listening to the entertainment of Charlotte and Anthony recalling every last detail of those two flat tires.

Fifteen minutes later, we arrived.

I welcomed Lia into the house, and her jaw dropped just like everyone else's always did when they stepped foot inside what looked like a home for the rich and famous. As soon as we entered, Brandy bolted at us, yelping and sliding on the hardwood floors as she always did. She bypassed me altogether and charged straight at Lia with all four paws in the air.

"That's Brandy," Charlotte yelled. "She'll bite you, but it won't hurt. She pinches like a little mosquito bite."

Lia smiled. "So this is Brandy."

"Yup. She's my aunt's dog."

Charlotte bent down and pulled at Brandy's curls as the dog sought out Lia's ankles and began her discovery phase. I picked her up.

"She's like this at first, then she'll calm down," I talked over the yelping, squirming, and biting. Brandy bit the air, spraying drool all over my arms.

Aunt Lola pointed a squirt bottle at her. "That's enough now, Little Bugger."

"That's an adorable name, Little Bugger," Lia said, attempting to lean in and pet her again. Brandy barked like she was a two hundred pound Mastiff. "Much more appropriate than Brandy."

My aunt moved in closer with the squirt bottle, and Brandy quieted, staring at her with big, brown, nervous eyes. "Willow, sweetest person on the planet, rescued this little bugger from a client who couldn't handle her. Thirty minutes later, she presented this little ball of trouble as a birthday present to me." Aunt Lola put down the squirt bottle. "I told her, I'm not living with a dog."

"I told her, I'm not letting her get killed at an animal shelter. She had the nerve to say no still," I said.

"Yeah, but tell her why."

I looked to Lia and smirked.

"They would have killed her at the shelter because she had a 'history'." I lifted Brandy to exaggerate an air quote.

"A history?" Lia asked, chuckling and trying once again to pet her.

Brandy barked at her again, growling lowly.

"Exactly," Aunt Lola screamed out. "She bit a hole through her client's wall. Look at the walls in this place. I didn't want some creature to come in and turn them into Swiss cheese."

"Only because my client's husband kept her boxed in all day and night." I rubbed the space between her eyes, and she blinked rapidly. "Look at this face. Is this the face of a dog who deserved to live in a cold, lonely cage waiting on a family to call her own?" I asked.

Lia stared at her with adoration. Brandy's tongue hung out of her mouth all crooked as she panted and dripped onto the patio floor. "She's a mess, and Dean's going to pull no stops on his dramatic defense when he comes to pick me up. He's terrified of dogs."

"We'll get her calmed down by the time he comes in."

Brandy fidgeted and squirmed. So, I lowered her to the floor and tossed her favorite toy toward the other end of the foyer. She ran after it, slipping and sliding until she gripped it in between her teeth and barreled her way back toward us. She ran straight for Lia, and instead of dropping it as we taught her to do, she pounced right up Lia's calves, spitting the toy out and caring only about her legs.

Lia jumped backward and a panic took over her face.

"Isn't she adorable?" A huge smile erupted on Charlotte's face as she giggled at Brandy who was now biting on Lia's legs. Brandy began to run in circles around Lia's ankles. Charlotte began chasing her and screaming. Then, Anthony joined in, laughing hysterically. And poor Lia, she looked at me with horror in her eyes.

"No," she said, hopping away from Brandy's stakeout on her bare ankles. She ran toward the living room and jumped on the coach, squealing as she looked down and found Brandy staring up at her with her crazed eyes. "Off, Little Bugger. Off," she said, now mounting the back of the couch to get away from Brandy's sharp snapping teeth.

I grabbed for Brandy, but she wouldn't let me catch her. "Get her collar," I yelled to Aunt Lola. "I can't grab her." I broke out in a sweat at that point, embarrassed and afraid for Lia. I'd never seen Brandy get that fired up over a new face before. I kept trying to land on top of her, but each time, she scurried away.

We looked like a three ring circus act. Me, belly flopping all over Lia's ankles, then Brandy throwing herself at her, and the kids hopping all over the couch in a fit of laughter. Meanwhile, Aunt Lola took her sweet time gathering up the collar as she hoarded the only defense, that squirt bottle, under her armpit, strolling around the kitchen counter.

"Kids, relax." I climbed to Lia's side and plucked up Brandy from the front and scooped her up and off the couch and into my arms again. She squirmed out of my grip again and headed back to Lia's ankles. Brandy jumped up and down, scratching her shins as she whined and her eyes grew large and bulgy.

Lia leaped off the couch and ran to the slider door. She opened it, slid through a crack just wide enough to fit through, and slammed it shut. Brandy acted like a little bugger for sure, panting, exposing her teeth, circling her big, scary eyes around Lia's face as if taunting her like a school yard bully.

I walked around the outside of the house to get to her. Lia sat on one of the pub style chairs near the pool bar, wiping her forehead and texting.

"I am so sorry." I sat down on the chair next to her. "I'm mortified. I've never seen her act like that before."

She put down her phone. "I texted Dean to warn him. He'd die. He would literally fall to the ground and keel over. The two of us would be doing chest compressions on him until we turned blue. It'd be something right out of a comedy show. Even more so than that scene probably already looked to you in there."

"You were adorable." I raised my face up to the sun, banking on its power to continue elevating me.

Her gaze tickled me from my head down to my toes.

"Have you ever seen such a lavish setup before?"

Lia glanced around the pool area, at the cabana with its lattice design in the far corner, at the kidney shaped water, at the stone pavers with its intricate patterns lining the pool's curves, and at the carefully selected plant life adorning the entire view. "I never knew flea markets could be such cash cows."

"Puts a whole new spin on psychics now, doesn't it?"

She circled back to face me. "That spin already happened for me long before I stepped onto this little piece of heaven on Earth."

My head twirled.

We sat for a while in the sun, sharing sweet smiles and flirty gazes, joking about Brandy, a.k.a. Little Bugger, and life as a psychic in a flea market booth. Then, Anthony knocked on the slider. We both turned to see the three of them staring back at us. My aunt, Charlotte and Anthony pressed their noses and lips up against the window and made faces at us as we sat in the rays of a setting sun. And "Little Bugger" continued to pant.

"Clearly, I screwed up that first impression." Lia grabbed a mini straw from the canister and placed it between her lips.

"Clearly." I matched her move, sticking one in between my lips too.

We playfully stared into each other's eyes. "I am a dog person despite what I looked like in there."

"I believe you." I tapped the tip of her nose and let my finger fall gracefully down her face, neck, and arm.

"They're all still staring at us." Lia's eyes twinkled. "Even Little Bugger is."

"Well, Little Bugger is going to have to learn some manners or else no doggy park for her."

Lia reached out for my hand, cradling my fingers with hers.

"You just have to come armed next time."

"Armed?" Lia released a soft laugh, as she circled my fingers in a slow, seductive dance.

"With a squirt bottle of course," I whispered, floating and giddy.

"Yes," she whispered back, leaning in closer. "Of course."

Everyone stared at us. I wanted her to kiss me. I traveled my gaze down to her lips and admired them before ascending to her hungry eyes.

She closed them, then brushed her lips against mine.

I sank into the comfort of her.

"They're still staring," she said, washing me over in her sweet breath. "We should make funny faces at them."

"Oh, I like the way you think."

"On the count of three?" Her eyes took on a wild, crazed look just like Brandy.

"One," we whispered. I loved how her breath warmed my face.

"Two." My insides warmed at the outdoorsy smell of her.

"Two and a half," she whispered, closing her eyes and brushing her lips against mine again.

"Two and three-quarters." I didn't want to break away from her.

We opened our eyes, latched on, smiled wickedly, and screamed, "Three." At which time we both jumped off the stools and began making funny faces at them. Lia pressed her face up against the slider, and Charlotte screamed out a laugh at a decibel I'd yet to hear come out of her little lungs.

Then, Lia cupped her hands to the glass. "Dean?"

I peeked in, cupping my hands too. Brandy snuggled in Dean's arms. She loved him, kissing his nose and his neck while he laughed and totally missed our funny faces.

"You told me that we'd need to revive him," I said.

"Total shocker to me too." She opened up the slider and walked into the kitchen with her confidence back in tow.

Brandy continued to pine over Dean, showering him in kiss after kiss.

Dean scratched behind her ears, and she cocked her head to the side as if in ecstasy. She snorted and leaned her head even further back, exposing her belly and neck to him.

"How did you get in here without being attacked?" Lia asked, walking up to him.

"Yoga afterglow, I would presume," he stated.

Lia reached out without reservation and petted Brandy in that spot between her eyes. Brandy stopped kissing and grunting, closing her eyes at Lia's touch.

Lia looked at me with a twinkle in her eye. "Little Bugger likes me."

My heart melted. I cupped my hands to my face and almost squealed.

Aunt Lola placed the squirt bottle back in its rightful spot near the microwave. "I love happily ever after moments."

I walked up to the trio, and kissed my little bugger's head. "I'm so proud of you."

She wagged her tail, and then kissed Dean's face all over again.

"Let me get a picture," my aunt said, pulling out her cell.

I swung my arm around Lia's waist to get us all in the picture, and then, the room blurred around me. I closed my eyes, trying to ward off the upcoming vision.

I opened my eyes, and stood at the beach watching two shadows digging in the sand. They kneeled in front of a sandcastle, molding grand towers as they laughed and tossed sand at each other. They worked and hummed songs, creating one of the tallest sandcastles I'd ever seen. I moved in closer to get a better look on its intricate design, and that's when I saw their faces; Dean and Lia.

The two stood and stared out at the sea, watching as the high tide rolled in off the coast and began to slowly eat away at their masterpiece. Peace surrounded them.

I closed my eyes and relaxed along with them, enjoying the splash of the ocean mist and the smell of salt water. Then, when I opened my eyes, I landed back in the kitchen watching Brandy lick Lia's face now. She bent her head back and laughed. "This dog is a mess."

I leaned into her, wanting to savor that moment when nothing else in the world mattered more than Brandy welcoming her into our world, and her being thrilled over that.

##

A little while later, after we drank some punch and ate cookies, the mechanic called to let Aunt Lola know her tires were fixed. "I need a ride."

"Say," Dean said, "Why don't me, you and the kiddos, go for a ride to get it? Willow can teach Lia a few yoga moves while we're gone."

Aunt Lola looked at me.

"That sounds perfect," I said without a blink of hesitation.

Aunt Lola and Dean shared a secret smile, before gathering up the kids and ushering them out of the house, leaving Lia and me alone to fill in the silence left in their wake.

She leaned against the wall and washed me over with her eyes.

God, she was sexy and mysterious. She filled the space between us with a sense of rawness, just barely hidden under the quiet cover of desire.

"Want to see the rest of the house?" I asked, riding on the fumes of my earlier confidence.

"I'd love to." She walked toward me.

I offered her my hand, and she slid it in mine, warming my skin.

"You've seen most of the main level, and the top is just bedrooms. You've got to see the basement. They threw no stops at it."

She followed closely behind me, so closely I could smell the honeysuckle on her and feel her breath on the back of my neck. I led her down the stairs and into the basement game room. My body lightened in contrast to the weight of knowing my hand touched Lia Stone's; her fingers cradled my fingers and heated my skin.

I led her into the main room that housed a pool table. The walls were decorated in old movie posters from the fifties, and classic theatre red draped walls. We walked past the popcorn machine and the candy counter. "Hungry still?" I asked over my shoulder.

Her eyes, half-opened and dreamy, teemed with a hunger, but not for popcorn and candy. My stomach flipped, and my legs turned soft and weak.

I turned forward again, leading her past the pinball machines and the Mrs. Pac-Man game, and straight through to the theatre room. "This is where we have movie nights. My aunt will stand up front and announce the movie pick, telling us details of the filming and the history behind the actors and settings. She is eccentric, if you haven't noticed," I said, turning back to catch her expression.

She looked only at me. The fancy movie chairs and the large movie screen did nothing to attract her attention. She focused on my eyes, watching me with a reverence I had only dreamed of.

I turned back to face the big movie screen. She leaned in closer, placing her chin on my shoulder and clasping her arms around my waist. I closed my eyes to steady the flutter of my heart.

We stood in that embrace for a few long moments before I braved around to face her.

She lifted the corner of her mouth into a smile. I loved her lips; they aroused me, those pouty lips with their wide v shape and plump curves. And her eyes. Oh, I adored her eyes, and could stare into them for hours without ever tiring or taking a break to blink if ever humanly possible. Her dark eyes sparkled, highlighting her golden flecks. As a teen, I had dreamed of her features, of brushing them with my lips in soft, romantic sweeps. I had known every line, curve, freckle and expression on her face. I'd never thought I'd actually be standing less than two feet from her. She had followed me into that basement knowing full well it would become quiet with our intimate desires and inner arguments to either stave off the hunger and the temptations or just embrace that moment when we were alone to do whatever the hell we pleased.

I moved into her space, commanding it as my own, reaching out for that moment when I led the dance, controlled the pace, and decided what I wanted and actually went for it.

Keeping company only with the shadows on the wall and the melodic hums of our heartbeats, my mouth watered, impulsed to taste her again, enjoy her softness, and inhale her light musk as it seeped into my lungs and embedded itself in the tiniest of nooks and crannies for safekeeping.

In the distance, I blocked out the sound of Brandy's nails hitting the floor, as she undoubtedly chased a toy around the living room, and zeroed in on only Lia and her mesmerizing pull on my heart.

Lia reached her hand out for me, and I slipped mine in it. She pulled me with a force that told me I had little choice in escaping that room, with its dim lights and hotter than hell temperature, without her first getting a chance to express the origin of that sly smile on her face.

She placed her finger on my bottom lip and circled it back and forth until my insides melted away all the residue of years of worrying if anyone would ever look at me with the kind of adoring look she gifted me with at that moment.

The lights from the movie projector room above peeked into the dim room, creating soft shadows on her face. I grazed her cheek with my fingers, sealing into its supple, comforting touch. My eyes closed, and she kissed my left eyelid, then swept across the bridge of my nose to my right one. I stiffened, afraid to somehow move and ruin the effect of her energy mixing with mine.

She cupped my face, teasing me closer, baiting me with the thrill of her. "I don't want to learn any of Dean's prescribed yoga moves," she said, hoarsely.

Her voice excited me, rounding up every last emotion my body could handle, landing me in that place of longing and desperation, and waiting for a witty comeback to emerge and carry us off to one of the quiet corners of the movie room where I could absorb the intensity of making love to a woman as beautiful as Lia Stone.

"I've had enough yoga for the day anyway," I whispered.

"I'm glad we're on the same page," she said in a low voice that turned me into a puddle at her feet.

Was I reading her signal properly? Did she want me to kiss her? Did she yearn for even more? My entire body softened and the most wonderful buzz drifted around inside of me, creating a sexy pulse in my heart, in my temples, along my shoulders, in my core, and far down into the lonely space between my legs. I was wet and excited, and about to burst if something didn't happen – and fast.

"What page are you on?" I asked.

Lia's chest rose and fell in quick beats. "I want to kiss you again," she whispered.

I swallowed past the always present fear of touching someone, especially in such an intimate way, and cradled my hands against hers, sinking into her loving gaze. "What are you waiting for, then?"

She eased closer and brushed her lips ever so softly against mine, bringing me into a state of absolute bliss. I kissed her back with a passion that was well over a decade and a half in the making.

She tangled her fingers around a strand of my hair as I proved with my curious tongue that, yes indeed, we were on the same page.

I leaned against her beating chest, gasping as she threaded her arms beneath my arms and lifted me toward the back wall of the movie room. She kicked the door shut, and leaned us up against it as she locked it. Then, she looked into my eyes. "So no to yoga," she whispered, nuzzling up against my cheek as she hugged me.

"Yoga is the farthest thing from my mind."

She eased into a subtle smile, looking very much like the young Lia I had first fallen in love with as a teenager, as she gazed down at me. "Does this have anything to do with the fact that I have zero self-control?"

"God, I hope so." I pushed her down to the ground and kissed her like I would die if I kissed her any less, free-falling into the comfort of normalcy for the first time in my life since sitting in that church pew so many years ago.

I eased into her love under the shadows of the movie room lights, exploring her body like a piece of fine art, one exquisite curve after another, bringing her pleasure. Her body softened under my touch, and arched when my lips discovered her earthy treasure. I poured all my love into her, responding to each of her moans with a hunger that slipped through reality's cracks and into a fantasy land all their own where the sweet taste of passion tested the strength of resistance and won, creating a ripple effect of gasps until she could no longer sustain any amount of self-control.

She panted as I continued to plant soft kisses along her trembling inner thighs. I caressed her hips and enjoyed the taste of her wetness, well past the final rock of her hips. Then, I just stared up at her, at her relaxed gaze and loving touch. She sat up and pulled me to her, kissing me with renewed fervor. My whole body quivered, desperately wanting her love to permeate me now.

184

She guided me down, and teasingly nibbled on my neck. I shivered with delight, eager for what was to come. She traveled around my body, taking in every square inch with a look of awe. I let myself go, surrendering all fears, and only leaving room for the sheer pleasure she created in me. She circled the outside of my breast with tenderness, and then heated my core with her tongue as she stroked the very tip of my nipple with it. She sent shockwaves through me with each slow, seductive pass across my sensitive skin.

I caved into the moment, rocking gently as she dared lower and set me on fire. My body convulsed under her touch, bringing me to a point of no return when my soul opened up and reached out for the exhilaration waiting on me. I seized it, clinging to it, and enjoying its fiery pulse until it lit up every last fiber in my being.

I panted just as hard as she had, riding the wild waves of a wake so powerful, I capsized. Arms spread out to my sides, I balanced against the residual trembles of Lia's love.

We laid back, cradling each other's hands and staring up at the ceiling with huge smiles on our faces.

"That was incredible," Lia said, breaking the silence first.

I could only respond with a light chuckle.

I rested by her side, enjoying the silence and the new bond between us. We remained in comfortable silence for a few lingering minutes, calming our beating hearts and coming back down from our high.

Then Lia asked. "How long do we have before everyone is back?"

I looked up above the movie projector hole to see the time. "Considering the Dean I've just gotten to know is highly talkative and questions every last detail, I'd say at least another thirty to forty minutes."

She tossed my clothes at me, and began to dress herself. "Good. You've got to teach me at least one or two yoga moves because otherwise, Dean's going to fish."

"Let him," I said with a spunky edge.

She put on her shirt and nuzzled up against me. "You don't want Dean fishing. Trust me. He gets all over-dramatic and high-pitchy."

I leaped to my feet. "Fine, let's move into the pool table room and do some downward dog poses."

Lia stood up and hugged me from behind. "You're beautiful, Willow." She nuzzled against my neck. "Absolutely delicate and beautiful."

I slipped into the comfort of her compliment, riding on the bliss of my newfound emotions.

Chapter Fourteen

Dean followed Yvonne's direction on holistic healing down to the last dotted I and crossed T. He was also becoming fast friends with Pat, who just like Dean, spent most every day at the center. When they weren't healing, Pat would ask Dean to tag along to his construction site visits, take him for coffee, or help him work in his yard. Apparently, Pat's wife baked the best chocolate chip cookies, which was the main reason Dean agreed to help.

Dean and Lia were helping me stock some shelves at Yvonne's one morning when he told us more about those cookies. "They're the most delicious things in the world. I crave them. Pat must think I'm a nut because I'm practically begging him to put me to work in his yard. The fresh air is doing me wonders. I can think, breathe and relax so much better than I do when I'm cooped up all day."

"Go ahead and rub it in a little more," Lia said.

"Please, you wouldn't know what to do with yourself if you allowed a little time for fun."

Lia pointed her finger at him. "It's a good thing I like this side of you."

"Yeah, yeah," he said. "Or else you'd fire me. I know. I've heard it before."

She punched his arm.

I loved watching them banter.

"I don't know how Pat's wife's handling his sickness," Lia said.

"She's very matter-of-fact with it. They've just accepted the fate and are embracing the rest of their time together. When he snuck out to get us some frozen Del's lemonade, she confided in me that he's now the husband she's always wanted him to be. He's attentive, nurturing, and even let's her watch Lifetime movies, which was a big no-no before he discovered he had three baseball-sized tumors in his liver."

"And the daughter? How is she taking it?" Lia asked.

187

"She's quiet. I've seen her maybe three times since I've been helping him out. He tries to joke around with her, but she's angry. She shoots him dirty looks and slams her door."

"She's going to regret that," I said.

"He said the same thing. He feels bad about that. So, he's eased up on her the past few days. He says he isn't going to push her anymore. That worked because just yesterday, she came out to the backyard and offered us cookies."

"Being around them must depress the hell out of you," Lia said.

"Quite the opposite. I've never felt so alive."

# #

Dean embraced the whole healing practice. He learned and practiced the techniques of Ayurveda healing, Yvonne's area of specialty. A few weeks into his treatments, he asked if I could bring Brandy to the center.

"Yvonne would kiss your feet if you could figure out a way. She's too worried that the State Board of Health will walk in and find her here."

"Do they show up often?"

"I've worked here for years, and so far I've never seen them step foot in here."

"I suppose it would be that one day when Little Bugger will be sitting in my lap, helping me overcome my fear of dogs, when they would walk in with their notebooks and glasses pulled halfway down the bridge of their noses." He shrugged.

"You can always swing by and take her for a walk. She loves being outdoors."

And so began Dean and Pat's arrival at my aunt's house every morning at seven a.m. to take Brandy to Lincoln Woods and get in their morning therapy of leash walking, sunshine, and fresh air.

"He's like a different person altogether," Lia said to me as she dug into her bowl of linguini and mussels at The Coast Guard House restaurant, about a month into Dean's holistic journey.

I sipped some Merlot. "I can't believe he ever had a fear of dogs."

"I have to give him lots of credit. He's been focusing on his bucket list since he found out about needing surgery. Getting over his fear of dogs topped that list."

"Why?"

"Because he knows I want to adopt one, and he knows I won't because of him. He tends to carry guilt around like a piece of garment."

"What else is on his list?"

"Simple things, really," Lia said.

"So, no climbing Mount Everest?"

She laughed. "Dean enjoys his pillow-top mattress and foot massager too much to part with them on such a trek." She stirred her linguini. "He listed very basic things like tour a winery, see Brandi Carlile in concert, go dance at a club, and enjoy tea and crumpets at an actual teahouse. The only big one as far as I'm concerned is his desire to become a certified scuba diver. If only he'd add 'getting over his fear of falling in love' to that list."

"He fears love?" I reached for a piece of bread.

She handed me the oil and herb dish. "He has told me the color of his bedroom walls as a child and the way fresh avocados from his tree tasted as a little boy in India, but he has never gone into great detail about his love life. He told me only a little. He fell in love with someone from India, and that guy moved to the States to complete his master's degree. He promised to return to Dean. Apparently, they kept in touch via Skype and Facebook, but then as Dean got further into studying for his civil servant exam, the guy fell in love with some Irish dude studying Electrical Engineering. Dean says he still loves the guy, and can't move on."

"Was that recent?"

"Years ago. But, to him it was yesterday."

I wiped my mouth. I once had a vision of him when I first dropped by Lia's office. In my vision, he flirted with a blonde man at the park. "Some people never get over that first love."

"Who was your first love?" Lia asked.

You were. I could only imagine how creepy that would sound. "Maybe I've never been in love, yet," I teased.

She smiled uneasily, and fidgeted with her linguine. "Hmm."

I didn't mean to change the vibe. I wanted spirited Lia back. I put down my fork. "I'm stuffed." I leaned in. "You're spoiling me rotten with all of this rich food."

She twirled linguini around her fork, then matched my lean in. "You've got to try this before you surrender."

I giggled, grateful for the return of her playfulness. I welcomed her fork of linguini, even exaggerating the gesture with a moan to which she visibly enjoyed.

"Let's get the check and get out of here," she said. "I'm dying to take a walk along the water with you."

Lia and I enjoyed a string of romantic nights just like that one. Of course, they started much too late because of her long days at the office.

Even though she looked exhausted, every date night she'd venture out to do something different. Sometimes we brought the kids along, and other times we left them with Yvonne and my aunt. My kids adored Lia, and began to whine when we told them we needed adult time. My heart melted when Lia would kneel down to their level and calm the whines with a good joke, a tickle, or an endearing promise that would instantly swipe off the frowns and rev the excitement. She was so patient with them, and genuinely concerned for their happiness.

One night she vented to me about Dean and his pressuring her to take time off of work to spend some time with him doing fun things outside the office. "I've got all of these clients who need my attention, and I can't afford to just stop working for a month so I can go hike a trail with him or fly in a hot air balloon."

She looked frazzled. "Maybe he's right. Maybe you need to slow down a little."

"No way. I can't."

"You can. It's just work. It's always going to be there. Work is one of those permanent structures in life. It's unavoidable."

"Unless you get fired."

"But, you'd still have to work, so you'd go out and get another job. Or like you, make up your own."

"I suppose you're right," she said. "I can certainly count on work to always be there."

"That's the spirit."

That talk helped because not more than three days later, she accepted Dean's offer to go to the beach with him, Pat, and his wife and daughter. They even invited me and the kids.

We piled into Dean's car and headed to Scarborough State Beach. Pat and his family followed behind. We arrived at the same time the rest of the state of Rhode Island decided to arrive. The kids danced around the hot sand, tripping over blankets and sneakers. Lia followed them, carrying the heavy cooler filled with sodas and ham sandwiches doused in mayonnaise that my aunt prepped for us. Dean and I walked behind, sharing a grateful smile.

Anthony claimed a spot near the general store and bathing house. I quickened my pace and skipped over to him. "This is perfect, Anthony."

"No," Pat said, dropping the cooler. "This is so not perfect." Just as he said that, a chubby kid wearing the wrong sized bathing suit sped by us en route for ice cream, no doubt, and kicked up dirt on our cooler. He pointed to the cooler. "See, not perfect."

I knelt down and wiped the cooler with the beach blanket. "See, it's no big deal. It's a little sand. We're at the beach. We're going to get sand kicked onto us. Today is all about relaxing. No stresses." I shook the blanket and the sand flew in Lia's face.

She spit it out. "You need to pay for that."

I laughed, and released my hair from my sunhat, shaking it out before settling my gaze back on her.

"That's not going to work," she warned me.

I strolled up to her, placing my finger under her chin and lifting her eyes to meet mine. She playfully refused, pointing her eyes down to a shell in the sand.

191

I kissed her lips ever so softly and whispered. "Think they'll miss us if we go hide behind one of those sand dunes?"

Lia looked over at Anthony, standing with his hands at his hips and gazing out to the sea like a man on a mission to have a fun day at the beach with his family. He looked proud, mighty, and confident, traits that would raise any mom's spirit, especially mine. "With that kid? Are you kidding me?"

Just then, another obnoxious kid sprinted past us and doused us in a fresh layer of grit.

Dean laughed.

Pat scooped up the cooler and hiked toward the shore. His wife and daughter marched alongside of him. "We came to build a sandcastle, and no way is some kid going to run by ours and crush it because he wanted a lemonade or an ice cream cone," he said. "Come on gang, to the seashore we go."

"To the seashore we go." Charlotte skipped up to his side.

They pushed forward and didn't stop walking until they came upon an open area near the rock dividers. Anthony strode up to them, opened his arms up wide, and said, "This is it. This is our spot."

Pat let him claim it, and we all watched as the pride resurfaced on his young face.

He dropped my cooler. "Fine choice, Anthony."

I scanned the area. "I suppose this is a little better."

"A little?" Anthony asked, his voice dripping in a sarcasm far too mature for his youth.

I took command of the scene, taking the cooler and reassigning it to the far right of our spot. "Yes," I said, glaring at Anthony. "You better not be making fun of me."

Lia dug her toe into the sand and scooped up a pile, then flung it at Anthony, no doubt, to break his rapid ascent into a fight with me. He scowled at her. "What did you do that for?"

She did it again.

"Stop," he screamed, pouting his chubby bottom lip at her.

192

So, she did it again. This time the sand twirled with the wind like a mini tornado, and that fascinated him. He began to laugh. Riding the wave, she ran up to him, scooped him up in her arms and began running in circles with him, kicking up sand and laughing like a wild woman who had gone completely mad. He began laughing like a child should, and then, me, Charlotte, and Dean grabbed each other's hands and spun in circles, hooting louder than them.

Pat and his family stared at us like we had lost our marbles. "You all are freaking crazy," he said before grabbing my and Charlotte's hand and joining in our craziness.

Before long, we sat on the blanket, secured by our sneakers and cooler and dug into a bag of potato chips. We crunched and slurped back sodas, getting tanned under that strong late summer sun.

Dean stared at the water with a seriousness. "Everything okay?" Lia nudged him.

He nodded. "It's fantastic," he said, tilting his head. "Absolutely fantastic."

She nudged him again. "You sound exactly like Yvonne."

He stared back out to the sea. "I take that as the highest compliment."

"As you should, man," Pat yelled out. "Yvonne freaking rocks."

Pat cracked me up. He was like a ten-year-old trapped in a forty-year-old body. He didn't care how people viewed him. He blurted out whatever struck his mind. I wish I could've stolen just a smidgeon of that confidence.

Lia traced her finger around his lump. "You know, maybe all the meditation is working. It's actually shrinking."

He shrugged. "I'm not even worried about it anymore. Willow says it's going to be fine. I believe her."

I smiled.

Charlotte screamed. "Anthony keeps throwing dirt on me."

A smile surfaced on Dean's face. "I love that little girl's scream."

Lia laughed. "Me too."

My heart warmed.

Anthony came around their side of the blanket. "Can we go in the water now?"

Dean stood up, and reached out for Lia's hand. "Shall we?"

"We shall." She climbed to her feet and reached for Charlotte. "Come on little one. Let's go have some fun."

She squealed. "Come on, Mommy." She pulled at my arm.

I readjusted my hat. "I'll watch you. I don't want to get my hair wet."

"Come on," Lia said, pulling Charlotte. "Maybe she'll come in later." She winked at me, and I offered her a silly gaze.

They spent time swimming, jumping and diving into waves, and getting seaweed wrapped around their ankles. Pat and his family walked off toward the boats.

I wondered if it would be their last walk on a beach together.

Would they get another chance?

I closed my eyes and listened to the water roll gently to the shore and to the seagulls squawking above.

Then, I heard some giggles. Before I had a chance to adjust my eyes, Lia had scooped me up and fled to the seashore with me screaming and flailing my arms. I kicked and punched her. "Put me down. Put me down right this minute."

She broke out into an out all jog, weaving around blankets and kicking up sand at other people's coolers, as if finally surrendering to the notion that the world wasn't perfect and that sand was messy, indeed, and belonged flying through the air at the beach and landing all over people's arms and legs and getting stuck in their hair. Just as we entered the water, we turned to find Anthony right by our side. Lia tore off my hat, handed it to Anthony and asked him to give us a moment.

He obliged like any good gentleman would, and stood next to Charlotte and Dean, safeguarding his momma's hat while she enjoyed being carried into the water by her girlfriend and being drenched from head to toe in salty sea water.

A few minutes later, we all began construction on our very first sandcastle together. We dug holes for trenches, laid the groundwork for the foundation, and built towers three feet tall. Lia showed Anthony how to carve windows, and Dean taught me and Charlotte how to build grand walls.

194

Within two hours, we sat admiring our work, while sipping on sodas and eating grapes.

"I can check off 'build a sandcastle with kids' from my list," Dean said, smiling.

"You and your list. You're acting like you're dying, and you're not," Lia said, flipping sand at him with her toe again.

"My friend, what you fail to understand is that I'm not doing this bucket list because I'm dying. I'm doing it because I'm alive, and because I can."

Lia squinted as if allowing his words to sink in, then looked to the sea in deep contemplation.

Then, Charlotte ended the moment when she stood up and screamed. "Watch this." She ran right into the left wall of the sandcastle, smashing it with her foot. "Ha. Ha. Ha. That was fun."

Lia stood up and grabbed her before she could land on top of the towers we worked so hard to build. She squirmed below her, kicking her feet and flinging sand every which way.

Dean jumped to his feet, and ran toward them. He laughed like a mad man, and right before he got to them, he leaped in the air and did a cannon ball right on top of our sandcastle, smashing it to smithereens. Charlotte roared out a laugh. Lia put her down, obviously dumbfounded and on the verge of a major rant, when Anthony and I ran toward it and kicked in its towers, walls, and trenches with our bare feet. The four of us stomped and laughed and tossed dirt at each other, while Lia stood on the edge of that circus show and watched us enjoy destroying a perfectly erected sandcastle. The more we tore it down, the harder we laughed. We clung to each other, spinning and screaming, enjoying the moment for all of its temporary glory.

And finally, Lia caved and joined our celebratory demolition, proclaiming, "We're crazy."

"Well, better crazy than dull," Dean yelled out before tossing more dirt in the air and spinning to catch it with his scrawny body.

The fun didn't end there.

Days later, Dean further talked Lia down from working so hard and invited us both out to tour Carolyn's Sakonnet Vineyard in Little Compton. We learned all about how they created their specialty wine, The Eye of The Storm, during Hurricane Bob as it churned up the vineyard's white and red grapes. We also learned about how the Sakonnet people once lived there. The land, according to their native tongue, was known as "the place where water pours forth." Dean and Lia stood mesmerized listening to the tour guide's spiel of fascinating history about how the queen of the Sakonnets, Awashonks, led her people with fearlessness. She forged strategic relations with Benjamin Church, an English settler, which blossomed into a lasting friendship and ultimately helped her lead her people to safety during the war.

Later, after our tour, we sat outside on a blanket in the grass and snacked on seared spiced tuna with sun-dried tomatoes, potatoes, olives and lemon as we enjoyed two bottles of The Eye of The Storm. Just as we were clearing up our belongings, Lia got a call from the office and freaked out. "What do you mean you lost the file? How do you just lose a file?" Her eyes blazed, as she rose and paced the grass beside us.

"Just fix it. I'll come in tonight after I'm done here." She put her cell away and sat back down, faking a smile.

"You're going in to the office tonight?" Dean asked.

Lia pointed her finger at him. "No talk of work. I've got a handle on it."

Dean zipped up his lips. "Fair enough."

Two days later, we went to see Brandi Carlile perform. We arrived early and stood right up front. When Brandi entered the stage, Dean and Lia squirmed as if about to pee themselves. I had never seen two people overtaken by fandom as those two were in that moment. They clung to each other and practically wept when she started jamming on her guitar. Brandi created a steam bath, arching her back and angling her muscles toward that instrument as if in ecstasy. The best part about that concert was the meet and greet after, when Brandi, wearing an adorable Fedora hat, kissed Dean's cheek. Dean squealed and nearly fainted.

196

Later on, we crossed off another one of his items when we completed our night out on the town by stopping by a club to dance. The club had round pedestal dance floor levels that several daring women stood upon and shook their behinds off, bumping and grinding against one another like sexy burlesque entertainers. At one point, Lia hugged me from behind, and we stared up at them as we created intimate bumps and grinds of our own on the dance floor below them. The air sat heavy with a sex vibe, smelling dangerous and animalistic. We tuned into only each other's moves, riding the exotic waves of sensual extremes as one force. I didn't know how much time had passed, but before I knew it, Lia pointed up to the pedestal above us and laughed at Dean, who worked his dance beat like he was Michael Jackson himself. Lia pulled out her phone and started filming, "He's going to hate himself in the morning," she said with an evil laugh only a friend with an embarrassing video could create.

As we drove home, she asked Dean to drop her by the office.

"You're going to work at one a.m.?"

"I'm addicted to it. What can I say?"

"I'm worried about you," he said. "You're acting crazier than ever."

"It's what I do."

A few days later, Dean dragged Lia out of the office and invited me along with them to a teahouse.

When we first arrived, an adorable lady sporting a bow-tied ponytail and an apron greeted us. She escorted us past shelves stocked with fine teas, teapots, and fancy utensils, up a spiral flight of wooden steps, and into a quaint room complete with lace curtains and eyelet tablecloths. The room smelled like an early spring day. She sat us at a round table next to an antique hutch decorated with exquisite china. I exhaled as softly as possible, fearing any rapid bellow of air would destroy the delicate ambiance.

She placed a cloth napkin on each of our laps and then explained the menu in one of those soothing voices that mothers use when tucking a child into bed. Then, she

197

retreated, leaving us alone to admire the old-fashioned wood carvings of the door and window trim, and antique photos of Victorian women with curvy hips and bountiful bosoms carrying flowers.

A few minutes later, she reentered 'our room' with a tray of individual teapots and cups. She placed the dainty, floral painted cups in front of us and explained the fine art of steeping a pot of tea, which was to allow three minutes for steeping before indulging.

As we diligently waited, she served us three tiers of scones and butter spreads, cute little sandwiches, and mouthwatering desserts dripping with fruits, creams and chocolates. I was in heaven. I felt like a little girl again sitting at the grown up table, allowed to use the best china. I even raised up my pinky finger when sipping.

I thoroughly enjoyed watching the two of them lift their petite teacups like dainty Victorians, complete with a propped up pinky as they sipped.

We giggled through half the afternoon. I never imagined myself sipping cup after cup of tea and snacking on crumpets like a little girl swaddled up in this charming dollhouse while the rest of the modern day world went about their busy day. As the sweet decadence of fruit danced on my taste buds, I looked over at Lia, who listened with patience to Dean ramble on about his new fascination with scuba diving. Apparently, Pat had equipment he no longer needed, and wanted Dean to have it.

"I have no desire," Lia said.

Dean responded, but his voice faded out. A dizzying vapor stole reality, and the room started to disappear.

I stood in Lia's office. She buried her head on the desk, pulling at her hair. She looked up, and tears were rolling down her cheeks. Defeated, she dropped her head back down to the desk and cried.

Something tapped against my leg and then I landed back at the teahouse. "What do you say, Willow?" Lia asked.

I collected myself. "About what?"

"Grilling steaks some night soon?"

"Of course. Sure."

"Eating a cow it is," Dean said, raising his tea cup to mark the decision.

I tapped mine to his, trying to erase the unease crawling up my spine.

# #

The next day, I picked up Lia at her office to eat brunch. She looked dazed and confused. "You slept here again, didn't you?"

She waved me off, and rested her head back against the seat. "It's temporary. Just a few more weeks."

"Until Dean comes back?"

"That, or until I drive myself insane." She managed a weak smile.

We picked Dean up, and then headed for brunch. We got through the scrambled eggs, scones, waffles, and spilled syrup, despite the kids being extra wild that morning. After that, we dropped Dean off at the center. "I've got to run in and get some files. Are you coming?" I asked.

"I am," Charlotte screamed and unbuckled herself.

"Me too." Anthony reached for the door.

"I guess I am," Lia said.

When we walked in, Yvonne walked up to Lia, grabbed her wrist, and took her pulse. "You look like a truck ran over you backwards and forward." She looked at her watch.

A funny smile sat on Lia's face.

She dropped her wrist. "You're getting a treatment."

"I don't have time. I've got a boatload of work to do at the office."

Yvonne crossed her arms over her chest. "The goal of Ayurvedic medicine is to prevent diseases. We all need it. You especially. I've never seen bags under someone's eyes like yours before."

Lia turned to me. "Save me from this?"

"She's right." I walked over to the front desk to get my files.

"I'll come in. I promise," Lia said.

199

"When you're done spitting out false promises, I'll be here." Yvonne shuffled away toward her treatment room, and Dean followed her dutifully.

"Thanks for the ride," he said. "Oh by the way, what time will you and Willow be picking me up tomorrow night for your birthday dinner again?"

Lia's face turned bright red.

"It's your birthday?" Charlotte asked.

Lia looked down at Charlotte and patted her head. "Yes tomorrow."

"Why is your face all red?" Charlotte squealed.

"Because she's old," Anthony said. "Old people hate birthdays. So shut up Charlotte."

"Anthony," I said, gritting my teeth. "Enough."

"Anthony's right," Lia said. "I'm going to be ancient tomorrow. We should celebrate my youth today instead."

"Oh, can we get ice cream?" Charlotte asked, jumping up and down.

Lia laughed. "I suppose we can hit Friendly's on the way back to my office." She looked up at me, and the color faded back to her normal tone. "Right?"

"I'll just slip into my treatment and let you two decide on the time for tomorrow," Dean said.

Lia turned red again.

Her red face hurt me, reminding me of those days at the campground when she refused to look at me or acknowledge my existence when others were around.

I ducked under the desk, pretending to gather files so I could hide my hurt.

A moment later, she leaned over the desk. "Hey, you."

"Hey," I said, easing myself up from the floor. "It's so dusty under there." I wiped the fake dust off on my pants.

She reached out for my hand. "So Friendly's for ice cream?"

"What about your work?"

Lia kissed me. "Eff it."

"Mommy and Lia are kissing in a tree, K-I-S-S-I-N-G," Charlotte screamed out. "First comes love, then comes marriage, then comes a baby in a baby carriage." She spun around, and Anthony tripped her with his foot.

Lia put her arm around me. "What do you say?"

I leaned into her embrace. "I promised to stop by the flea market to bring my aunt a coffee. So, right after that maybe?"

She scratched the back of her neck. "Oh, the flea market?" Her face flustered again. "Can you go after you drop me back off at the office?"

The kids wrestled on the floor.

The phone rang.

The music changed tempo.

Lia's face grew redder.

My heart tore open.

She didn't want me around her family or them to be around mine. "Of course."

An uncomfortable vibe sat between us. We both took refuge in the kids' laughter.

"It's not that I don't want to go with you. It's just that ever since Dean's leave of absence, I can't keep up with the workload. So, I need to get back to the office sooner than later." She spoke with a vulnerability to her voice, one that instantly took away my defenses. I rallied around that vulnerability, using it for everything it offered to bandage my wounded ego.

She needed me, and I needed to step up and help her.

I placed my finger under her chin and turned her to me. "It's temporary."

"I know it is." She nudged my finger from under her chin. "I know he's going to be fine. That's what's so frustrating to me. He can be so dramatic. He's taking this way beyond where it needs to be. Even the doctor called his lump unremarkable. Yet, he's going to all these crazy extremes."

"What extremes?"

"He broke his coffee habit. He meditates six times a day. He comes here every single day of the week to get treatment for something that is unremarkable. He asks me to drop everything to go live out his silly bucket list. He's not dying. Yet, he wants me to stop working to have fun because he has a one percent chance of dying. Hell, I could walk out the door and get slammed by a biker going too fast. I've got clients yelling at me because I can't get their projects done, and he's expecting me to go to concerts and teahouses and to the beach to build sandcastles."

"You looked like you were relaxed and having fun. That's a good thing."

"I'm losing control over my business and staff. We don't have time to have all this fun."

Her imbalance caught up to her and she feared losing Dean to his newly expanded mind. "He's living life."

"He's being ridiculous." Panic trailed her words.

"He's learning to be proactive."

"He walks your aunt's dog every day not because he is still overcoming a fear, but because he wants to know if she senses anything else. She brings him comfort."

She said that as though my aunt was the most ridiculous woman in the world. "So, let him be comforted by her."

She watched the kids chase each other around in circles, tensing by the second.

"I can guarantee you that if he knew how upset you were right now, he'd be devastated." I rubbed her arm.

She pulled in her bottom lip. "I don't want him to know."

"He might already sense it."

"Is my stress that obvious?"

I laughed to release the pent-up pressure. "You're a mess."

She lolled her gaze back to me, and this time the laughter returned to her eyes. "De-stress me."

"We just need five minutes, and I can tell you a few ways you can help yourself."

"Is it wacky?"

"Ayurvedic medicine is not wacky."

"With a name like that?"

I eased my hand into hers and led her to the chairs near the front window display. "It's thousands of years old. So, it's obviously helped someone out."

She sat down next to me, stretching her eyes. "What the hell. It can't hurt, right?"

"It's all in the breathing."

"Breathe in, breathe out?" she asked.

"Yes, it's called pranayama breathing. By practicing this technique, you'll calm yourself."

"I can't even pronounce it."

"All you need to do is close your right nostril with your thumb and inhale through the left nostril as you count to four. Then, hold your breath for another four counts. Then, lightly close your left nostril with your ring finger and release the thumb from your right nostril. Exhale through the right side. Then, repeat this alternating between left and right nostrils."

Lia nodded like I just told her about the fine features of a washing machine on the store floor of Lowes.

I demonstrated.

"That is seriously the most ridiculous thing I've ever seen."

"May not be sexy, but it works."

She batted her eyelashes.

"Then, there's Abhyanga, which is rubbing the skin with herbal oil," I said, gently massaging her forearm. "You'll increase blood circulation and draw toxins out of the body through the skin. I can help you with this one whenever you need."

She eased into my touch. "Go on."

"Another technique is Rasayana," I said softly. "That is the practice of using mantras during meditation combined with herbs to rejuvenate your spirit."

Lia's cheeks swelled up in an obvious struggle to maintain seriousness.

I pinched one of her cheeks, and she sealed her eyes shut. "No giggling."

"I will not laugh," she said.

I pinched a little harder, and she remained stoic. "I'm totally impressed."

"As you should be."

I continued. "There's also yoga, of course. Yoga will improve your circulation and digestion, reduce blood pressure, cholesterol levels, anxiety, and chronic pain."

She opened her eyes. "Sounds like yoga takes the prize for most benefits. I may need some one-on-one help with that one too, I suppose."

"Of course."

Lia's eyes twinkled.

"Then, there's pancha karma."

"Sounds kind of kinky," she said, swallowing a laugh.

I playfully slapped her leg. "Honestly, my kids listen better."

We both looked over at them as they continued to wrestle and pull each other's hair. "That's eerily accurate."

I turned her back to face me. "As I was saying."

She stared at my lips.

"Eyes are up here," I teased.

Laughter sat in the crinkles of her tired eyes.

"Pancha karma will cleanse and purify your body, helping to restore your balance. That one you'd need Yvonne's help with. That's the main focus of Dean's treatments."

Lia cocked her head as if about to ask me a serious question. "Can we just have ice cream? A nice big, heaping three scoops with hot fudge and nuts?"

I placed my hands on my hips. "You're a bad student."

"Ice cream is just easier."

"Can we come too?" Charlotte asked, running up and pulling on Lia's arm.

She hugged her. "Of course. I wouldn't dare celebrate ice cream without you two."

"Does that mean we can come to your birthday party tomorrow too, then?" she asked, looking up at Lia with her big green eyes.

I pulled Charlotte off of Lia's arm. "That's enough now, honey."

Lia cleared her throat, as if looking to fill the space with something other than the obvious awkwardness.

I walked over to their toys and began to place them back in the backpacks.

Lia knelt down to help. "My family is weird."

"Oh, don't worry about it." I faked a chuckle.

She clasped her hand over my wrist. "I want you to come. I really do," she said, nodding as if trying to convince herself of the same thing.

"Yay," Charlotte danced around us. "Can we go then, Mommy? Can we?" She threw her arms around me.

"How can you say no to that?" Lia asked.

I answered with a blink and reserved smile.

Chapter Fifteen
Lia

The night of my birthday dinner, I met Dean, Willow and the kids at her aunt's house. They stood outside on the front lawn waiting for me. Dean piled into the backseat with the kids and Willow took the passenger seat up front near me.

Willow and Dean joked around with the kids as I drove, taming my nerves. I warned my parents that I invited Willow, Charlotte and Anthony. My mother asked their ages and what they liked to eat. My father had no reply.

I was playing with fire, getting deeply involved with Willow. It would be just a matter of time before something or someone pulled us apart, and the closer we got to my parent's house, the more I kicked myself for putting any of us in a position to suffer through the night ahead.

When we first arrived, my mother ushered Anthony and Charlotte into the front door with a gentle, loving sweep. She offered the kids milk and cookies, my father's stash. My father emerged from the basement stairs, carrying a box of sangria and flashing an eyeful at my mother. "Oh shush, you cookie hog," she said. "Go into the living room."

He passed through the archway separating the two rooms and greeted me with a nod before lifting his eyes to meet Willow. "It's been a long time."

Willow extended her hand. "It's a pleasure, Mr. Stone."

He eyed her hand, then reluctantly shook it.

All of a sudden, Anthony ran into the living room sporting a set of playing cards. "Check this out. Solitaire."

My father eyed him like he carried the Ebola virus.

Anthony dropped to the ground with his new cards. "This is so cool. The cards have all the characters from Star Wars."

My father cleared his throat and scanned Anthony nervously. "I'll just go in the kitchen and help your mother."

Just then, Anna walked in with her kids in tow. She stopped as soon as her eyes landed on Willow. She shifted her feet, as if contemplating her escape. Her kids darted past her and straight toward the kitchen.

"Hi Anna," Willow said, sweetly.

"Hey." Anna's face turned white. She walked past us.

"Where's Jeff?" I asked.

"He's working." She looked around the room as if afraid that the walls would collapse around her. "I'm going to see if Mom needs my help." She took off to the kitchen.

The three of us sat in the living room and watched the Red Sox while Anthony continued playing by himself, and Charlotte explained to my mother how she used seashells for the windows on her sandcastle.

A little while later, we gathered around the dining room table like one big, awkward family.

We dug into the basket of garlic bread like we'd survived a week in the desert without food or water. My mother loved the hunger. I could tell by the glow in her eyes as Anthony took a second piece even before biting into his first one.

"How's work for you, Lia?" My dad asked, warming up.

"It's crazy busy." I plopped a pile of spaghetti on Anthony's plate. He reached out for it, licking his lips. Their eyes popped out of their little faces at the sight of homemade spaghetti and garlic bread. Did Willow just feed those kids frozen dinners?

"Anything worth earning is not going to come easy," he said.

"I'm certainly not complaining, Dad."

He bit into his garlic bread, avoiding my eye. *Why did I challenge him?*

"Lia runs a great business, sir," Dean said. "She credits you for teaching her how to do it successfully. I've never seen a person work harder."

He acknowledged that compliment with a nod. "Why thanks, son."

"Willow," my mother said, "What is it you do for work?"

Both my father and sister cleared their throats.

I cringed as my teeth sunk into the buttery bread.

"I'm a yoga instructor," she said.

I cradled my hand on her kneecap, grateful that she saved us from unnecessary assault.

"Mommy, you're a psychic like Auntie Lola, right?" Charlotte asked.

"Sweet Jesus," Anna mumbled.

Willow swung her arm around Charlotte. "Just eat your bread while the adults talk."

"Wine anyone?" I stood up, knocking over the Italian dressing. It pooled around the salt and pepper shakers.

"Our glasses are filled to the top, Lia." My mother pointed her eyes for me to sit back down.

I gulped mine down, then topped it off before sitting.

"So, a psychic?" my mother asked.

The alarm of impending disaster wailed in my head, signaling for me to jump in and save Willow. "She's a yoga instructor. Let's leave it at that."

Willow clicked her tongue and took refuge in her spaghetti.

My mother folded her hands under her chin, taking in the full load of my attempt to sway the conversation. "I see."

"In many cultures, psychic ability is revered," Dean said. "It's a lack of understanding that drives most people to fear it."

"Seriously," I said, tersely. "Let's just drop it."

He dug into his spaghetti. "This is quite delicious Mrs. Stone."

"Why thank you, Dean. I cooked plenty. So, don't be shy."

He twirled it around his fork and smiled at her before stuffing it into his mouth.

"I smell something burning," Anthony said.

I sniffed the air and smelled smoke, too.

"I have to say," Anna said, buttering her bread. "I find it fascinating that—"

"—something is burning." I stood up.

My mother sprang to her feet too and ran to the kitchen. "Oh shit," she yelled.

My father pushed back from the table and ran to the kitchen. The two kids shot panicked looks at us. Willow grabbed Charlotte from her seat and ran out the front door with her, yelling back for Anthony to follow her. Instead, he jumped out of his seat and ran toward the smoke-filled kitchen. Dean ran out of the house screaming.

Anna and I ran after Anthony. She tripped over my mother's stack of study bibles near the edge of her recliner. I kept running toward my father who stood in front of the smoky oven with the phone already pressed his ear. Smoke billowed out from the burners and the oven door. My mother screamed for him to do something. He screamed back, "I'm trying."

Then, he screamed at the 9-1-1 operator to hurry up and get a fire truck to his burning house. "The kitchen's on fire," he yelled. "Tell them to hurry."

"Oh my God, the kitchen's on fire," Anna yelled.

The kitchen was not on fire. The oven was on fire. "Dad," I yelled out over his frantic screams at the poor innocent person at the other end of that phone call. "Relax."

He turned to me and his eyes grew big. "Don't just stand here. Get your mother and that kid out now."

I grabbed him by the shoulders and shook him. "Calm down."

He wrestled out of my grip, still pressing that phone to his ear. "What's that you say?" he yelled into the phone. He turned to the stove. "Yeah, it's still on." He nodded. "Yeah, okay," he said, turning to me. "Turn it off," he yelled at me.

If a group of aliens could've seen us then, they'd turn their spaceships right around the strange planet with the crazy people flipping out over a little smoke billowing out of a stove top burner. I reached around him and turned off the oven.

"Okay, okay," he said into the phone. "Just tell them to hurry."

The smoke continued to pour out of the burners.

210

Panic surfaced on Anna's face. She opened the spice cupboard, pulled out the baking soda and started flinging it all over the stove.

"For goodness sake," my mother yelled. "Stop her," she begged me.

My family was crazy.

Even Anthony stood back with a look of bewilderment at the scene unfolding in front of him. Something he'd be able to write about in his summer journals for school. Come that fall, my family would be the laughing stock of Lincoln Elementary school as he confessed his greatest summer adventure. Who would've known it'd take place right here in the kitchen of Betty and Stan Stone?

My father took the baking soda from Anna and waved it around that stovetop like he fought a three alarm fire with it. He emptied the whole box. The black stovetop turned into a winter scene complete with smoke from a fire nestled safely within the confines of a well-protected oven.

He bent over at his knees, huffing and puffing in defeat of the massive wildfire he must have imagined raged in the fiery inferno of his hearth and home.

"You warned me not to come. Good thing I didn't listen," Anna said, rubbing my father's back like a saint sent to save us from hell.

My father didn't argue with her fact.

I turned to walk away, and ran right into Willow standing in the kitchen doorway, carrying Charlotte on her hip and taking in the whole scene. Angst sat on her face.

My father shooed her and Charlotte back out to the dining room. Anthony and Anna followed. My mother and I remained planted in the kitchen, amongst white soot and the remnants of whatever still smoldered in that kitchen oven. With her hand still caressing her chest, she whispered, "I hope nobody wanted more garlic bread."

I grabbed that oven handle and yanked it open. I stared down at seven black circles still smoking. My mother wrapped her arm around my shoulders and together we stared at them. "I'm sure glad you were here tonight," she said.

I clasped her hands in mine and sighed. I loved my mom so much.

By the time the fire department arrived with their axes over their shoulders, trudging through the living room with their helmets and masks on their faces, the panic simmered and we were left with a tinge of embarrassment for having those brave firefighters gear up only to find burnt garlic bread on the middle rack of my parent's well-protected oven.

Later on, long after the smoke cleared and Anna and my father's panic had been packaged back up and returned to its hiding spot, we sat down again, sans the rest of the garlic bread, and tried once again to enjoy a dinner.

About the time we dug our spoons into the cannolis, Charlotte banged her cup against the table. "Mommy, read his mind," she said pointing to my father.

My father's eyes grew larger. Anna bowed her head as if in prayer. So, I jumped in to save the moment again, wishing for another harmless fire. I tapped Charlotte's wrist, shushing her. "That's enough now."

"It's okay," Willow reassured Charlotte. "Just eat your dinner."

To that, Charlotte and the rest of us shushed for the rest of the arduous meal, pretending that my father and sister didn't mind sharing the table with a psychic who identified as a yoga instructor.

Once we finished up, Willow and Dean thanked my mother and father.

On our walk down the path, the three of us watched the kids skip ahead, excited to be going home with playing cards and a new book.

"Well, that was awkward," Dean said.

I elbowed him.

Willow power-walked to the truck.

The kids kept the conversation going all the way back to Willow's aunt's house. Even Dean sat silent in between them.

When we arrived, Dean took off.

"I'm going to tuck the kids into bed," Willow said. "Wait for me if you can? We need to talk."

"Sure," I said. "I'll come and help you."

She put her hand up. "Please don't." She backed up. "I'll be back in a few minutes."

I did as she asked. I stood under the harsh glow of a bright lamppost and respected her wish.

# #

Ten minutes later, Willow stood before me, hugging herself and squinting. "For most of my life, I carried the burden of a cursed life. Seeing my mother look at me with horror when I was a kid pained me like you can't imagine. My own mother feared me. She always kept a safe distance from me, and never asked about my day the way she did with Mary Rose. In church she saved the seat next to her for my sister, pointing me toward the end of our row. My father and sister, to this day haven't returned my calls, invited me to a holiday, or even met my kids because they're afraid of me. The only person who has ever accepted me for who I am is my Aunt Lola because she gets it. She believes in me. She knows I'm not a freak."

I shivered from the coldness in her eyes.

"Most people who have tried to get close to me, have asked me to suppress my ability. They feared my mind. They never introduced me to their families. They viewed my ability as outrageous, and instead of trying to understand it, they asked me to put it away like old paperwork. Out of sight, out of mind."

Her voice, covered with sternness, chilled the air between us.

"For the longest time, I thought I had something critically wrong with me. Why else would no one want to get close to me?"

I moved in to touch her.

She backed away. "Do you know how much it hurt me that you couldn't even look your family in the eye and tell them the truth about me? You were embarrassed for me."

"My family just doesn't get it."

"You don't either."

"Don't say that."

"I can't pretend not to be a psychic." She charged forward in her stance.

How could I tell her that I grew up in a family that ridiculed her ability because we didn't know how else to deal with it?

"Not everyone is going to understand what you do. It scares people."

"Does it scare you?" Her voice shelled out an attack.

I bent over at the knees and sighed before looking up at her and trying to figure out how to deal with the uneasiness. "It's different what you do," I said, trying to sound rational.

"You're embarrassed of me. Admit it. You were embarrassed of me at your family's dinner table, and my kids saw it. You can't even hide it. It's engrained in you. Your face says it all. I've been running from that exact look all of my life, and I'm tired of running. This is me. And I've had plenty of time to come to terms with that."

"I just wanted to protect you."

"Here's the thing, Lia. I don't need protecting. This is the real me. I help people. I'm not embarrassed of that. In fact, I love it." She turned from me and walked up her path.

"So that's it," I yelled. "You're just going to walk away from this without trying to figure it out with me?"

She stopped walking and faced me. "We have nothing to figure out. I can't be anyone else but me. I don't want to be. You can't handle that."

She turned back around and continued to walk up her path, leaving me tangled in the truth of her words.

I ran after her. "Look, I'm sorry."

She spun and faced me. "I thought you were different. But, you're still that scared person you always were, worrying about everything you could lose instead of gain – just like your sister. And frankly, I'm not interested in that kind of small-mindedness."

She marched away, leaving me with a biting sting.

# #

I drove. I just kept driving all night, up and down the interstates that snaked through Lil Rhody. I drove up north to the far reaches of Burriville, and when that didn't calm me down, I drove south to Newport. I listened to classical music, then reggae, and upgraded to rap, which helped me push out some of the anger poisoning me.

Me? Small-minded?

I never should've gotten involved with her.

I had predicted correctly, the first fight had marked the end of flutters and the emergence of bitter-tasting regret for putting myself in a position to hurt the way I did in that moment.

As dawn broke, I drove home, took a shower, then headed into the office to get my mind off the bitterness piling up inside.

Work was my go-to friend when all else failed. It patiently waited for me to embrace it each day, and rarely let me down. It let me strike it with harsh blows, yell at it, argue absurdities, and it responded with keeping a consistent presence over my life. It never shoved me out of the way, knocked me down, or refused to yield when times got a little rough. It remained there by my side, encouraging me when the rest of the world turned its back. It offered me good news, joy, and an escape from the harsh realities of life and all its stupid, illogical complexities.

I walked into my office and waited for its comfort to take root. I needed its comfort. I needed its distraction. I needed it to massage out the knot left behind by Willow's blow.

I sat at my desk and listened to the soft hum of the water cooler right outside of my door. I normally loved the peace. I hated it in that moment. I hated how I could hear every single solitary tick of my clock. Its ticks grew louder and bolder by the second. I hated the way my chair kinked up on the carpet, refusing to roll on my command. I hated that my cups left stains on my desk. I hated that the angle of the building blocked my view of Waterfront Park.

215

I escaped the anguish by looking at my phone. It blinked red with a new message.

I placed my hand on the receiver and listened to it. "Lia, it's me. Mr. Allen. I need your brilliance again. I just opened up another company, and this one is going to need some special care. Call me ASAP." His excited voice did nothing to tame the beast inside of me.

I hung up the receiver, and dropped my head onto a pile of paperwork that I needed to get through that morning.

That kind of call would've excited me in the past. Dean and I would've camped out at the office and brainstormed while drinking sangria and munching on popcorn. Instead I wanted to throw the phone against the wall.

I stood up and paced my floor, trying to reason with myself.

I was very open-minded. I listened to her explain that silly breathing and herbal oil lesson, and even smiled through it all.

What did Willow expect? That I take out a full page ad in the *Providence Journal* stating 'my girlfriend is a psychic'?

And who the hell wasn't afraid to lose out in life? I hated the breakdown part of anything. I hated that everything always had to be so goddamn temporary.

I paced and argued with myself for well over an hour before landing back in front of the pile of paperwork again.

I couldn't focus for shit.

Overwhelmed, I pounded my fists against my desk as I sank into a mild breakdown.

# #

I spent three days trying to get my brain rewired around the thing I loved most, my work. My workload increased in pressure, and my mental capacity faded when I needed it to be at its sharpest.

Willow took over my mind and steered it far off the road I needed to be on at that point. I hated that she questioned my outlook. I hated that she viewed me as small-minded. I hated it most of all because, deep down, I feared that maybe she was right.

216

I continued to circle around that dread. When the phone would ring, I'd answer it on a huff, aggravated to be interrupted. When a new contract surfaced on my desk, I'd buckle under the weight of all the work ahead. When someone on my staff would knock to ask me a question, I'd be short with them.

The more I tried to focus, the more my mind shut down.

On the fourth day, the day before Dean's surgery, he called me up to check on me again. I reassured him that all was fine. I didn't want to burden him with my selfish problems.

"Do you remember what you promised me today?" he asked.

Effing pizza. "Of course I remember."

"I'm outside waiting on you."

I covered my mouthpiece and sighed. I just wanted to hide under a rock. "I'll be right down."

#

We sat in a booth at Pizza Hut, both contemplating between ordering deep dish or hand tossed. A mother entertained her three young children at an adjacent booth and struggled her way through the tantrum her youngest boy broke into. She propped him on her hip, tapping her foot. Our waitress whizzed past her without taking notice. The tapping of her foot intensified, coupled with a growl at the boy who screamed with the power of a newborn baby entering the world and taking his first real lungful of air.

She yelled out to the waitress, who pummeled through the room, weaving through tables toward the front of the restaurant where perhaps her oasis awaited her behind the waitress stand. She looked about twenty years old, but struggled through the air as if carrying the weight of one hundred tumultuous years.

"I wish I could grab her by the shoulders and reassure her that she knows nothing of real stress," Dean said.

I shrugged, not able to judge.

217

She raced back through the restaurant, and past our table, stopping to tell us she'd be with us when she could.

"A foot trip would save her," Dean said. "It would stop the world for ten valuable seconds and allow her a chance to catch up with herself. She needs a break."

"She's obviously too busy for a break," I said, absently.

"That's the problem these days. We're all too busy, aren't we? We work ourselves to the bone and for what? To find out one day that we may have caused ourselves to get sick with cancer? So then we end up spending the rest of our days fighting for our lives instead of traveling a bit slower through it and enjoying it."

"Are you talking about you or Pat?"

"All of us. We're all vulnerable."

"How is Pat?"

He ran his fingers through his hair. "He's aged ten years from one day to the next. His wife told me he didn't want to have any more treatments with Yvonne. He doesn't have the strength."

"We're all going to get there one day, my friend. He's just arriving earlier than us."

He nodded. "It took a tumor on my neck to see how good I have it. What's it going to take you?"

I considered his sentence as I played with my straw. "I'm fine."

"You look frazzled. You've got roots that are over an inch long right now, something I've never seen on you before. You're not wearing makeup. Since when do you not wear makeup? Your shirt is all wrinkled. You're not fine."

"We're not here to talk about me. We're here to enjoy a pizza and beer as we planned."

The waitress buzzed past us, spilling lemonade all over the floor. "One day that waitress is going to stand back and it'll dawn on her that when life tossed all sorts of shit in her path, she reacted to every single morsel of it with disgust, and as a result it seeped inside of her and left her with the grit of her stupid meltdowns over botched pizza orders, spilled beer, and forgotten crumbs on the tabletops of a neighborhood Pizza Hut." He paused. "Thirty minutes from now, no one is going to remember the crumbs, the beer, or the pizza. They'll be on their way to other ventures, causing someone else the stress of their existence by expecting both reasonable and unreasonable demands on someone outside themselves."

Just then, the mother stormed up to the waitress stand and yelled at the frazzled girl to get her the check. "Please tell me I'm not like her," I said.

We watched the frantic scene play out in front of us. The mother grabbed for her takeout box as the waitress punched the cash register keys.

"You kind of are." He tapped my hands.

The sincerity in his tone caused a small cry to escape.

"Tell me what's wrong," he said.

I fought to stay silent, to keep the night about him, but the genuine concern in his eyes reached out and pulled the news right from my heart. "Willow ended it with me the other night."

He clasped his fingers over mine. "I figured that might be coming."

"Really?" I pulled my hands away, but he pulled them back.

"Are you really going to argue that with me?"

I could only imagine how the scene played out to him. "So, I'm screwed up."

"Hmm. Screwed up is rather harsh." He cupped his hand to his chin. "Sounds more like you've got yourself an imbalance."

"An imbalance." I scoffed. The word rang sharply, deafening me to everything else but the bitter sting it left behind.

"And you didn't believe her back then." He sat back with a smug look on his face.

"It doesn't take a psychic to predict such a normal thing. Aren't we all a little imbalanced?"

"She risked coming to your office and dragging herself through a muddy pile of embarrassment to tell you just how imbalanced you were. I highly doubt she was referring to a little imbalance, just like I highly doubt you're suffering from just a little imbalance."

I let out an exhaustive exhale. "You always have to be right."

"Newsflash, my dear. I always am."

I pulled my hands back and tossed a straw at him. "You're lucky you're having surgery tomorrow."

"On your tongue right now are a few sarcastic choice words just dying to leap out at me." He blew his straw wrapping at me. "They're burning a hole on that tongue, aren't they?"

I kicked him.

He kicked me back.

"I hate when you're right," I said.

"I always am."

Chapter Sixteen

Dean's surgery was scheduled for eight o'clock in the morning. I drove him to the hospital, and arrived an hour earlier than necessary. Yvonne met us there. The intake nurses prepped him with an IV, as Yvonne massaged his shoulders to help relax him. "Easy in, easy out. And you better not think that once you come out of this with nothing more than a tiny scar on your neck that you're going to stop coming in for proactive treatments. Because if you do think that way, I'm going to drag you in by your skinny little ankles."

"I'll have you know, these skinny little ankles have swung from a bungee cord recently," Dean said.

"What?" I barged into their conversation.

"Yes. Pat and his daughter and I partook in some bungee jumping three weeks ago."

"Brave soul." Yvonne shook her head.

"I also took Little Bugger to the dog park all by myself, and didn't freak out when thirty dogs came running up to us to sniff our little girls' behind."

"Must be nice to have all that time off," I joked.

"A person should play hooky for months at a time at least once in his lifetime. Or at the very least live as though he were going to die in a few weeks."

"You are not going to die," I said. I turned to the nurse. "Could you please tell the man he's not going to die?"

She shuffled off, muttering something about needing to get more sterile tape.

Dean stared at her as she walked away, dropping his jaw in dramatic fashion.

"You're not going to die."

Just then, the doctor walked in, introduced himself to us again, and examined Dean's lump again. "It's just a small unremarkable mass still. Maybe even slightly smaller than I remember. It'll be a simple procedure. We'll get you in there nice and comfy, then I'll perform the simple procedure and you'll wake up in recovery. You'll drink some juice, and they'll put you in a room. If you want to stay the night, you're welcomed to. Some patients thrive and want to go home the same day. We'll see how you're feeling and decide later on."

He spoke so casually, like he was removing a zit from Dean's neck.

He bid us farewell and the nurse came in to wheel Dean away.

I kissed his forehead and told him to enjoy the drugs.

He looked like he would throw up.

"Knock him out with the good stuff," I said to the nurse, who wheeled him away still wearing her weak smile.

A few minutes later, Yvonne and I sat in the waiting area in quiet contemplation.

I broke the silence. "How's Willow?"

She pointed her eyes to me. "Getting on with life, as you might expect."

I sunk in my chair. "It's that easy for her?"

She leaned forward, placing her hands on her kneecaps. "She's gotten used to this game."

"Game?"

She bowed her head. "What else is she going to call it?"

"It was not a game to me."

She sat back and folded her hands in her lap. "She's been treated like an outsider all her life. She wanted you to be different." Discomfort sat on her face. "I did too."

"I am different. I'm not like everyone else. I care for her. I don't want people to treat her like she's a freak of nature. The fact is, though, we live in a world where people judge, and I just tried to protect her."

"Protect her from being herself? That's like having your loved ones protect you from being gay." Raising an eyebrow, she rose from her chair. "I'll be back. I need to stretch my legs."

222

I watched her walk off until she disappeared around the corner of the waiting room.

I stood up and fumbled with the spoiled byproduct of an illogical argument. I walked over to the window and stared down to the parking lot. Rain poured down, and people were jumping over the puddles it created.

I was not like everyone else.

I was just trying to protect her.

The world could be hateful.

I pulled out my cell. I needed to call her. I needed to hear her voice. I needed her to know that I was not the bad, judgmental person I showed myself to be the other night.

She picked up on the third ring. "Hey."

"Hey," I whispered.

"How's Dean?"

"Still in surgery."

"Oh. That's not why you're calling?"

I leaned my head against the window. "I miss you."

Silence.

"A lot."

More silence.

"I'm sorry for the way I acted the other night."

Still more painful silence.

"Are you there still?"

"Lia, I meant it when I said this isn't going to work."

Embarrassment and regret settled over me. "I just—I just wanted to apologize. That's all."

"Listen, I have to go. I've got a client that just walked in the door. Please let Dean know I'll be visiting with him soon."

She hung up, leaving a trail of bitterness for me to confront.

# #

An hour later, Yvonne returned and offered me a smile. "I'm sorry about earlier. I guess I tend to get a little protective too."

I sent her a knowing look before we resumed our sitting position.

Soon after, the doctor walked through the double doors I had been staring at all morning.

We shot out of our seats.

"The surgery got a little more complicated than I suspected. The tumor was deeper, and denser. Which means more recovery time, and possibly some short term paralysis on the right side of his face. He won't be leaving today."

My limbs went numb. Yvonne put her arm around my waist. I clung to the doctors every facial move, waiting on more. "You said he would be able to go home today."

Yvonne gripped me tighter.

"He'll likely be in here for another two days. I had to put in a drain, and I want to monitor it."

"You said it was unremarkable and smaller than you remembered."

"It's still unremarkable."

"I don't understand then. Is he going to be okay?" I asked.

He relaxed into a grin. "He's going to be fine. The tumor looked like a benign growth. We'll send it to the lab to be sure. You'll be able to see him once he wakes up and we take him to his room," he said, then walked away.

Yvonne patted my back. "Take a breath."

I did as instructed, ten times over.

# #

A few hours later, I walked into Dean's room with a cherry coke and a box of animal crackers, his favorites. He smiled, and half of his face rose while the other remained still. I tried my best not to stare.

I sat down on the edge of his bed. "How are you?"

"I feel fantastic."

"Bullshit."

"I no longer have to worry about that tumor taking up refuge on my neck. It's rather freeing."

His cheek didn't move, and it freaked me out. I wondered if he didn't know half of his face drooped.

"You'll be scuba diving before you know it."

"Perhaps I should get the movement back in my face before I start planning my first dive?"

Relief washed over me. "Oh thank God you know about your droopy face. I didn't want to have to break the news to you."

"The doc said it might take a few days."

I patted his arm. "Well you still look handsome, my friend."

Just then, the door opened wider. "Oh don't go filling his head with lies," Pat said, entering the room in a wheel chair.

He looked like a frail old man as his wife pushed him in.

"My face looks rather awesome this way," Dean said, exaggerating the side that did work. "If my face stays this way for five more days, and I can convince Lia to take me to a Halloween party, I bet I'll take the top prize for best zombie costume."

Pat waved him off. "She's right. You're too damn handsome to be ugly. Even with a droopy face. If I wasn't married and straight, I'd be all over you, buddy. All over you, I tell you."

"Well, Pat, that would be my pleasure."

His wife and I laughed. Then, Dean joined in.

"Easy does it," Pat said. "You're going to go and get the misses all jealous, and then what am I going to do for the last few weeks of my life?"

We stopped laughing as a group, as if unified under the same sad conclusion that he probably had a week or two left to crack such jokes.

Dean exhaled. "Thanks for coming. I know it wasn't easy."

"Yeah, yeah," he bowed his head.

His eyes hung heavy.

His wife wrapped his jacket around his shoulders, rubbing his arms.

He looked back up. "How are you doing, man? They treating you okay in here? Are you chomping on those scrumptious ice chips?"

Dean's smile strengthened. "I'm doing just fine."

"You plan to remain out of work for a little while longer, I hope?"

Dean shrugged. "I'll be fine to go back in two weeks."

"Why the rush?"

"It's time."

Pat looked at me. "He's only going back because in his mind, he's obligated. Let him off the hook. Tell him to take some time to do a few more of those things he wanted to do."

"Pat," he said. "Stop."

A lump formed in my throat.

"No," Pat said, grunting. "Hang on." He bowed his head and groaned, clutching his belly.

"He's okay. He just needs a moment," his wife said.

We froze and waited for him to recover.

He cleared his throat and looked back up. "As I was saying. The guy told me you work like dogs. You've got to stop working yourselves like that. Take a vacation. Enjoy yourself. Work smarter instead of harder." He paused as if waiting on me to say something. "Just slow down for Christ's sake."

He coughed and gasped, clutching his stomach again.

For the love of God, please don't let him die right here.

He wagged his finger. "Listen. I've got a beach house in the Outer Banks. We spend every Thanksgiving there. Every single one. We're not going to make it this year, so the ghosts will be very upset that no one is there to entertain them. So, here

226

is the key." He pressed his fingers against its shiny surface. "Go down there and cook the best fucking Thanksgiving Day dinner you can manage. I mean go all out. Cook everything from scratch. Put on some Billy Joel and sing your hearts out while you chop potatoes and turnips, cut slices into the turkey and stuff garlic cloves in it, bake apples pies, and drink lots of wine. Bring everyone with you, including Little Bugger. Just get the hell out of Rhode Island for that week and enjoy yourselves.

Dean and I looked to each other.

"For me. Please," he whispered, clearing his throat. "Promise me," he said more sternly.

I jumped in. "Dean promise him, will you."

"I promise. We promise."

Tears streamed down his wife's cheeks.

I grabbed the key and handed her a tissue, fighting back my own tears.

"It would mean a great deal to him," she said.

I cradled her arm, and searched Dean's eyes for tears. Sadly, not even a dying man initiated them for him.

Pat drew a long inhale and said, "I'm tired. I'm really tired."

His wife stood tall. "Let's get you back home."

She unlocked the wheel brakes. Dean climbed out of his hospital bed, and, with his IV stand by his side, rolled his way over to Pat. "Thanks for coming all the way here." He leaned in and hugged him.

"Anything for you, man." He sniffled and wiped his eyes as Dean stood up.

I bent down and hugged him too. "Take care of yourself."

"Take care of that girlfriend of yours," Pat said. "She's crazy about you."

I nodded as if I had any right to do such a thing.

He tensed his chin as his wife rolled him away. He glanced from me to Dean and flashed a look of acceptance that told us he understood that this part of his journey was coming to an end. For the briefest moment, I caught sight of a tinge of regret staining his tired eyes.

Long after I left the hospital, and deep into the night, I couldn't get that look of regret out of my mind, the regret of a man not quite ready to leave his journey and move onto the next, wherever that might be.

#

My father called me later on that night. "We wanted to see how Dean is making out with his surgery."

"He's doing remarkable." I smiled at my word choice.

"Good. We're glad to hear that."

I didn't want to talk to him. I was still upset with how he treated us on my birthday. "I should go, Dad. It's been a long day, and I'm tired."

"Listen kiddo, another reason I'm calling is because, well, your mom said I was rude to Willow the other night."

I swallowed hard. "You kind of were."

"I'm sorry about that. All that psychic stuff is weird. I don't like to hear about it."

I ran my hand over my face. "Well, that was obvious."

"I don't like things that I don't understand," he said. "That's how people get hurt. They play with fire, not understanding its power."

We were more alike than I realized. "The only thing you need to understand is that Willow is a nice person who's not out to hurt anyone."

"I guess time will convince me because as they say, proof is in the pudding. Especially with these kinds of things for me."

"Sometimes you just have to trust, Dad."

#

Just one day after Dean's release from the hospital, Yvonne called me to tell me that Pat had passed away at his home, comfortable with his wife and daughter by his side.

I cleared my throat and asked if I could do anything.

228

"Go check on Dean and make sure he's going to be okay."

"I sure will."

#

I stopped by Dean's apartment as soon as I hung up with Yvonne. Little Bugger sat on his lap curled up in a ball. "Yvonne dropped Little Bugger off yesterday to keep me company," he said with a full smile. He paused a video playing on his iPad.

I sat down next to him. "No more droopiness, I see."

"All gone." He petted Little Bugger's head.

"What are you watching?"

"One of Pat's recordings from a talk he did at Yvonne's a couple of months ago."

I leaned over and pressed the play button. Pat stood before a room chocked full of people. They were laughing at something he just said. "I'm telling you, it was kismet. The week after my doctor told me I had only a few months left to live, my wife took me to the flea market to get my mind off of everything. I love those places, man." A grin spread across his face.

I looked over at Dean who sported a grin of his own.

"Of course, she hates flea markets." He winked at her in the front row. "She invited me to go anyway. So, we walked into this crazy place and ran right smack into a psychic set up with a stack of tarot cards and colorful signs. She took one look at me and called me over. My wife tried to pull me away, but I was like, 'No babe, let's see what she has to say.' So I walked over to her and handed her a five dollar bill and asked for a palm reading. She stared at my hand like she was reading the f'ing Wall Street Journal's stock options. I started sweating, you know?" He wiped his hand across his forehead.

The crowd laughed.

"With this serious tone, she looked at me and told me I was going to live a long ass life and that I was going to have three children. I tossed her another ten dollars and she kept going on, talking about how I was going to go back to college and get a degree in finance and my children were all going to get married and have a couple

229

children of their own. She colored my future like a fucking rose parade." He laughed. "We walked away from that crackpot psychic completely entertained."

I clenched my jaw, bracing for something hurtful to come barrel rolling out of his mouth about Willow. Even Dean scoffed. "Oh, hell, don't go there Pat," he said. "I can't listen." He aimed for the pause button, but I pushed his hand out of the way.

"Shh," I said.

Dean cocked his head. "Fine," he muttered.

"So, we walk further into the flea market and what do we see but this adorable blonde lady standing behind her psychic table."

"Aw," Dean said.

I smiled, and leaned in closer.

"I say that respectively knowing my wife equally crushed on her." He turned to her. "Didn't you?"

"Just get on with the story," she said.

The crowd chuckled.

He opened his arms up wide. "Willow. Sweet Willow. I wanted to have more fun with this. I mean, maybe she was going to tell me I would win the lottery and spend the rest of my life traveling from one exotic bar to another slurping fruity drinks straight from a coconut." He smirked and waited on the audience to respond. "Okay, so no one here is into slurping drinks from a coconut. Whatever, peeps." He paced the floor. "So I walked up to her and asked her for a palm reading. I handed her twenty bucks because that's what her sign said. She wouldn't take it. She stared at me with this look of innocence and peace." His voice softened to a mere whisper. "It was surreal, like time stood still for the three of us."

He pulled in his lower lip, as if struggling to maintain his grip on humor. "I asked her to read my palm, and she shook her head no, saying she didn't need to. She just continued to gaze at me and offer me peace. 'I'm dying,' I told her. She nodded. Just a sweet simple nod."

He looked over at Willow who sat to the far right. "She handed me a card to the wellness center and told me Yvonne would take good care of me. Up until then, I never trusted people. But for some reason, I trusted her. I took that card and called her, ending up here where they've helped me manage my treatments with dignity."

He looked around the room wistfully. "So the moral of the story here is—and I have to tell you this so I don't go to my grave with the regret of not revealing it to you—is never, I mean never, go to the first psychic table you see in a flea market. Imagine the mangos I could've bought with that fifteen dollars I wasted?"

Dean and I laughed along with the crowd.

"He's a nut," Dean said, staring at the video in awe. "He certainly knows how to elevate the credibility of psychics like Willow to a much-deserved level."

He sure did.

I leaned against Dean, as we continued to watch the last minutes of Pat immortalized in his unfiltered, childlike manner.

"In all seriousness," he said, folding his fingers under his chin like a steeple. "I'm here today because the cookies are f'ing awesome." He laughed at himself in his usual obnoxious tone.

I would miss that laugh.

"Okay, okay, I digressed." He refocused, pacing the floor again.

"So why am I here today? You're all looking at me like I've got all the answers." His shoulders dropped slightly, as he settled into a serious gaze. "I don't. But I do have a pretty good handle on a few things. For instance, I hear people all the time saying things like 'I don't have time to take a pee, let alone sit with a friend and talk, take the dog on a walk, or cut up an apple and sit on a park bench and enjoy the sunshine." He exaggerated the words. "Well listen up, people," he yelled. "Wake up call." His voice grew bigger than the room. "Odds are you have a hell of a lot more time than I do."

My heart beat wildly, waiting on his words.

231

He stared out at the sea of quiet people. "You have a chance to get this right. Do you know how lucky you are?" Desperation clung to his words. "You can wake up in the morning and get it right. You can right all the wrongs. Hell, it would take me another ten years to right my wrongs," he scoffed. "I wish someone would've told me my fate sooner. Hell, Willow," he said dramatically calling out her name. "I wish I would've met you ten years earlier so you could've warned me to stop being such an asshole to people." He grinned at her. "It's alright, doll, no pressure." He winked.

The crowd remained still.

"I'm going to cut to the chase here." He scanned the rows of focused onlookers. "Shed the regrets, people," he yelled. "Put them in a hole in the ground and burn them. Light the little f'ers on fire and get over them because if you don't they'll eat you alive." He exaggerated every last word of that sentence.

He pointed his finger and looked directly into the camera. "No regrets." He bowed his head, and walked off camera.

Dean and I sat still, staring at the iPad.

"Wow." Dean bowed his head.

"Talk about lighting a fire under people's butts."

"We've all got regrets, and we need to take care of them while we can."

"We sure do." I stared at his clenched jaw and wondered if one of those regrets was wasting so much time working for me.

I eased back, striking the match to one of those regrets before it got out of control and ruined a perfectly good man's journey in life. "That thing Pat said in the hospital about work. What was that all about?"

He regarded me carefully. "That was nothing."

"You need to be honest with me." I pointed my finger at him, swallowing the lump in my throat. "If you weren't working for me, what would you be doing with your life?"

He stroked Little Buggers eyelids. "What kind of question is that?"

I clasped onto his wrist. "Answer it. Please."

"No," he shook his head. "I refuse. It's a ridiculous question."

"Dean," I said, squeezing his wrist. "Please be honest."

He stared down at my firm grip around his wrist.

I wouldn't let up on it. "Tell me what you would do differently with your life."

He squeezed his fist. "You're cutting off the circulation to the rest of my arm."

I didn't ease up still. I needed all the leverage I could gain.

"Well fine," he said, snippety. "For starters, I'd work a normal eight hour day. I'd do yoga every morning and possibly find myself taking up something fanciful like oil painting with my free time. I'd also take vacations, most likely to scuba resorts and then maybe alternating those with hiking a new mountain. Lastly, and most importantly, I'd get a solid eight hours of sleep every night."

Tears stung the back of my eyes and began their descent down my cheeks. "I never knew you were so miserable."

He touched me gently on the shoulder with one hand and wiped my tears with the other. "I'm far from miserable."

I wrestled with my tears. "You spent the last five years repaying me with your loyalty, working like a dog," I said.

"You have worked us like dogs. I can't disagree." He continued wiping my tears. "You know, you don't need to continue filling that void anymore. There's more to life than work. Start balancing yourself better by embracing the fun too."

"I'm glad at least you've learned to have fun. I hope you continue to have fun because it's more than deserved. You paid your debt a long time ago, Dean."

He blinked, and in that blink I saw the birth of a watery, peaceful recognition. "Repaying you has been my greatest honor."

His admission placated to that part of my heart that needed to be told the truth. He had in fact been repaying me.

"You're going to be a hard one to replace," I said, spilling more tears.

"Are you firing me?" Shock spilled out of every fine line on his face. His chin quivered.

I leaned back. "I thought you were just quitting. Weren't you?"

"Quitting?" His voice rose high, and his eyes grew more watery. "Lia, working for you has been my greatest honor." He wrestled with his quivering chin. "I love working with you." A tear escaped his dewy eyes and rolled down his cheek. "I can't imagine a life when I'm not working with you. You may as well sweep me out to sea if I'm not working with you." He punctuated each sentence with a sniffle.

Tripped up by the clutter of untold truths, I stared at him for a long moment. "Pat delivered a sharp truth, though, that we can't deny. You are miserable."

He jerked forward. "Pat also said 'fuck' a lot. Who are you going to believe? A man who flung the f bomb around every two words or me, your most loyal and grateful friend?" He swiped the tears rolling down his face as if angry with them.

I had no words. The tears came faster than I could catch them.

He grabbed my hands. "I hope you understand how important it was to me that, even though it went against your grain to not work those days when I dragged you around the state to have fun, that you did anyway." His voice broke. "You proved our friendship is more than just a fluffy word, by doing that for me. You proved that our friendship actually means something to you. You got me through this ordeal."

"I did?" My voice sounded small.

"Yes," he said with a cry clinging to the edge of his voice. "And I'll continue to wonder, as I always have, why you're so generous to me." Uncertainty filled his voice.

"Because—because I love you, my friend." I kissed his forehead.

He lifted his head just high enough for me to see tears and relief fill his eyes, before resting against my shoulders and breaking into his first adult cry. I patted his back, nurturing him and helping him to dissolve all the stress he carried.

I held him, sheltering him in the safety of one of life's most basic human emotions. Out of those tears would come a strength that would change him; an emotional shift that he desperately needed so he could finally release a lifetime accumulation of emotional baggage off his narrow, yet fully capable, shoulders.

He trusted me, and that trust allowed him to let go of all that trapped him.

He started to mumble something. "Eight hours a day, no more."

I stretched back, and he revealed a satisfied, watery grin.

"Eight hours?"

He arched his eyebrow at me. "And three weeks of vacation a year."

"A little demanding, are we?"

He grew serious again. "You know, I'd work twenty hours a day if you needed me to."

I pinched his cheek. "That's why we're going to institute seven hour days with mandatory one hour lunches."

"No more twelve hour days? No more midnight oil burning?"

"No more."

"Then, we'll need to hire more staff to keep up."

"Then more staff it is."

He tilted his head, coyly. "Can we hire a handsome blonde who knows his way around a computer system?"

"Oh? Someone in mind?"

He shrugged and his face turned red.

I punched his arm. "Well? Is there?"

"Well," he danced his head around. "I keep running into this blonde at the park who got laid off this summer. He says he's good with his hands." A silly grin took over his face.

"Finally. Your mind is in the gutter like the rest of us. Halle-freaking-lujah!"

# #

That night, I re-watched Pat's video. He did elevate Willow's credibility, which was more than I'd ever done for her. No wonder she bolted from our call. She knew, just as I did, that no words would take back the hurt I caused her by not believing in her the way she deserved.

235

I thought about what my father said regarding proof. What proof had I shown to Willow to show her I was not small-minded, and that she could trust her heart with mine?

She needed to know without a doubt that I wanted to understand her, and that living life without her in it felt empty on a level I'd never experienced before. She needed more proof than shallow words.

Suddenly, it dawned on me just how I could prove that.

##

After spending the night researching my idea online and coming up with way too much drivel, I decided to pursue the old-fashioned route of research and go to a bookstore the next morning.

I walked right up to the information desk and approached an older lady with reading glasses pulled down to the middle of her nose.

"Where can I find books about psychics?"

"Follow me," she said taking off her reading glasses and leading me to the far wall.

"These four shelves here will have plenty of choices." She smiled and walked off.

I browsed and browsed, looking at every one of those books. I spent four hours kneeled down on that floor, finding the perfect one that would help me understand how Willow's beautiful mind worked. I selected a thick book, five inches to be exact. It detailed lots of research, history, and personal stories, enough to answer many questions and arm me with the knowledge to lift the credibility factor for what I was about to do.

Later on, I set up my video camera and recorded what I hoped would convince Willow just how open-minded I could be, and how much I admired her.

##

The next day, I walked through the messy aisles of the flea market, on a direct route past the mango man, past the Avon table, past the stacks of t-shirts and underwear selling for three dollars a pack, and straight ahead to Willow's booth. Aunt Lola was reading the palm of a middle-aged Hispanic woman when she saw me enter. She motioned for me to head to the back of the booth. She offered me a wistful smile as I passed her.

I pulled back the booth curtain and Willow stood alone eating straight from a can of peaches. She fell into an uncomfortable smile.

"Hey you," I said, entering her private domain.

She half-smiled. "Hey."

I walked up to her. "I know you probably don't want to see my face right now, but I needed to come here and see you."

She shook her head and her hair spilled down around her shoulders. "It's sad about Pat, isn't it?" she asked.

I wanted to hug her and remove the awkward energy from between us. "Yeah, it sure is."

Her face turned pink just as it did the day I first kissed her in the pool room. She dug into her canned peaches. "Do you want some? I could put some on a plate for you."

I moved in closer, and took the can of peaches from her, placing it down on a folding table. I cradled her hands and told her what I came to tell her while the words still sounded good in my head. "I don't want to be small-minded. I don't want you to view me that way. I want to change that. I want to be that person who isn't afraid to go against the grain and face some fears of the unknown."

She inhaled deeply. Her eyes watered.

"I brought something with me that I want to show you." I opened up my tote bag and pulled out my iPad and opened up to the video.

She hugged herself and watched.

"Hey, it's Lia Stone and I wanted to share some fascinating things I've recently learned about psychics." The camera zoomed in on me. "Number one – I learned that psychics rely on free-flowing energy and information, which means if a person isn't interested in a psychic knowing what's going on in her head, it's highly unlikely for that psychic to get in it." The camera zoomed back out slightly. "Number two – A psychic works by a strict code of ethics and is not about to destroy your life by telling you traumatic information without good reason. If bad news is a concern, a good reader will be there to guide you through and help you avoid the news from ever materializing by providing her insight." The video faded to the next angle. "Number three – Psychics offer credibility. Governments and law enforcement agencies throughout the world have used verified psychics to help them out with investigations, and they've had remarkable success rates." The camera caught my defined pause. "Number four - Psychics have shaped world history. Kings and rulers throughout the ages took the insights of psychics very seriously. They based political decisions and arranged marriages on the advice of psychics. This influence is dated back to the Shakespearean era."

The screen faded out and opened back up. "Lastly, number five - A psychic doesn't walk around the world being a psychic all the time. She needs rest. For a psychic to tap into her ability, she needs to focus deep into her subconscious mind. A person can't maintain that focus all day long. If she did, she'd go into extreme exhaustion and require lots of mental health therapy."

The camera zoomed back in. "So, there you have it. Psychics are phenomenal people whose insights have helped many throughout the ages. They are no different than you and I, other than they have incredible self-control and ability to tune out the chaos and tune into the peace of their inner voices, an ability we all have, but few are able to master. I happen to be madly in love with someone who has mastered this. She's remarkable, and has so much to offer those who are fortunate enough to be blessed with her friendship and love."

Willow cupped her hands to her face, staring at the screen. Her eyes were wide and full of tears.

"Right before walking in here," I said. "I emailed it to my entire distribution list because it's important people have the facts about things they don't understand."

"You sent it to everyone on your list? Including your father and sister, too?"

"Yup. They're on there."

I cradled my hand to her trembling shoulder. I turned her to face me, using my thumb to wipe her tears. "I'm so sorry I doubted you." I squeezed her shoulders. "You are so mysterious, so unique, and so interesting to me. I got scared because no one has ever been that to me. No one has ever moved me to challenge life the way you have."

Gratitude played out in her beautiful eyes, reflecting a brilliance that lit up her entire being.

I reached down to her hand, lacing my fingers in hers. I brought them up to my lips, kissing them softly, lovingly, and respectfully. "Up until a few days ago, I didn't know anything about psychics." I reached for my tote bag and pulled out my new thick book. "I've been reading this nonstop, so I could come to you and say I am certifiably knowledgeable about everything and anything psychic related."

She lifted her eyebrow.

"Of course, I'm not yet. I got a little overzealous in my planning. I didn't realize how long it would take me to read seven hundred pages." I smiled weakly. "I look forward to reading every last page. I want to be a part of your journey."

She relaxed into a lopsided smile. "I'm very complicated."

"I love that. I don't ever want you to be anyone else but you, complicated and all. I love you just the way you are."

Her eyes twinkled. "I'm madly in love with you too."

I kissed her forehead. "My tummy just fluttered."

She giggled in the way I loved, like an innocent girl discovering the beauty in a flower for the first time. "So you really want to understand me?"

239

"I really do."

"I suppose we can take baby steps."

"Fine. Baby steps. Micro-baby steps. Whatever it takes to never be small-minded again," I whispered.

"It's impossible for you to be small-minded now. You've just expanded your mind by filling it with a bunch of knowledge."

I closed my eyes and hugged her, embracing the glow of another regret set on fire and extinguished. I savored the warmth and compassion spreading between us.

"My mind is craving more expansion," I whispered, placing my cheek against hers.

She smiled and whispered into my ear. "How much more?"

I rested on her playfulness. "So much that it'll take a lifetime to complete."

She stretched back slightly and took in my flushed face. She bit her lower lip and stared deeply into my eyes. "We better get started then, no?"

I giggled and pulled her in close again, basking in her warm breath. "Take me there. Please," I whispered.

She kissed me with a deep passion, opening my mind to new possibilities that extended far beyond my old understandings of how the world, with all if its mystery and surprises, truly operated.

Thanksgiving Day – several weeks later

On Thanksgiving Day, we blasted some Billy Joel, poured tall glasses of wine, and cooked up the biggest feast any of us had ever attempted before. We chopped pounds of potatoes, turnips, carrots, and apples, as we teased about Dean's singing and Yvonne's inability to grasp the concept of vlogging as the kids filmed her, in between hunting for ghosts. She froze whenever the camera pointed at her.

We decorated the table with an elegant white linen cloth, a beautiful fall arrangement of flowers, and china that Pat's wife had insisted we use, because as she put it, *that's what Pat would've wanted.*

Just as I opened the oven door to place the dinner rolls in it, Dean reminded me that we still had to get the box of pastry out of my trunk that my mother had packed for us. "I'll grab it," he said, dashing off.

A minute later, he entered and placed the huge box on the counter.

I wiped my hands on my apron, and broke into it. "God, I hope she baked a blueberry pie."

I peeled back the box flaps and saw a bag of Doritos, a two liter bottle of Coke, and three pies.

I lifted up the Doritos and smiled. "Well what do you know?"

I found a note stuffed between the pie boxes. "Your father baked the apple one. Oh, and about the Doritos and Coke, Anna said you'd understand," my mother wrote.

Dean rested his chin on my shoulder, hugging me from behind. "I fully expect complete details about what that all means at some point this weekend."

I tapped his arms, which were squeezing me too tight. "Complete details you shall get, my friend. First, let's eat. I'm starved."

I headed into the dining room, enjoying the freedom of knowing that life's course was correcting. Yvonne and Aunt Lola began lighting the candles. Willow busied

241

herself, separating Anthony and Charlotte. Little Bugger panted, circling under the table, already looking for scraps. Dean slid out my chair for me. "Ma Lady," he said, bowing.

I welcomed his chivalrous act with a gracious nod.

I sat before my friends and raised my glass. "To Pat."

"To Pat," everyone chimed in.

"To Pat, a man," Dean continued, "who taught us the finest lesson in life, which is to live, whenever possible, without filter."

"Here! Here!" We cheered, then we dug into our scrumptious feast.

I took in the smiles and jokes, reflecting on how life came together for us all. I no longer worried about the small things in life I couldn't control, like how others perceived me.

Life wasn't perfect, and so we lived it anyway. Rain poured on wedding days, traffic snarled when people were in a rush, satellites broke down during playoff seasons, and people messed up when we needed them not to.

That was life.

It tossed us loopholes, and we had to work to find a better way. Life would continue to throw us challenges, and it wouldn't be the nature of the challenge that decided our fate, but more so how we interpreted and responded to those challenges that decided it.

All those times we built sandcastles and watched the sea swallow them up, I bowed out, powerless. Now I've come to accept that no matter how strong I build a sandcastle, the sea will always rightfully reclaim it.

The tides would continue to roll in and swallow the proverbial sandcastles we painstakingly built in life, be it a marriage, a career, a friendship, or a family, but that offered no reason to stop building them.

We were meant to shape and reshape our lives, and allow the tides of change to roll in and redefine those landscapes. The constant flow protected us from stagnation and the perils of growing too comfortable with the here and now.

The biggest lesson I had learned since meeting everyone at that table, including Pat who hung out with us in spirit, was that the secret to enjoying a beautiful life would never lie in the strength of saving it, but solely in the magic of building it.

The End

NOTE FROM THE AUTHOR

As with all of my books, I enjoy giving a portion of proceeds back to the community by donating to the NOH8 Campaign www.noh8campaign.com and Hearts United for Animals www.hua.org. Thank you for being a part of this special contribution.

A SPECIAL REQUEST

If you enjoyed reading this story, I'd be so grateful for your favorable review of it. Just a sentence or two saying what you liked about *Sandcastles* will help others discover it and help me to serve you better with future books! (www.amazon.com/author/suziecarr)

Made in the USA
Charleston, SC
31 October 2015